THREADS OF EVIDENCE
THE COMPLETE CASES OF
RIORDAN, VOLUME 1

THREADS OF EVIDENCE

THE COMPLETE CASES OF RIORDAN, VOLUME 1

VICTOR MAXWELL

INTRODUCTION BY
TERRY SANFORD

COVER BY
LEJAREN HILLER

ILLUSTRATED BY
F.M. FOLLETT

POPULAR PUBLICATIONS · 2021

PUBLISHING HISTORY

"Introduction" appears here for the first time. Copyright © 2011, 2021 Terry Sanford. All rights reserved.

"The Plainly Marked Track" originally appeared in the August 8, 1925 issue of *Flynn's* magazine (Vol. 8, No. 7). Copyright © 1925 by The Frank A. Munsey Company. Copyright renewed © 1952 and assigned to Steeger Properties, LLC. All rights reserved.

"The Work of an Artist" originally appeared in the September 5, 1925 issue of *Flynn's* magazine (Vol. 9, No. 3). Copyright © 1925 by The Frank A. Munsey Company. Copyright renewed © 1952 and assigned to Steeger Properties, LLC. All rights reserved.

"Threads of Evidence" originally appeared in the September 19, 1925 issue of *Flynn's* magazine (Vol. 9, No. 5). Copyright © 1925 by The Frank A. Munsey Company. Copyright renewed © 1952 and assigned to Steeger Properties, LLC. All rights reserved.

"What the Cipher Told" originally appeared in the October 24, 1925 issue of *Flynn's* magazine (Vol. 10, No. 4). Copyright © 1925 by The Frank A. Munsey Company. Copyright renewed © 1952 and assigned to Steeger Properties, LLC. All rights reserved.

"The Honest Thief" originally appeared in the November 7, 1925 issue of *Flynn's* magazine (Vol. 10, No. 6). Copyright © 1925 by The Frank A. Munsey Company. Copyright renewed © 1953 and assigned to Steeger Properties, LLC. All rights reserved.

"Another Use for Water" originally appeared in the December 5, 1925 issue of *Flynn's* magazine (Vol. 11, No. 4). Copyright © 1925 by The Frank A. Munsey Company. Copyright renewed © 1953 and assigned to Steeger Properties, LLC. All rights reserved.

"Three Out On Christmas" originally appeared in the December 12, 1925 issue of *Flynn's* magazine (Vol. 11, No. 5). Copyright © 1925 by The Frank A. Munsey Company. Copyright renewed © 1953 and assigned to Steeger Properties, LLC. All rights reserved.

"Mister Somebody Else" originally appeared in the January 9, 1926 issue of *Flynn's* magazine (Vol. 12, No. 3). Copyright © 1925 by The Frank A. Munsey Company. Copyright renewed © 1953 and assigned to Steeger Properties, LLC. All rights reserved.

Visit argosymagazine.com for more books like this.

TABLE OF CONTENTS

INTRODUCTION BY
TERRY SANFORD

AS A VORACIOUS reader who once owned a mystery book store, I found myself in a position years ago where I had read almost all of the works by my favorite authors. New authors were filling some of the gap but not quickly enough and I felt like that robot, Johnny Five, in the movie *Short Circuit:* I needed input! If you can't go forward, then why not try backward? I was fortunate to have two world-class pulp magazine collectors living nearby and they guided me into the pulp scene years before the Internet made it so much easier.

I soon discovered *Flynn's, Detective Fiction Weekly,* and its various incarnations. They were very affordable and I began amassing a pile of them. There were a dozen or so authors I soon was reading avidly. One of them was Victor Maxwell, whose Sgt. Riordan tales really impressed me as being intelligently written. Take the subject of interrogation, for instance. Now sweating a subject under a bright light in a darkened room was strictly Hollywood. Beatings from telephone books and rubber hoses did happen in the old days but you won't find that in a Riordan tale. Instead, you find, just as you do today, an investigator lying to a suspect to try to extract a confession and you find the cops concerned that a smart lawyer might shred their case in court. What was so remarkable about this was that these stories were written from 1925 until 1944. Now that is foresight!

A few years ago, I wrote an article for Steve Lewis's on-line *Mystery*File* where I highlighted some of my favorite *Detective Fiction Weekly* authors, including Victor Maxwell. I mentioned that Mr. Maxwell's name was thought to be a pseudonym and no other information about the author was readily available.

A couple of years later, Steve and I were contacted by a nice gentleman named Don Wilde who happened to be the step-grandson of the author known as Victor Maxwell. Mr. Wilde had Googled the pen name and discovered my article. He was excited to see some recognition of his Grandfather and mentioned that he had some ephemera that had belonged to the author. I asked if any of it was for sale. After several conversations, he offered to give it to me! What a bonanza for a Victor Maxwell fan!

Victor Maxwell was indeed a pseudonym. The author's

real name was known but forgotten after so many years had passed. Maxwell Vietor (1880–1950), a long-time newspaper man wrote as Victor Maxwell. Mr. Vietor was born on July 7, 1880 to Edward W. and Agnes C. (McCahey) Vietor. Edward Vietor was a medical doctor and, within a few years, so was his wife. Edward was the founder of the Brooklyn Bird (watcher's) Club, which exists today.

In January of 1882, Dr. Edward Vietor was summoned to a local residence where ten year-old Bessie Thayer had become gravely ill after eating some candy she bought at the neighborhood candy store. Although Dr. Vietor was the third physician to see the girl that day, his was the correct diagnosis: arsenic poisoning! The girl died in his presence.

Dr. Vietor subsequently testified at a Coroner's Inquest where it was resolved to turn the matter over to the police. There is no conclusion to the case that I've been able to find. Is it likely that this became a story that was mentioned from time to time in the Vietor household and fueled the imagination of young Maxwell? Perhaps.

At some point prior to 1910, the Vietors divorced. Dr. Agnes Vietor and Maxwell moved to the Boston area. Maxwell graduated from Phillips Exeter Academy in 1898. He then attended MIT where the records show, "Maxwell Vietor ex. '02 has been granted a leave of absence for one year by the faculty, in order to take up practical railroad work with the Boston and Maine R.R." Like many a college kid before and after him, Max soon realized that manual labor was not a Hispanic gentleman.

During the next ten years, Maxwell moved back to New York and began his newspaper career, first with the *Sun* and then with New York City News, a news distribution service. There was a sojourn to Wilmington, Delaware and there he may have been an "advance man for a show" as he stated once in an autobiographical piece.

By 1910, the Census Bureau shows him back in Boston, residing with his mother and employed by the *Boston Globe*. It was about this time Maxwell married Helena Haworth and the young couple soon moved to the Vancouver, Washington and Portland, Oregon area.

During 1911, Maxwell made a haphazard attempt at keeping a diary. Some of the entries deal with personal matters but many of the pages just bore the letters, "P.P." Later in the diary those initials were spelled out as "Purple Pulp." This was a humorous reference to his newspaper writing as he hadn't yet begun to write for the pulp magazines.

While the Vietors were expecting a child and Max was employed by a Portland newspaper, he continued to seek better opportunities. The diary notes a job offer from a Helena, Montana newspaper which he turned down. He also took the test and was considered for a position as a county motorcycle cop but the diary's June 10th entry reads, in part, "The motorcycle blows up!" The couple

welcomed their daughter, Alice Mildred into their life on August 15, 1911.

In 1915, tragedy struck the Vietor family. Helena's car was discovered parked by a bridge spanning the Columbia River gorge, but Helena was gone! The river flows into the Pacific Ocean from that spot, which was used by many suicidal people over the years. There was no trace of her after that day. Max would never remarry.

The January 20, 1916 issue of *The Popular Magazine* published the first Victor Maxwell story, "The Little Girl Who Got Lost." A second story appeared in the August issue of the same pulp.

Family history tells us that there were times when Max wrote for the pulps full-time and one of those periods may have been in 1917 when eight stories appeared in *The Popular* in an eight-month period.

At some unknown point in his life, Max ran for Sheriff according to him. He won the Democratic nomination but lost the election. He admits to have done some "high class gumshoeing for the state involving Wobblies" which explains a letter found in his effects from the Governor of Oregon, Ben W. Olcutt and dated April 5, 1920. The body of which reads:

"I am in receipt of your report of April 3rd, which I have read with interest. In this connection and in passing I wish to say a good word for the work you have accomplished for the state in the capacity of special agent and for your highly intelligent and understandable report made in that connection."

Reporting must have lured him back as the pulp stories ended until his first appearance in *Detective Fiction Weekly*

(hereinafter: *DFW)* in 1925. He credits his future rela-
tionship with *DFW* to Don Thompson who was a fairly
prolific *DFW* writer who convinced him to give it a try.
And try he did, as that first story became the first of exactly
one hundred appearances in the detective pulps, thanks, in
part, to a novelette that was serialized in three successive
issues of *DFW.*

Max found a home there. All but seven of his detective stories were published by *DFW.* What prompted the inquiry is lost to the ages, but in March of 1931 Max apparently wrote the editor of *DFW* asking if he thought their readers might be tiring of Sgt. Riordan. At this point in time, Max had sold them over fifty stories in five-and-a-half years. Editor Howard V. Bloomfield wrote Max saying that he did not think anyone was tired of Riordan and strongly encouraged Max to continue on or send in even more!

In addition to the detective stories, Max wrote three non-fiction articles for *DFW.* There were a smattering of other stories published in *The Popular, Railroad (&) Railroad Man's Magazine, Short Stories* and *Street & Smith's Complete Magazine.*

With his daughter grown and married, around 1938 Max moved back to the Boston area where his mother resided. He would finish his newspaper career at the *Worcester Telegram—The Evening Gazette.*

His hearing was going and he would be completely deaf in his last few years. He switched from reporting to editing copy and would communicate with his co-workers via handwritten notes. His last pulp story was in the January, 1944 issue of *New Detective Magazine.*

In 1950, increasingly worse back pain was plaguing Max. He went to the Mayo Clinic finally for help. Their diagnosis was inoperable cancer. From the clinic, he returned to the Pacific coast to be with his daughter. Just two weeks prior to his death, there was a heart-breaking exchange of letters between Max and his last employer where he was told that he was not eligible for a pension from them.

He died at a Portland hospital of a heart attack on October 4, 1950, survived by his mother and daughter. His residence, *the farm*, remains in his family to this date.

—Terry Sanford

THE PLAINLY MARKED TRACK

Old Tightwad's Safe Was Looted,
And Captain Brady Trailed The
Black Sheep By An Auto Tread

1

A CALL FROM "OLD TIGHTWAD"

"**WELL, RIORDAN, I'M** glad that's over," said Captain Brady of the detective bureau, as he hung his best, newest and most gold-braided uniform in the locker and donned the old suit in which he was more familiar to members of the department. "This being a bodyguard to a distinguished member of the President's cabinet may be all very well, and bring you in glory and cigars, but it doesn't get you anywhere save out of bed.

"Here it is two o'clock in the morning of a Sunday, and I'm just getting off duty—like it was the old days when Saturday night never ended till Sunday dawn. Don't call me till Monday morning unless somebody cracks open a bank or something."

Sergeant Riordan nodded and smiled, filled his pipe and lighted it, and settled into his place at the desk, where during Brady's absence he was titular head of the bureau. Spreading an early edition of the morning paper before him, he was just glancing at its headlines when the telephone rang. He picked up the receiver, spoke a few words, listened to some more and then turned to his chief, covering the mouthpiece of the instrument as he did so.

"It's old Ladd," he said. "Asked if you were here. I told

him I didn't think so, but that I'd look in the locker room.
He wants you."

Captain Brady swore silently. "Find out what he wants,"
he whispered.

Riordan turned to the phone again, then turned back.
"It's no use, chief, he wants you and wants you bad. I told
him I'd see what I could do."

Brady finished changing his clothes, jammed an old
hat down on his forehead, bit the end off a cigar and then
walked over to the telephone.

"This is Cap'n Brady," he said. "Sergeant just caught
me at the door—what was it you wanted? Oh, Mr. Ladd,
yes. That so? Uh-huh. All right, soon as I can get my car
started, Mr. Ladd."

He hung up the receiver and looked wistfully at Riordan. Then he gazed up at the ceiling of the office, noted
the same old cobwebs in the corner and the crack that
ran diagonally across the room, from the outer wall to the
partition that separated the private office from the outer
one. Then he looked down at his cigar, lighted it and puffed
silently. Finally he looked at Riordan again.

"A policeman," he said, getting his holster from the
locker and taking off his coat, so he could strap it over his
shoulder and around his chest, "a policeman, Riordan, gets
promoted for just three things. One is pull, one is when the
man higher up dies, retires, or is fired, and the third thing
is using his head. They made you a sergeant when they
boosted me to be captain. Take off your uniform and put
on your old clothes, get one of the boys to sit in here and
come with me. I'll be waiting down in the garage."

Riordan, used to the ways of his chief, called in Maddox

*Mrs. Sawtelle hesitated a moment, then
removed her own domino.*

to take charge of the desk, slipped out of his uniform and
into his street clothes, and a few minutes later was seated
beside Brady as the latter guided his own machine out
from behind headquarters building. He knew better than
to ask questions, for Brady spoke when he wanted to and
only then.

He surmised the call was to either Ladd's Emporium
or to the Ladd residence, and he knew it must be important, because "Old Tightwad" Ladd was probably the most
influential man in the city, and one of the richest. And
he knew very shortly they were not bound for the Ladd
residence, for Brady was driving the car into the business
district.

There was one car standing before Ladd's Emporium
and Riordan recognized it at once as Ladd's limousine.
Beside it stood the patrolman on the beat, talking to the
chauffeur, and in the doorway of the Emporium was Old
Tightwad himself and the night watchman. Brady pulled
up behind the limousine and hopped out, motioning to

Riordan to stay in the car. He walked quickly to the door-way, where Ladd drew him and the watchman inside.

"You stay here, Childs," said the merchant to his employee, "and you, captain, come with me, please."

He led the way through the silent store, its showcases swathed in covers and its aisles but dimly illuminated by the night lights, hurried back to the stairway and mounted to the second floor, going thence to his private office back in a far corner of the building. Entering he switched on the lights, motioned Brady to a chair, shut and locked the door and began pacing back and forth before his desk.

"Yuh want to call the Fidelity Company and tell 'em there was a leak in the water pipes, or something, and that's why the watchman isn't ringing in regular," said Brady. "Otherwise you'll have a pack of agency men down here when they notice the boxes ain't being rung."

Ladd stopped in his pacing, snatched at the telephone and followed the detective captain's suggestion.

"Lucky thing, Brady," he said, "that they know I have a habit of coming down here at night. Otherwise they might think it queer, me calling up at nearly three in the morning."

Then he resumed his pacing again. Brady waited three or four minutes and then spoke.

"Now that we're alone, as you might say, Mr. Ladd, suppose you tell me all about it."

The merchant stopped his restless walk.

"Safe's been robbed," he said. "Thought it might be, so I came down after the good-bys had been said at the train to the guest of honor. Inside job, Brady. Somebody who knew that the Saturday night cash would be in the store and who knew Childs's hours on the boxes.

"All Childs knows is that when he was on the fourth floor he heard an automobile start, and looking out of the window, he saw a car driving away from the freight entrance in the back. He came down here to telephone me and met me as I was coming in."

Brady looked at the safe from where he sat.

"Combination?" he inquired with a rising inflection.

"Whoever it was knew the combination."

"How much gone?"

"I don't know—can't tell till I get the returns from the bookkeeper Monday morning. Three, four, maybe five thousand. The amount doesn't make any difference—I'm carrying plenty of burglary insurance."

"What are you worrying about then?" asked Brady.

"You know," said the merchant levelly.

"I'm a captain of police, Mr. Ladd, and I don't know anything."

The merchant fidgeted on his chair. Suddenly he swung round and slammed his hand upon his desk, and with his back to the detective shouted:

"It's my son, Brady. My God! You don't know what I'm up against. I love the boy. He's always been wild. He was fired from three colleges. He never spent more than one term in any preparatory school. Finally I took him in here with me. Nobody knows that combination, Brady, but my wife, my daughter and my son. My wife was with me all night. I saw my daughter at the ball of honor the Chamber of Commerce gave for the secretary. I called up the house the minute I got here, and the servants say the boy hasn't been home all night!

"That's why I called you, Brady, and asked you to come here alone. I can't stand it any longer. If it—if it's the boy, Brady, I'm through. If it's the boy, I want you to get him and put him away. But you've got to be sure first. And if it's the boy, you've got to arrest him under some other name and railroad his trial—I'll fix the district attorney.

"If it's the boy, damn it, he's got to suffer this time; I can't cure him, though God knows I've tried. He's been thrown out of two schools under suspicion. If my son is a thief—"

"Just because he knows the combination," said Brady, "is no reason, Mr. Ladd, to blame him—"

"Brady, he's in debt up to his ears. He begged me for money, but I told him to get out of it as best as he could, that I was through putting up for him. He's always after me for money."

Captain Brady sat thoughtful for many minutes. Finally he sighed gently.

"All right, Mr. Ladd, I'll see what I can do," he said. "Does Childs know about it?"

"No—he may suspect something is wrong, because he saw you come in, and because I asked him about the automobile. He didn't see anything else—just a car driving away. He said the lights were out. It's so dark in the back of the store that he couldn't see the license number from where he was on the fourth floor. If you want to question him, you can tell him I was nervous about silk thieves, or something like that. I suppose you'll want to 'finger-print' the safe?"

Brady shook his head. "No. If it was a good man did

the job he wore gloves. If it was—if it was an amateur, we can pick up his tracks another way. And then finger-prints don't prove much in the sort of a case you think this may be—there's too many alibis possible. You call me up Monday, Mr. Ladd, after you find how much is gone. I'll report when I get anything. I'll be going now; I want to have a look around."

"I'll make it right with you, Brady. Much obliged for coming down."

2

"A HEN'S ON"

AS THE NIGHT watchman let Brady out, he asked if there was anything wrong.

"Not a thing, as far as I can see, Childs. Guess the old man was nervous about that auto you told him about—likely it was some fellow and his girl parked for a spooning time in the alley. Good night."

Once in his car, Brady swung the machine around, circled the block and stopped at the entrance to the alleyway leading to the freight entrance of the Emporium, so that the glare from his headlights illuminated the roadway.

There he got out and walked slowly up the alley, looking at the auto tracks in the dirt that had accumulated there. Right beside the loading platform was the impression of where a car had stood for some little time, with the tread of the tires plainly marked. Brady studied these tracks, and suddenly bent forward, drew out his flash light and focused its beam upon a certain spot. Then he waved to Riordan.

"You go back to headquarters as quick as you can drive," he said, "and bring a couple o' pounds of plaster of Paris and a can of water. Make it snappy—and when you come back you stop just the way the car is now, so the lights will shine in here."

Riordan and the car vanished, leaving Brady crouching in the darkness. The detective captain, looking up at the dark pile of the rear of the Emporium, shook his head slowly as he saw the lights switched off in Ladd's office. "His son," he said to himself out loud. "His son—he suspects his boy. A man must have a peculiar mind to suspect his own son of robbing him—especially a man like him. Lock him up, he says—only under another name. 'I'll fix the district attorney.' He would, too."

Ten minutes later the headlights of the car flashed in the alley again and Riordan appeared with a package and a five-gallon can filled with water. Brady took the plaster of Paris, sprinkled it plentifully over a part of the tire tracks beside the loading platform and then, pouring some of the water into the palm of his cupped hand, let it gently soak into the plaster.

Riordan, watching, grinned. "I guess I brought plenty of water, chief," he said with a chuckle.

"Maybe, lad—maybe it will be enough."

From time to time Brady poked the top of the plaster pile gingerly. He repeated this at intervals for twenty minutes. Then the door of the receiving room of the Emporium was suddenly opened and a voice said:

"Don't move or I'll drill you."

Riordan tensed, but Brady gave no sign of surprise.

"Put up your gat, Childs," he said, speaking evenly. "It's me—Brady. I'm investigatin' something for the old man."

A beam, from a flash light shot out of the dark, explored the stooping figure and then Childs laughed.

"Gosh, Brady," he said, "I thought I had 'em this time. Want any help?"

"Not a bit. Go ring your boxes."

The door of the freight entrance slid shut slowly. Brady poked the plaster pile again, then lifted the whole thing gingerly and wrapped it in his handkerchief. Stowing the cast in his coat pocket, he reached for the five-gallon can of water and, swinging it, shot its contents over the tire-marks, obliterating them completely.

"You brought just enough," he said to Riordan. "Come on. You drive me home, for I don't want to break what I've got in my pocket. It'll be good and hard by Monday, and then we can clean it up and see what we've got. In the meantime, son, you keep your mouth shut. Forget it, understand?"

"I never saw a thing, chief," laughed Riordan.

MONDAY MORNING CAPTAIN Brady deposited on the top of his desk a plaster of Paris cast, painted a slate gray, that looked surprisingly like a section of automobile tire. It had rugged markings on its tread, and in the very center was a great tear, as if the heavy rubber had been ripped off down to the fabric by a terrific skid.

This was painted a dirty white, the more to accentuate it. The cast was put in such a position that no caller in the office could escape noticing it. The newspaper reporters, on the regular morning visit to the captain of the detective bureau, spotted it at once and wanted to know all about it.

"It's a curiosity, boys," answered Brady, to their questions. "A friend of mine gave it to me. It's a cast of part of an automobile tire that got considerably torn up. That's all—there's no story."

Brady knew reporters. That was all that he would tell them, and five minutes after they had left a steady procession of police officials of all sorts began coming in to his office to "pump" him about the cast of the auto tire. None of them got any satisfaction, however, except Captain Minor, of the traffic bureau. To Minor Brady gave a sheaf of photographs of the cast.

"You give these pictures to the boys," he said. "Tell 'em to keep their eyes peeled for a tire cut up like that. Tell 'em if they see a car with a tire like that on it, to bring the driver in here. Get me, Minor? Have 'em bring the guy in here. I want to talk to him."

"Sure, I get you. But what's the dope?"

"You bring the guy that drives that tire in here, that's the dope. If you get him, there may be something more. And you might have the boys show the pictures to any auto salesmen or tire agents they know. Any line you get on that tire, you bring to me, savvy?"

When Riordan came on to relieve his chief for the night, he, too, noticed the cast.

"That's good work, chief," he said.

"Yes," said Brady. "I spent all of Sunday cleaning the sand off it and painting it. You didn't know I was an artist, did you?"

And that was all Riordan could get out of the older man.

After his chief had left for the night, Sergeant Riordan studied the cast closely for a long time. Then he went on with his routine work, only to get up every now and then and take another look at the model of part of a tire.

He, like Brady, entertained many callers who came in to look at the cast and to inquire about it; but to all questions, Riordan answered that he didn't know anything about it—it was something the captain had dragged in. Along about nine o'clock in the evening young Cliff Sterrett of the Morals Squad dropped in and took a squint at the curiosity.

"That's the same kind of a tire as Jimmy Rathbun had on that car he drove in the races out at the track," he said. "I'd know that tread anywhere."

"So," commented Riordan casually.

"Yeah, he told me at the time he had the tires specially made back East. He said a tread like that would give him lots of traction."

"Racing tires, eh?"

"Yeah, you know, I was out at the track looking for gamblers. I knowed Jimmy a long time—he's working down at the Ajax auto shop now. Quit racing, he has. They say he's a swell mechanic."

Riordan nodded. After waiting awhile to see if his information would get a rise out of the sleuth, Sterrett left. Five minutes later Riordan called up Brady and imparted the information to him.

"You're a good kid," said Brady. "But don't say anything. You'd better lay off early to-night and put somebody else on. I may want you to-morrow. Show up at noon."

Riordan looked at his watch, did a little work and at half past ten put Maddox on the desk again and went out. He dropped into the Panama Billiard Parlors on his way home, bought a near-beer and sat down at one of the side tables to drink it. Very shortly he was joined by "Lucky Tom" Ruble, who operated the place. They chatted about one thing and another, all in the sporting line, and finally the subject of automobile racing came up. Riordan made some comment about the Indianapolis speedway, Ruble told an anecdote or two, and then the sleuth said:

"By the way, I suppose you'll put on some more races here this fall? I hear you cleaned up big on them last year."

"I dunno," answered Ruble judiciously. "Once with them things is almost enough. These here hippodrome races, you know, is all framed. There's a gang of riders go round the country, see? They come into a town and get some wise guy, like me, to put up some cups and to back the thing.

"The gate, of course, is split with the winners—and then there's some side betting. There was a lot of betting on Jimmy Rathbun last year—local guy, you know, and all that. They made a come-on out of him. He had no more chance than you. In the first place he didn't know the racing game, and in the second place they doctored his gas. Once for them things is about enough for me, I guess. Happen again, the home boys might get suspicious; you know how it is."

"Rathbun put up any money," asked Riordan.

"Somebody did," said Ruble. "That special car he had built must have set him back considerable. Besides that he had a lot of money bet on himself. I never knew Rathbun was any million-dollar guy, so I didn't say nothing. But somebody backed him, and somebody got trimmed."

All of which Riordan recounted to his chief next day at noon, and Captain Brady seemed much pleased with the information.

"You got a good head on you, Riordan," he said. "A good head and a close mouth. That's what you want in this police business. Let the other fellow talk. Well, you sit down and read the funny papers or something for a spell, till I look over these reports and then we'll go riding. I got a hen on, and I want you to help me count the eggs. Two heads are better'n one, you know—and you got a good head on you."

3

FINDING THE TIRE

BRADY SCANNED HIS reports and routine papers for some minutes, and then laid them aside, pulled shut the roll-top cover of his desk and swung round in his chair.

"You had your lunch?" he asked Riordan.

"No, chief. Just got up out o' bed. Had breakfast, though. Hot cakes and coffee and bacon and biscuits and peach pie with ice cream on it—you see, whenever I get up early like this, it sort of mixes up my meals."

Brady nodded sagely as if considering the information.

"I've had lunch, too," he said "Ate round at the Emporium's lunch room, on the top floor. There's a jane up there I used to know once. I was asking her about young Ladd. Maybe you don't know it, but we're working on the robbery of Ladd's safe—up in his private office, where I was Sunday morning while you waited outside.

"Old Tightwad says four people knew the combination—himself, his wife, his son and his daughter. He don't know where his son was that night, the rest of 'em he's catalogued. Seems he thinks the boy is a wild blade. He's got him working in the store as superintendent of delivery, trying to tame him down.

"This here jane that I knew, says all the girls in the place are trying to make a hit with young Bob Ladd, but that he don't notice 'em none, acting always like he had something on his mind and was too tired to think of two kinds of trouble at once. You might say my lunch wasn't very profitable, outside of that. They don't serve you much for twenty-nine cents."

"The old man thinks it was an inside job, eh?" said Riordan. "That's why he's so quiet about it, I suppose. Who are you goin' to put on the kid?"

"Nobody. If the lad did it, he'll tip his hand. But I'm not sure he did."

"Why?"

"Well, from all I can hear, the lad's a good sport—wild all right, but a good sport. And a real sport don't usually rob his own nest. He may rob the next guy, but not his own folks. Not of money, that is."

"Has he got an auto?" asked Riordan.

"The Ladd garage is a quarter of a block big. There's more cars in it than a taxi-cab company would have. I guess he's got one."

"Had anybody check on their tires?" Riordan pointed to the cast on top of his chief's desk.

Brady shook his head. "I don't figure the fellow who tapped that safe was a plain fool," he said. Then he rose, put on his hat and motioned Riordan to follow him. The two went down to the police garage, climbed into Brady's machine and drove off.

It seemed to Riordan they were circling about aimlessly at first, but presently Brady straightened out on his route and drove rapidly to the Ajax agency, pulling in to the shop entrance. To a floorman who came up, he said he wanted to see Jimmy Rathbun.

The mechanician soon appeared. He was a bright-looking youngish chap with an open countenance. He looked inquiringly at Brady and then swiftly surveyed his car.

"Trouble?" he asked.

"None at all, Rathbun. I'm Captain Brady of the detective bureau. This is Sergeant Riordan. We got to have a small, quick car for use in trouble, and one of the motorcycle men told me you had that old racing machine yet that you used in the races last fall. Want to sell it?"

"I'd sell my shirt, captain, if anybody offered me a fair price."

"Well, what's the racer worth?"

"I dunno, captain. I'll have to ask my partner. You see, that old bus is a sort of a cooperative concern. That is, it was."

"Who's your partner and where can we find him?"

Rathbun thrust his tongue into his cheek and hesitated. Then he said:

"He don't work days—he works here nights. I'll see him this evening. Meanwhile I tell you what you do— if you want to. You run out to my houses—2141 Laurel Avenue—and tell mother to let you in the garage. The car's there. You look it over and see what you want to offer for it.

"The engine's in good shape, but one of the tires is just about gone. I was coming down town in it the other night to go to a show and got caught on the railroad crossing. I had to jam the brakes on to keep from pushing a freight train over. One of the tires caught on a spike or something in the crossing and darned near tore apart."

"All right, Rathbun, we'll go look at it and make you an offer. See you later."

Brady backed his machine out of the shop and drove in silence to the address he had been given. There he and Riordan climbed out, rang the doorbell and waited. There was no answer, apparently Rathbun's mother was out. So they made their way to the rear of the house, found the garage unlocked and went in.

The racing car, revealed as they opened the swinging doors of the shed in which it was kept, was speedy looking, but neither officer thought of that. They both looked at its front tires—of the same patterned tread as the plaster mould in Brady's office. Both of the same mind, they stepped back to the rear wheels, Brady on one side, and Riordan on the other.

"Same here," said Riordan.

"Come and take a look," said Brady. Riordan stepped around the machine and gasped. There was no tire at all on the rear wheel on Brady's side—the rim was resting on the ground. Under the car was a tipped-over jack.

"Give a hand and shove it ahead," said Brady, "then we'll be sure."

They pushed the machine forward until the parts of the tires that had been resting on the ground were exposed. The three tires were whole and unmarred.

"And he said his partner worked nights," murmured Riordan. "We just ought to talk to his pal, eh, chief?"

Brady shook his head. "Not yet, son," he answered. "We'll push this car back the way it was and then I want to telephone. We'll drive to the nearest box—there's one down the block—I noticed it as we came up."

They returned the car to its original position, made a silent, quick, but careful survey of the garage, and then departed. At the call-box Brady alighted and rang headquarters. Riordan listened.

"Gimme the dicks," he heard his chief say. "Who's this— Grimes? This is Brady. Hop one of the boys down to the Ajax agency shop and get hold of the mechanic there, Jimmy Rathbun. Bring him to my office. I'll be in by the time you get him there."

Returning to the car, Brady turned on the siren and "stepped on her." In less than ten minutes his machine whizzed into the headquarters garage and a minute later he and Riordan were upstairs in his office.

The first thing he did was to pick up the cast of the torn tire and place it in his coat locker. Then he sat down. Riordan was about to say something when the door was thrust open and a traffic officer pushed his way in, leading a chauffeur in private livery.

"Cap'n Minor, sir, said for us to bring in anybody driving a car with a tire like that in the pictures he gave us, sir," said the officer. "This bird was driving a big car with a tire torn just like that, marked the same way and everything. He put up a squawk about coming in, captain; said he was Mrs. Millicent Sawtelle's private driver and was on his way to pick her up at the Belmont Hotel."

"Very good," said Brady. "Leave him be here and return to your post. I'll tell Captain Minor about your good work—you're Benedict, if I make you right."

"Benedict's my name, captain. Yes, sir."

As the traffic man closed the door behind him, Brady turned to the chauffeur.

"What's your name?"

"James Wilson, sir."

"Who do you drive for?"

"Mrs. Millicent Sawtelle, sir."

"What's the license number of your car?"

"Five, eight, two, ought, nine, sir."

"Look it up, Riordan."

The sergeant turned to an auto register and quickly found the number. "That's it, chief," he said.

"Where were you going when the traffic officer stopped you?" Brady asked of the chauffeur.

"To the Belmont Hotel, sir. Mrs. Sawtelle phoned for me to be there at two o'clock. If you please, sir, if there's anything wrong, will you let me phone for a taxicab to meet her—she's very particular."

"You can get there at two o'clock if you talk straight, Wilson. Otherwise you can't get there or phone. Now listen, I want to know how you came to have that torn tire on your car. You know damned well it isn't Mrs. Sawtelle's tire. And don't try to stall me about it being a spare you picked up in some shop."

"Mrs. Sawtelle told me to put it on, sir."

"She did, eh? Well, why would she tell you to put an old, rotten tire like that on her car? Has she gone broke all of a sudden, that she can't buy new tires? Last I heard, Mrs. Sawtelle's husband was still one of the richest men in town."

"It's Gawd's truth, captain. She came to me Monday morning out at the garage. 'Wilson,' she says, 'there's a tire on the front porch I wish you'd put on the big car. Keep it there till I tell you to take it off.' I done what I was told, sir."

4

THE SHADY PARTNER

BRADY LOOKED AT the man closely. "Suppose I lock you up for half a day, do you think you can figure out a new one?" he asked.

"S' help me Heaven, captain, it's the truth. You don't think I'd frame up a fool lie like that, do you? I could think of a lot better story. I've seen some crazy going-ons from the Sawtelles, captain, but this has got 'em all beat. But I get paid for minding my own business and driving the car, so I should worry."

"Monday morning, eh, she told you to put it on?"

"Yes, sir."

"The car downstairs now?"

"Yes, sir, I drove round here with the traffic cop riding beside me. I had to—he said he'd drill me if I didn't."

"And he would have," commented Brady; "he's a bad hombre, he is. Eats chauffeurs for breakfast every day. Well, I tell you what you're going to do. We'll go downstairs— or you will—with Riordan here, and drive round to the garage in back of headquarters. There we'll take that tire off and give you a good cord tire, same size, like we use on the patrol. And if Mrs. Sawtelle wants to know why you changed tires, you tell her. Go on, now, and get out of here."

Riordan and the chauffeur left and Brady swung round to his desk, opened it and pressed a button. To the doorman who answered, he said:

"Bring me Sunday's *Chronicle*."

A few moments later he had the paper, brought in from the bureau files, and at once he opened it to the society section and began to read. He was still reading the columns devoted to the doings of the alleged upper crust of the city's inhabitants, when Riordan returned, carrying the torn tire with him.

"Lean it against the desk," said Brady without looking up.

Riordan placed the tire at the side of the desk with the tear down next the floor. Brady went on reading, until a knock sounded on the door.

"See who it is, Riordan. You notice the difference between my boys and them traffic hounds, don't you? My men knock, them speed demons just rush in."

"It's Grimes with the Rathbun lad, chief."

"Bring Rathbun in here."

The mechanician entered, fingering his cap nervously. Brady swung around and looked at him.

"That your tire there?" he asked, pointing beside his desk.

Rathbun advanced, picked the tire up, spread it apart and turned it around.

"Yes, sir," he said. "There's my initials inside of it. I always mark my casings that way—with red ink."

"Well, I suppose you wonder how I got hold of it, don't you? It wasn't on your car. Riordan and I went out to your garage to look that racer over. It had been jacked up and this tire was gone. It just happened I run across the tire on another machine down town. Now you and me are going to have a talk."

"Am I under arrest?" demanded the mechanician.

Brady frowned. "Now listen to me, young man," he said. "Don't you go getting onto a high horse. I'm captain of the detective bureau and under the law I got a right, when investigating a crime, to go pick up any person I think may be connected therewith, question him and hold him for forty-eight hours for investigation.

"I'm investigating a crime right now and I've had you brought in here for questioning. You're not accused of anything and you can talk or not, just as you want to. But it shall depend on how you talk, how long you stay here. Get me?"

"I guess so."

"Well, that's good. Now who's this partner of yours who has an interest in that old racing car of yours and who works nights?"

Rathbun considered awhile.

"I guess I don't answer that one captain," he finally said levelly.

Brady got up, walked over to the locker and drew out the plaster cast. He held it before Rathbun, then bent over and turned the tire over until the tear was on top.

"Compare them two," he said. "What do you make of 'em?"

The mechanician's interest was awakened at once. He examined the painted cast closely; then his own tire. He fingered both, comparing them minutely. Then he looked up puzzled.

"That's a cast of my tire," he said.

"Wrong," snapped Brady. "That's a cast of a print in the mud that some tire made. Riordan and I took the cast Sunday morning."

The puzzled frown on Rathbun's forehead deepened.

"I suppose you want to know where I was Sunday morning?" he said.

"Nope—I want to know who this partner of yours is."

"I haven't got any right to tell you, captain." The answer was immediate and firm.

Brady leaned forward. "Listen to me, Jimmy," he said not unkindly. "This partner of yours is evidently a good friend—your pal. You don't think he's done any wrong. I don't know that he has either. But Riordan and I made that cast near where a crime had been committed.

"You admit that's your tire and you're convinced that the cast proves that your tire was on an automobile near where that crime was committed. You've told me you couldn't sell your car until you consulted your partner. Get the drift? Now, in order to clear this thing up, I want to know who your partner is."

"He's an all-right guy," said Rathbun. "He works nights down at the Ajax shop—from half past six in the evening until two in the morning. Punches the time clock. He wasn't mixed up in this at all."

"What's his name?"

"I won't tell you."

"Don't be a fool, Rathbun. I can get him, same as I got you. All I've got to do is to send a man up to the shop tonight and bring him in. You tell me his name and maybe I won't have to."

The mechanician considered this. It was so palpably

true that he began to view the proceedings in a different light—his face showed that. At last he spoke.

"I'll tell you, captain," he said. "He's young Robert Ladd. He doesn't work under that name, though. At the shop they've got him listed as Robert Laddson. Ladd's been pretty good to me in times past, and he came to me shortly after he was fired—after he left college—and said he had to have some extra money and wanted to work for it.

"I got him a job as helper at the shop on the night crew. He's bright and quick and they've advanced him. He's assistant to the night foreman now. I know they say he's been wild and all that, but take it from me, captain, he's a real guy. And straight. He made me promise not to tip off who he was and I never have until now."

Brady's face softened and his eyes smiled. He got up, put one hand on Rathbun's shoulder and extended his other hand for a hearty grip.

"Jimmy," he said in his kindliest tone, "you're all right. You've done young Bob Ladd a big favor. And me. I admire your grit and I'll keep your confidence. Nobody's going to bother you nor Bob any more—nobody from this office. You can tell him, if you want to, how I've treated you—all about your call here—but you assure him it's all right.

"And I thank you for the information. I hope you won't bear any ill feelings toward me; we have to do our—work in our own way. You can go any time—but I want to keep this tire for awhile. When I get through, I'll bring it back to you."

"I'm sure relieved, captain," said Rathbun. "And I don't hold anything against you. I'm glad you're so sure Bob's all right—for he is. But I wish you'd tell me what this crime is, that you speak about. I didn't know the tire was off my car—I'd like to know who took it."

"So would I, Jimmy. When I find out, maybe I'll tell you. By the way, did you lose much when you lost that race last fall—much money, I mean?"

"I didn't lose very much, captain. Just my savings."

"Bob Ladd lose some?"

"Well, yes, captain, he did. He put up most of the money—I always figured that was why he wanted to go to work and earn some."

"How much do you think he dropped?"

"I don't know, captain. I never could get him to tell me how much he bet on the race; but I guess it was plenty."

"This fellow Ruble, down at the Panama Billiard Parlors—did he lose much?"

"I don't think so, captain—he was stakeholder. I don't reckon he bet anything."

"Well, I hope you win next time. Much obliged for the information, Rathbun."

When the office door had closed behind the mechanician, Brady motioned Riordan to a chair.

"What you think of it?" he asked.

"I'd say it don't look so good for Bob Ladd, chief."

"You haven't got as much head as I thought you had, Riordan. Or else you haven't studied this."

Riordan looked surprised. "It's open and shut, isn't it, chief?" he asked. "Ladd knew the combination to the safe, he had an interest in the car with that tire, he knew the store, he needed money, and we found the imprint of the tire in the alley back of the store?"

5

A CALLER AT HEADQUARTERS

THE TELEPHONE ON Brady's desk rang sharply.

"You answer it, Riordan. Tell 'em I'm out—and I'm going out, too. I'm going down across the street to get some cigars. Take the message."

When Brady came back Riordan was walking up and down the office. The captain looked at him and grinned. "Wasn't it Mrs. Sawtelle?" he asked.

"She said she was, chief. I don't know the lady's voice. She said she was Mrs. Sawtelle and she wanted to speak to you. I told her you were out. She said to tell you she was much obliged to you for giving her chauffeur a new tire when his blew out in front of the police station and to send her a bill for the tire and she'd pay it."

"Yeah, I thought she would. And she will, too." Brady's face grew suddenly hard. Then it softened into a smile again.

"And you still think it looks black for Bob Ladd?"

"Why, yes, chief."

"You poor dummy. Now listen to me. Who's Millicent Sawtelle? She's the wife of Jake Sawtelle, investments and mortgages, and the sharpest business crook we've got in the city. Everything within the letter of the law, but that's all.

She's one of our society queens, always giving bridge and Mah Jong parties, and also got a roulette wheel.

"Lots of money, all the time. And she tells her chauffeur to put this old tire on her car. What for? So we'll find it. She knows we're looking for it. And she wants us to find it. Why? So as to alibi for the party that tapped 'Old Tightwad' Ladd's safe. How alibi—because Sunday all day and all Sunday night she was out at the Country Club with her car.

"And if her car and that tire were out there, how could they be in the alley back of the Emporium? Her alibi is in the papers—and here on the society page is a whole column all about the party she gave out there and the impromptu auto races they had on the track by moonlight."

"Young Ladd is in her set," protested Riordan. "Maybe he owed her money—gambling money. Framed the tire stuff with her—"

"You poor fish, he was working in the Ajax shop Sunday night. When I went out to buy cigars, I telephoned out there and the timekeeper says yes, there was a gang working overtime."

"But he could get somebody else to punch his card for him—young Rathbun, his pal, for instance."

Brady snorted. "You think just like a harnessed bull," he said. "You got an idea in your head and you try and make everything fit it. Do you figure if a fellow as clever as young Ladd is, and a woman as clever as Mrs. Sawtelle is, were in cahoots, they'd go get a marked tire like that and plant tracks and alibis all around? No, sir, they'd know there were too many people mixed up in it.

"There may have been two on this job, but that was all.

Personally, I think there was only one. If your dope was any good, Mrs. Sawtelle, Bob Ladd, Jimmy Rathbun, the chauffeur—they'd all have been in it. And Rathbun and the chauffeur talk straight and reasonable. Their talk is reasonable and true, because it is just the opposite of what you'd expect if your line was right. Use your head."

Riordan puzzled over his chief's discourse. "Well," he asked at length, "what are you going to do about it?"

"Wait," said Brady. "Just wait—and nose around a bit. All you got to do in a case like this is wait and use your head—not go off at half cock and try to 'make' the first guy you might suspect. This thing was all planted for a big roar—news in the papers about the robbery and all that. Well, there wasn't any roar. The papers don't know that Ladd's safe has been tapped.

"There was no noise. Yet the people interested are going ahead and shoving alibis under our noses. They want to lead us off the scent. All we've got to do is to wait and pretty soon we'll get the lead we want. If I can wait, you can. So wait, boy, and use your head."

"But, chief, if she told the chauffeur to put that tire on her car Monday morning—Mrs. Sawtelle, I mean—how would we think it was out at the Country Club?"

"Because she figured we'd question *her*. She don't know yet that the chauffeur spilled the beans. What did she say he'd told her? That he had a blow-out in front of the police station. You don't suppose any servant is going to tell the madam that he's been pinched and brought in, do you— not if he can alibi out of it? She figured the blow-out was a streak of luck.

"She was hoping one of the cops would pick up the car

when she was in it—then she could pull a lot of high-tone stuff about being embarrassed and how she wasn't here when the thing happened. She was figuring there would be a roar, I tell you. That tire was used as a plant—to leave tracks in the alley. The chauffeur isn't going to tell her that he was dragged in here and that he told us she was a nut. He's got his job to look out for—so *he* invented the story about the blow-out to save *his* face."

"Then you think the Sawtelle woman had a hand in the robbery?"

"No, but I think the robber told her part of it and made it worth her while to play in the game.

"Well, then, why ain't it Bob Ladd?"

Brady threw up his hands. "You're hopeless. Forget Bob Ladd—and if you can't do anything else, wait and see."

IT WAS NEARLY midnight. Sergeant Riordan, sitting in Captain Brady's office, and in charge of the first night relief work, shook his head and gave it up. There had been little to do throughout the evening and he had ample time to think over Brady's remarks. Brady was regarded as a great man, he knew, but he was sure Brady was getting old. There was no reason to his theories; that is, no valid police reasoning, of the sort with which Riordan was most familiar.

The doorman entered and said there was a young man outside who wanted to speak to the officer in charge. "Captain Brady, he said, he preferred to see. I told him the cap'n was home to bed and that you was in charge. He wants to see you. He wouldn't give his name."

"Show him in," said Riordan.

The man withdrew and a moment later the caller entered

the office of the commander of the detective bureau. He was clean-cut, good looking, but pale.

"Would it be possible for you to get in touch with Captain Brady," he asked. "I have something very important—"

"Tell it to me," interrupted Riordan. "I'm in charge here. I know most all of Captain Brady's cases; I'm his sergeant."

The caller hesitated a moment and his eyes roved over the office, and then became fixed on the plaster cast of the tire, which had been restored to its place on Brady's desk. He looked at it a long time, then shifted his gaze, and caught sight of the tire itself, leaning against the side of the desk. He slowly drew himself together and then spoke.

"I'm Robert Ladd—or Laddson. I've come here to give myself up."

Riordan could not help but feel elation. But he tried not to show it.

"Yeah—and for what," he asked.

"That—that job there," said his caller. "The thing you've got that tire-cast for. I did it. I've been thinking about it a long time and I've decided to give myself up, plead guilty, and have it over with at once. All I ask is that you call me Laddson in whatever action you may take, and keep it as quiet as possible. I want to save my family."

Riordan's elation began to ebb. He could not just tell why. But instead, a feeling of protest against this thing began to steal over him.

"Very well, Mr. Laddson," he said. "Sit down and let's get it all regular. Now just what is it that you want to plead guilty to?"

The young man looked a trifle more worried. "You are

holding that tire as evidence in a criminal case, are you not?"

"We are."

"Well, I am the man you want in that case. I committed the crime which you are investigating. Afterward, I escaped in the automobile that Captain Brady was talking to Jimmy Rathbun about to-day. When I—when I had gone away, I happened to think that this particular tire was strikingly marked and I took it off the car, put on a spare tire, and threw this tire away. I threw it where you found it."

"You what?"

"I say I threw that tire away. I threw it where you found it."

Sergeant Riordan leaned forward in his chair.

"Listen," he said. "Don't try to kid me—especially on this case. It's on my nerves. What did you say you did with that tire?"

"I threw it away to hide my tracks. I threw it where you found it."

"Well, it was a darned good throw, young man. We found that tire on a woman's automobile, right down town in the shopping district. How did you happen to pick her car to throw it on to—and what did you do with the tire that was already on her car when this one of yours knocked it off?"

In spite of himself, young Ladd laughed and ended it in a sob.

"Never mind the tire, man," he said. "I committed the crime. I plead guilty."

Riordan stroked his chin. "To all the booze, and everything?" he asked.

His caller seemed suddenly relieved.

"Yes, yes," he said quickly. "I took the booze in my car. It was my booze; I bought it, and was going to sell it. I'm a bootlegger."

"That's funny, too," continued Riordan. "There wasn't any booze in this case—none at all. Try another one."

"Well, I did it, whatever it was. If you didn't get the booze, that isn't my fault."

6

AT THE MASQUERADE

RIORDAN TIPPED BACK in his chair and regarded the broad toes of his heavy shoes.

"As a matter of fact," he said slowly, "I don't think you did it at all. You're trying to shield somebody."

"I'm not—I did it, I tell you."

"Well, then, answer me this—and come clean on it—whose car did we find that tire on?"

The young man looked earnestly at Riordan for a long time. Then he asked:

"As man to man, sergeant, if I tell you whose car you found that tire on, will you give me your word to accept my plea of guilty?"

Riordan did some thinking. Finally he said:

"I'm a man of my word, Mr. Ladd. If you tell me whose car we found that tire on, I'll accept your plea."

His caller paled noticeably.

"You found it on my sister's car,"

"Ah!" The exclamation escaped Riordan's lips involuntarily.

"Remember your word," said his caller. "You must accept my plea—leave her out of it."

"Get a chair and sit down, son. That's it. Relax. Your

troubles are all over now. Take a long breath. There, that's the stuff. Unbutton your vest and feel real easy, because you and I are going to have a talk." Riordan reached into Brady's desk and drew forth a box of cigars. "Here, have one of these?—soothe your nerves. Here's a match."

The sergeant took his time in putting the cigar box back in its place. Then he leaned forward.

"Now listen. You and me is pals, see? You're afraid your sister has done something, and you want to shield her. That shows you're a real man. You've shielded her before, I guess. However, that's all aside from this. Now listen to me—we haven't got a thing on your sister. If I didn't read the papers, I wouldn't know you had a sister.

"We found that tire on Mrs. Millicent Sawtelle's car. She had it put there. We got nothing to worry your sister about at all, see. She's all right—and she's got a fine brother.

"But I want you to come all the way, now that you've come so far. I want you to tell me what you were so afraid of. What do you know about this Sawtelle woman? Just between you and me, tell me. Remember, your sister isn't in this at all—officially."

"Are you sure, sergeant?"

"You bet I am. Cap'n Brady and me, we've checked on all your family. Know where your father was, where your mother was, where your sister was, where you were. And we got pretty good evidence where Mrs. Sawtelle was at the time we're interested in. What do you know about her—real inside stuff, I mean."

Young Ladd looked at the end of his cigar, then watched the smoke curl up toward the ceiling.

"I'll tell you, sergeant. She's a—a devil. She's teaching a

lot of young girls and boys to gamble and to drink and to be fast. The young folks think she's what they call 'smart,' and they imitate her. Just because her husband is a prominent man here and she's in society, they think what she does is clever. They can't see—oh, you know.

"They gamble at all the parties she gives. I believe half of the young people in her set owe her money. I think her card playing is crooked. I've heard she's got a roulette wheel, and if she has, I'll bet that's crooked. My sister goes there a lot—and she's lost money. She's come to me for help, she's afraid to go to my father. I've done what I could.

"Back last fall my sister owed Mrs. Sawtelle pretty nearly two thousand dollars, all from gambling and jazzing around. Then these automobile races came on and Jimmy Rathbun thought he could win. We backed him—my sister and I. I gave him all the money I had and Sis borrowed all she could get—and pawned some of her jewelry—and we backed Jimmy. He lost.

"Father thinks I'm a black sheep—I guess I raised a good deal of hell when I was younger—but I've tried to settle down. I've been working nights to get extra money—father's cut off the allowance I used to have and doesn't pay me more than enough to live on at the store. I've been trying to get sister on her feet, so she could break away from that Sawtelle crowd.

"But she's in trouble again—I don't know how much, she won't tell me. And when Jimmy told me that you had him down here—about that tire—well, I figured the only thing I could do was what I did. You see I figured Sis had taken the car out and gone and done something. I was the black sheep; I was willing to take the blame. I figured I could stand it and I hoped the shock of the thing would straighten her up. That's the whole of it."

"You're all right and here's my hand, son," said Riordan. "Now you go on home and go to bed and to sleep and don't you worry. And what you've told me to-night is all forgotten, see? Only you tell your sister this for me—and I mean it. You tell her to cut out that Sawtelle woman and do it quick. That's all."

For a long time after Ladd left the office, Riordan sat plunged in thought, repeatedly shaking his head. Then he turned to the telephone and told the exchange operator to waken Captain Brady. When he got his chief on the line, he said:

"Put on your slippers, captain. I'm coming up to talk to you. I want to tell you that you're right and I was wrong—and I can prove it."

Ten o'clock the following Saturday night Captain Brady and Sergeant Riordan, resplendent in their best uniforms, stepped from a taxicab at a drug store near the Sawtelle home, crowded themselves into a telephone booth, and Brady called up Police Chief Olmstead.

"This is Brady, chief," he said. "Did Mrs. Sawtelle ask you to send anybody up to her masquerade to-night?"

"Sure she did, Brady. I sent Reynolds and Peterson up there. With a mob like that in the house somebody's got to be on watch."

"How many men did she ask for, chief?"

"She didn't specify. She just asked me to send somebody up. What's the big idea, somebody crack the place?"

"Not yet, chief. But I want you to send me and Riordan up there, too."

"Well, go on up. I won't stop you."

"That isn't the idea, chief. I want orders to go—I got a reason. I want you to remember, too, that you ordered me to go there."

"Something doing, eh, Brady? Well, all right—go up to Sawtelle's and take a man with you."

"Much obliged, chief. And don't you ever forget that you ordered me to go up there. Good-by."

Chuckling like two schoolboys, the officers walked from the booth, turned into the street, and made their way to the brilliantly lighted Sawtelle mansion. As they neared its entrance, they both slipped black domino masks over their eyes. The footman at the door and the butler within gave them hardly a glance as they entered the hallway, in which shrieks of laughter and strains of music were echoing—there were many uniforms that night among the guests.

7

FOUR MINUTES AND $4,000

THE TWO POLICEMEN moved slowly here and there among the guests, into this room and that, replying with laughter to the quips thrown their way by other masked and costumed figures, and for a brief space they even stood about a long table, at one end of which a croupier was manipulating a roulette wheel, while throngs crowded about, some to watch and some to play.

There was real money on the board, in coin and currency. Finally the two approached a man in clown costume standing near a sideboard on which were various kinds of liquid refreshment.

"You Reynolds or Peterson," said Brady. "The costume's so good I can't tell."

"Reynolds," replied the clown.

"I'm Brady—maybe you recognized me. Which one of these here is the madam herself?"

"That one over there in green—with her back all bare and not too much on the rest of her," answered Reynolds, pointing a big hand at the most daringly dressed woman in the throng. "How'd you know me, cap?"

Brady laughed. "I'm a dick, ain't I?" he answered and with Riordan walked away. A moment later he was on one side of the figure in shimmering green and Riordan was on the other.

"I'm Captain Brady, of the detective bureau, Mrs. Sawtelle," he said speaking quietly, almost in her ear. "Don't make a fuss, but move quickly. Sergeant Riordan and I have got to see you in private for a minute at once."

She turned to the gorgeously uniformed officer and let out a squeal of laughter. "Oh," she exclaimed, "the policemen have arrested me and are taking me away," and as her guests shouted with glee she led the two officers, though seeming to be led by them, from the big room, across a hall and into a smaller chamber. Outside they could hear the shouts of mirth from the guests at what they all regarded as a clever bit of buffoonery.

Brady whipped off his mask at once and Riordan did the same. Mrs. Sawtelle hesitated a moment, then removed her own domino, and faced the officers inquiringly.

"Is something the matter, captain," she asked.

"Something very much is the matter, Mrs. Sawtelle. Otherwise I would not have disturbed you. Chief Olmstead sent me and Riordan here. I will be brief. Miss Florence Ladd has been gambling in this house for a long time and you have been winning money from her, putting her in more deeply all the time. Recently you put the screws on her. Driven desperate, she entered her father's store last Saturday night, while most everybody in the city was at the reception to the distinguished cabinet member we had as our guest, and robbed the safe.

"You were at the Country Club at the time. Early Monday morning Miss Ladd came to you, gave you the money, and asked you as a favor, to put a tire she left on the porch on your car. Possibly she told you why. You did. Now I want you to go get that money and give it to me. Then we'll forget all about it."

Mrs. Sawtelle's face was hard. "Do you know what my husband will do to you, captain, for this attempt at blackmail," she asked coldly.

"I know what he won't do, Mrs. Sawtelle. He will be too busy defending you and your guests. There is gambling going on here to-night. Four police officers, more or less disguised, are among your guests. They have seen it. They are so posted that they can at once seize the evidence.

"You are also violating the prohibition laws. They have evidence of that. I have the house surrounded and in five minutes, if I do not countermand the order outside, half the policemen in the city will rush in here and place everybody under arrest. Your parties and your behavior have reached the limit—passed it.

"But, to save a foolish young girl, and her family, I will countermand these orders, if you give back that money. After you have given it back, it will be a good plan for your health, I think, if you take a trip to Europe or California. I will wait here four minutes for your return. At the end of four minutes Riordan and I will go to the front and rear doors to see that nobody leaves this house in the confusion."

"I haven't the money here," she said. "I will get you a check."

"Checks won't do, Mrs. Sawtelle. Riordan and I will wait here four minutes—it is now a quarter of eleven, exactly."

She looked at him steadily for several seconds, but Brady was looking at his watch. Riordan was looking at Brady. She turned and walked through the door. Neither officer moved. Two minutes later she was back, a black leather wallet in her hand. She gave it to Brady, who thrust it in his hip pocket, pulled his uniform coat down over it, donned his domino, and turned toward the door.

"I want a receipt," she said, her voice stopping him.

Riordan whipped out a pad and pencil.

"How much is here," asked Brady.

"Four thousand, five hundred dollars," she answered coldly.

Brady scrawled upon the pad, tore off the sheet and handed it to her. Then he opened the door and Riordan followed him out.

Mrs. Sawtelle looked at the sheet of paper in her hand, and laughed grimly:

> Received of Mrs. Millicent Sawtelle four thousand five hundred dollars, being payment in full for one automobile tire furnished her chauffeur.
>
> MICHAEL RIORDAN.

Outside Brady and Riordan hailed a taxi and sped to the home of Ladd—"Old Tightwad"—owner of the Emporium. A maid who answered their ring said Mr. Ladd was in the library. He rose to greet the two men.

Brady handed him the black wallet. "There's your money, Mr. Ladd—that was taken from the safe," he said.

Old Tightwad opened the wallet, then he looked up in surprise.

"There's too much here, captain," he said. "We checked up Monday and the thief only got three thousand nine hundred and eighty. I was expecting you to call every day and get the amount."

"I was busy getting the money, sir. Well, if there's too much, you'd better give the balance to your son, Mr. Robert, sir. He needs it. He had nothing to do with the robbery, sir. He's foreman of the night crew down at the Ajax garage, working every night so as to pay his debts. I think you have misjudged him, sir."

The merchant winced, as if he had been struck a blow, then smiled slowly.

"Are you sure, captain," he asked.

"I can prove it, sir—I had to prove it to myself."

Old Tightwad took a deep breath. "Oh, captain," he said, "that's better than getting the money back. You can't know, captain, how I've suffered—"

"And you don't know how he's suffered, Mr. Ladd, if you'll pardon my saying it. I think you two have misunderstood each other, sir."

The merchant fingered the wallet awhile, then placed it on the table. Then he tensed.

"The thief, Brady—who was it?"

Captain Brady's voice was low as he answered:

"Man to man, Mr. Ladd, I'm not going to tell you. It wasn't your boy. It wasn't a natural-born thief, either. It was somebody who was in a jam, and who was being threatened with blackmail by a real crook. We've got the big crook—run 'em out of town.

"Let the little fellow go, like we're going to do, Mr. Ladd; and don't make another mistake, like you made with your son. The thief, I think, has learned a lesson—and you got enough more back there, to make it worth your while to forget it. And you've found your boy is all right. Let it go at that, sir—and you'll be doing the best thing."

THE WORK OF AN ARTIST

*Sergeant Riordan Undertook To Defend
His Nationality And Incidentally
Settled Another Important Matter*

1

DEFENDING THE IRISH

ARTIST—One who shows trained skill or rare taste coupled
with inspiration in any occupation.
(Unabridged.)

WHEN CAPTAIN OF Detectives Brady entered his office at
headquarters Monday morning, he was surprised to find
Sergeant Riordan, his right-hand aide, who had charge of
the detective bureau during the first night relief, washing
his face at the basin over in one corner, while the appearance of the old lounge in another corner indicated that
it had been occupied as a bed during the early morning
hours at least.

"Why didn't you call me," snapped Brady.

Riordan sputtered, dashed the cold water from his eyes,
and turned round.

"Call you? What for, chief? Something broke?"

"Why, I suppose so—you don't usually work overtime
for fun."

Riordan laughed.

"This isn't overtime—I just stayed here so's to be up in
time. I got a case in court."

"Huh?"

"Yes, chief. Drunk case. I promised him I'd show him, and I'm going to keep my word."

Captain Brady put his coat in the locker, tipped his uniform cap on the back of his head, sat down at his desk, and reached for the report basket. After glancing over the slips perfunctorily, he swung about in his chair and faced his aide, who was now combing his hair.

"I guess you know your business, son," he said. "But you'd think there were enough harnessed bulls to handle prohibition drunks, without you going into court. The fellow hit you, or something?"

"He did not," responded Riordan emphatically. "He lurched into me at half past eleven Saturday night right in front of the door downstairs as I was going out to lunch, and he called me a 'flat-footed Irish mick.' Then he went into some needless and insulting remarks as to my ancestry.

"I hooked him round the neck, lifted him inside, dragged him across the floor, booked him as drunk and disorderly and using foul and obscene language in a public place, and turned him over to the doorman to lock up. He's had a nice rest over Sunday, and this morning I'm going to ask the judge to give him some more."

Captain Brady smiled quietly.

"Anything else doing?" he asked a moment later, looking up again from the reports.

"Nothing but the usual run, that I saw, chief. Moffett and Lewis went out on a call down town, I heard, but they haven't phoned in yet. Want to come into court with me and see if I've forgotten yet how to handle a case?"

"I'll just do that, me lad. I'm curious to see this drunk

*Brady snapped a viselike grip onto the man's
feet and he fell to the garage floor.*

party that's riled you so much you'll lose your beauty sleep
over it."

In police court the drunk in question was notable chiefly
for the fact that he didn't look it. In contrast to the rest of
the Monday morning line he was well-dressed, clean for a
man who has spent two nights and a day in jail, and not at
all disconsolate looking. He spotted Riordan the moment
that officer entered the court room, and nodded pleasantly
to him.

Riordan gave no sign of recognition, and waited in
the rear of the room with Brady till the case was called,
when both officers went forward to the "bridge" before the
magistrate, the captain of detectives purely as an interested
spectator.

The judge looked over his glasses at the prisoner, then
at the docket.

"B. Smith, you are charged with being drunk and disorderly, and with using foul and obscene language in a public

place, contrary to the ordinances for the peace and quiet of the city. Do you wish an attorney?"

"No, your honor."

"Officer, be sworn. Do you solemnly swear buzz-buzz-buzz-urumph, so help you God? What is the nature of the offense?"

Riordan had raised his hand and lowered it as the mumbled formula that passes for an oath had been muttered by the magistrate, and at its close spoke quietly.

"Your honor, this man, very drunk, lurched into me Saturday night at the door of headquarters as I was going out to lunch, made insulting remarks to me and called me a vile name. He was pretty messy, judge, and I locked him up. I can bring the desk sergeant and the doorman as witnesses, if your honor wishes."

"The prisoner may want witnesses, officer," said the magistrate, cocking his head. "B. Smith, do you desire to hear corroborative witnesses?"

"No, your honor. I plead guilty. I am very sorry I insulted the officer, judge, and I humbly apologize to him. I had had a few drinks at a little party, your honor, and having once flaunted the law I thought it would be funny to insult a police officer. Insane idea, judge, but I was drunk. I am very sorry, after spending two nights in a cell."

Captain Brady leaned forward. "If it please your honor," he said, "I would like to ask the prisoner a question. Where did you get this liquor?"

"At a little party, captain—just a few friends. Social time, you know. I was going away and they came to see me off."

"Answer the question," snapped the judge. "Where did you get the liquor?"

"Down at Joe Loeb's, the plumbing shop—I guess the captain knows where it is."

Brady showed more interest. "Judge, your honor," he said, "I'd like to have you give this man a little jolt—long enough so we can investigate his story."

"Ten days," said the magistrate.

"But, your honor," spoke up the prisoner, "I am able to pay a fine. I would much prefer to pay a fine. I can give the captain here my name and address—"

"Ten days. Next case."

Brady and Riordan wheeled and left the court room as the patrolman stationed at the bridge dragged B. Smith to the corridor leading to the city jail. Once back in the detective bureau office, Riordan gave vent to his surprise.

"What's the idea, chief? Did you think the judge was going to weaken? I was all set to make a speech myself."

"No, I didn't figure he'd weaken—or you either. I saw blood in your eye, you were that wild. But if Joe Loeb's staging parties in his dump, he's through, and I don't care whether's he's a stool pigeon or not. I got no use for stool pigeons, anyway. You go on home and sleep your peeve off now you've got hunk, anyway. Me, I got work to do."

He plunged into the mass of papers at his desk as Riordan went out, and was still making reports when Moffett and Lewis, two of his staff, came in after knocking for entry.

"Mornin', chief," said the former of the two. "Got a call down to Wolff's jewelry in the Empire Building. He claims he was touched for two trays of jeweled rings and a leather pouch of unset ice some time since closing time Saturday night. Says he put the stuff in the safe when he locked up and it wasn't there this morning when he opened up.

"Me and Lewis went all over the place and there ain't a sign of a jimmy nor nothin'. Place is protected by A.D.T. wires all around, and no alarm come in. Nothing mussed up, and the safe's got a time-lock on it. Personally I think he's a liar or else it was an inside job. There ain't a sign of entry in the place."

"You know better than to accuse Wolff of an inside job," said Brady. "You've known him longer than I have, and I know him like a book. He's so honest he'll run out on the street and give you your change if you go away and forget it. What's the idea of talking inside job about him?"

"Well, if it ain't that, chief, there's a real wise bird in town."

"That's possible. They come once in awhile. Make out a report on it, and I'll take a look-see after awhile myself. And stay on the case and see what you can get. Look up his clerks, and all that."

2

THE LAST CALLER

THE TWO SLEUTHS departed, leaving Brady to his reports and thoughts until he was interrupted again, this time by Special Agent Byrnes of the Protective Association.

"Hello, chief. I've got a good one. Seven thousand bucks in unset diamonds and maybe a thousand dollars worth of rings taken from old Wolff's place Sunday or Sunday night and not a scratch to show for it."

"Yeah," said Brady. "Coupla my boys are working on the case."

Byrnes laughed. "Better put a couple more on. Better get Sherlock Holmes and Nick Carter, too. Burglars me eye. Why, the old wolf did it himself. He's been having a hard time meeting his bills lately. Insurance is what he wants, and what he don't get. To get insurance you gotta show there was a burglary, forcible entry and all that."

"Well, what'd you come to me for, if you're so sure," Brady growled.

"I want to get your report to back up ours, chief, that's all. We got to have it, in fact."

"Well, come back in four or five days. I can't make you any report till I look at it, and I'm busy on something else right now. But I'll do this, Byrnes—I'll bet you a good dinner and the cigars Wolff never pulled an inside job in his whole life and never will."

"Why won't he?"

"Because he isn't that kind. I know him. You'd better do a little work on that case, and not go off at half-cock. Come back in four or five days, if you're stuck, and I'll give you a lift, maybe."

Byrnes, a little less confident looking, went his way. Captain Brady slammed his desk shut, went down to the police garage, started his car and rolled down to Joe Loeb's plumbing shop.

Loeb greeted the glittering uniform of the detective captain with considerable awe. He did not like to have uniformed officers come into even the front of his plumbing shop, which was all it should be. As to the back room, it was one of his unwritten laws that uniforms were barred.

"Good morning, captain. And what's on your mind?"

"Put on your hat and coat, Joe, and lock up. You're going with me."

"But, captain, I got a call to fix—"

"If you want, Joe, I'll drag you out."

Mr. Loeb slowly donned his coat and hat, followed Brady out to the sidewalk, locked the door behind him, and climbed into the front seat of the auto beside its driver.

"Listen, captain," he said, as the machine was tooled through the morning traffic. "You know what the chief said. As long as I run a quiet place and come through when I was asked to—"

"Quiet place," snorted Brady. "How about the party Saturday night that spilled a fighting drunk on to the street?"

"Saturday night? Party? You got me wrong, captain. There was only three men in my place Saturday night—a couple of the boys come in early to get a quart apiece to take fishing, and along about eleven o'clock or maybe later another man I know is all right come in and got one drink. And he choked on that and spilled most of it on his clothes. You got me wrong, captain, I'm telling you the truth."

Brady made no reply. At headquarters he beckoned to the doorman and pointed to Loeb.

"Take him upstairs and book him to me for investigation," he said, and then drove off; this time to the Empire Building, on the main floor of which was Wolff's jewelry store, a relatively small and modest shop, but one which had long been famed in the city for the quality of its goods and the fair dealing tendered its customers. Old Anthony Wolff, the proprietor, spotted Brady as soon as he entered the door and came forward at once.

"You come right upstairs, captain," he said.

"Captain, I am so glad you have come. The things they are saying already, it is dreadful. It is worse than the loss. Though just now, if I do not get the insurance, I cannot stand that either. I am in a bad way, captain."

A balcony ran around the shop, the first floor of the building being high-ceiled to accommodate a mezzanine floor in other parts. At the rear of the balcony was Wolff's private office, in which was a sturdy, modern safe which took up so much room that aside from it the only furnishings were a small table and a few chairs. From one side of the office a door opened into a workshop. Wolff closed this door, then closed the door leading to the balcony, and sitting nervously on the edge of a chair, looked up appealingly at the detective captain.

"Tell me, Mr. Brady," he said, true anguish in his voice, "you don't believe I have done it—that I have robbed myself, do you. That is what they are all saying. Even your two men, though they did not say it, they looked it as they went out of here."

"Wolff, if you were starving to death you wouldn't steal a bowl of milk from a cat. That's what I think. Now tell me about it."

"Oh, Captain Brady, you make me so glad. You believe me, I know. But, God help me, captain, I don't know why you should. I almost think I have gone crazy and done this. As they say, there is no mark of entry. And the safe has a timelock. And the wires—everywhere. And no alarm. Oh, captain—"

"Here, here, Wolff, pull yourself together. Of course you didn't do it. Now stop talking about that. Going over that won't get us anywhere. You answer my questions, remembering all the time I got to know everything if I'm to help you. Now, what time did you close up Saturday night?"

"About eleven, captain. I'm not sure just when, maybe a little after."

"And who was in here then?"

"Nobody, captain. I was all alone. Ambrose, the last clerk to leave, went home about ten. It was raining, and there was no trade. Usually Saturday night, after the theater, I do some business. But it was raining. So I told Ambrose to go, that I would lock up.

"Who was in here after that?"

The jeweler hesitated. "I am trying to think, but it is so

hard, captain. Yes, I have it. Very soon after Ambrose went out there was a young girl came in. She wanted to look at wrist watches. But she only wanted to pay eleven dollars and I have none that are worth less than twenty. She went out. I sat at my desk downstairs, under the balcony in the back, you know where it is, reading the paper.

"The spring was on the front door and the buzzer was connected. Nobody came for a long time, then about half past ten the buzzer sounded and I got right up. Mr. Hemmingway, the superintendent of the building, it was. He came in and got his boy's watch; he had left it that morning to be repaired.

"That was all the business I did. I saw it was a bad night, so I started to put things away. I put the rings from the back showcase in the safe. It was two of those trays that were—that are gone, captain."

"Who else came in?"

"I had no other customers."

"Who else came in?"

"Captain! You don't believe me?"

"Sure I believe you, every word. Who else came in? Who came in after Hemmingway went out, when you were putting things away?"

The jeweler studied the pattern on the carpet and suddenly looked up with incredulity on his features.

"How did you know there was somebody else, when I had forgotten it, captain. How did you know?"

"Who else came in?"

"Mr. Trelawney. You wait here a minute, captain, till I run down to my desk."

The jeweler left the room and Brady leaned forward and

examined the safe carefully. He did not touch it, but his eyes traveled over every inch of its front, over the combination knob, over the concealed hinges, around the edge of the partly opened door. He was still looking at it when the jeweler returned, carrying with him a large decorated card.

"Mr. Trelawney came in," he said, taking up the answer to the question as if he had not been interrupted. "He is a salesman for novelties. Also he makes these himself. He has made several for me. I asked him to work out a certain design in this one, and he had just finished it and brought it in. He wanted the money, he said, as he was going out on the road."

The jeweler stood the card against the safe door—it was an advertisement, in pastel shades, of engagement rings, beautifully drawn and lettered; just the kind of card to put in a jewel shop window, nothing gaudy or bold about it, but as artistic a bit of work as the silver and gold amid which it was designed to stand.

"Well, what, did Trelawney do?" asked Brady.

"I had just put the trays in the safe," returned Wolff. "The buzzer sounded and I pushed the door of the safe to, but not shut, and hurried downstairs. I was there as he came in. He had the card wrapped in paper and stood at the counter while he undid it. I saw it was all right and gave him seven dollars for it. He thanked me, said he was going out on the road and could use the money, and went out. I—"

"Where did you get the seven dollars?"

"Out of my pocket, captain. I always carry enough to meet small bills. He bade me good night and went out. He was the last person in the store—but me."

"You saw him go out?"

"Certainly, captain."

"Then what did you do?"

"I walked back to my desk downstairs, put the card on top of it, turned the light on it to examine it for a minute, then went upstairs, set the time-clock on the safe for this morning, shut the door, and locked it. I remember twirling the combination knob. Then I put that bar there across the workshop door at your side, turned the switch that sets the burglar alarm, put on my hat and coat, got my umbrella, turned out the lights, opened the front door, set the lock on that, closed the door, and went away."

"Did you go home?"

"Not right away, captain. The rain stopped just as I got to Washington Street, and the air was cool and nice. So I walked out Washington Street to the Boulevard and then back again to the interurban depot, where I got the quarter-of-twelve train home. I was tired from being in here all the long Saturday and thought the walk would do me good."

3

A "PLUMBER'S" STORY

CAPTAIN BRADY PULLED a cigar from his pocket, carefully cut the end off with his penknife, and lighted the brown roll.

"The whole place is wired, is it?" he asked.

"Everything but the workshop, captain. They charge so much a room. The workshop opens off this room, and that bar on the door is wired, so I did not have the workshop wired. There is nothing in there but a lathe and some tools. All the jobs—all the work, you know—we lock up in the safe at night."

"Who is this Trelawney party?"

"He is a novelty salesman, captain. I have known him three years. I met him at Mendlebaum's one day when I was over there. These cards he does himself, side line, he calls it. I have been up to his rooms at the Grand Hotel. He is unmarried, a quiet man. Plays checkers very well, but I have beaten him. He does not work for any jobber or firm—buys his own stuff wholesale, and then sells it. His selections are always good, his stuff moves quickly."

"And there was nobody else in the place Saturday night?"

"Nobody, after Ambrose left, except as I have told you. A girl to look at wrist watches; Mr. Hemmingway, to get his boy's watch, and Mr. Trelawney. I would have forgotten him if you had not questioned me."

"Where were the diamonds—in what part of the safe?"

"I will show you, captain."

The jeweler swung open the door of the strong box. "On this side here, near the door, I keep my gems in packets, so I can get them easily when showing them to a customer. On this other side, here, I piled the trays with the rings. The two trays on the top were taken."

Brady looked about the interior of the safe, then carefully examined the inside of the door.

"Moffett and Lewis took finger-prints, I suppose?" he asked.

"Yes, captain. On the safe, on the front door, both."

"Put that bar on the workshop door and connect it up—I want to see it."

The jeweler did as requested, and Brady examined the connections closely.

"Now take it down, let me go in the workshop, and then put it up again," he said.

The jeweler disconnected the wiring, opened the door, spoke a word to the workman within, and again closed the door with Brady on the inner side. The detective captain examined the door, pushed on it, then stepped back and looked about the little shop. It was a close, stuffy room, the only opening aside from the door being a small window scarcely three feet square, that opened onto a narrow airshaft. Its panes were thick with dust.

"What time did you go home Saturday?" he asked the artisan at the lathe.

"Noon. I only work half a day Saturday. Did the boss lose much?"

"Who told you about it?"

"Oh, there was a million dicks in here already this morning."

"No, he didn't lose much."

Brady rapped sharply on the door, and Wolff opened it for him, then left it open and followed him out on to the balcony.

"You go on downstairs and peddle your junk," the detective captain said cheerily. "And don't you worry none. And forget I'm in here. I want to loaf around this here gallery a bit. Tell the clerks if they see a strange man in uniform up here not to be scared, that it's only a cop."

"You have an idea, captain?" asked Wolff hopefully.

"Not the faintest idea in the world. That's why I want to hide up here. I'm ashamed of myself."

The jeweler shook his head sadly, hesitated a moment, and then went downstairs into the body of the store. Captain Brady moved along the gallery a way, and then, leaning on the railing, looked down at the store below.

The clerks, told of his presence by Anthony Wolff, naturally supposed they were being watched, and moved about nervously at first. But as customers came in they forgot the face hanging over the railing above them, and soon went about their duties as usual. All knew there had been a robbery, of course, but they had been able to pick up little of the details.

Brady, after perhaps twenty minutes' study of the shop below him, began to shift his position, an inch at a time, along the railing. His eyes still gazed down at the scene below him, passing over every square inch of the surface beneath—show cases, floor, vases standing in the corners, the top of Wolff's desk, and the other various furnishings of the store.

And still he kept inching along, around the gallery. So slowly did he move that it was fully an hour and a half before he had made the circuit of the place and reached the end of the rail at the other side of the stairs. Then he straightened up and walked down to Wolff's desk.

The proprietor, waiting on a customer, saw him and, excusing himself a moment, hurried back.

"When do you clean up the store—sweep and dust?" Brady asked.

"Usually first thing in the morning, captain. But this morning, when I found what had happened, I told the janitor never to mind. I did not want anything disturbed—you understand."

"You got a head on you, Wolff."

"You have seen something, captain?" Hope lit up the jeweler's face.

"I don't know whether I have or not. I'm coming back this afternoon. Don't you let that janitor touch anything in here till to-morrow morning. In the meantime, don't you worry about what people may say. I'll take care of the papers. And don't you believe anything you see in them, either."

Brady left the jewelry store and drove back to headquarters. Once in his office he told the man on desk duty in the outer room to "round up them reporters and send 'em in." The task evidently was not difficult, for Brady was soon surrounded by a group of keen-eyed young men who had been waiting eagerly for a chance to question him as to details of the robbery of Wolff's place, which was only barely alluded to on the "slips" which they were privileged to see.

"Well, boys," smiled Brady, "I know what you want. You can say that Wolff's store was bumped off some time Sunday or Sunday night, and several thousand dollars' worth of unset gems taken. We haven't finished listing the stuff yet. The job was very plainly the work of two men, one tall and one short, the tall man getting into the place by standing on the short man's shoulders and crawling through a window in the rear of the place—"

"But, captain," broke in the reporter for the *Chronicle*. "There isn't any window in the rear. The store backs right up against the elevator shafts in the Empire Building."

"All right, me bucko, if you know more about it than I do, hop to it," said Brady. "I'm just tellin' you what I think about the case. If you don't think the guys got in that way, figure out some other way. All the stuff they took was low grade junk, taken from the show cases, the real good stuff being locked up in the vault. The police are working on the case and expect to make an arrest after they have combed the pawnshops and telegraphed to Chicago. That's all I got to say."

"In other words, cap," said the *Ledger* reporter, "you don't know anything about it, is that it?"

"You ought to be a dick, boy," laughed Brady. "You got a head like a tack. All I can say at present is that the police are co-operating with the Protective Association on the case, and if there's anything to be given out, get it from Byrnes. Me, I'm dumb."

The reporters laughed and filed out, and Brady reached for the telephone. To the operator he said:

"Bill, wake up Sergeant Riordan at four o'clock and tell him to come down here on the run. But don't do it till four o'clock."

Then he hung up and twirled round in his chair to face the desk officer, who was standing in the door.

"What now?" he snapped.

"Joe Loeb wants to see you, sir. He's been beefing in jail for an hour. Don't want to see the chief, wants to see you. Says it's important."

"All right, drag him down here."

Presently entered the pseudo-plumber. He had one very large and ripe black eye, otherwise he was less dejected than when Brady had turned him over to the doorman to be locked up. Brady could not help smiling.

"Well, well, Joe, where did you get that?"

"It's him, cap'n. The dirty squealer. And he's a liar, too. I betcha he's a Federal man."

"Yeah? Who? What's it all about, anyway?"

"The feller I told you about, cap'n. You know I said there were only three men in my place Saturday. Two of the boys to get a quart to take fishin', and this other guy. The minute they turn me in I lamped him in the corridor. 'You dirty stool,' says I, makin' a rush at him. 'You're the guy told the cap'n my place was full of fightin' drunks Saturday night. An' I thought you was all right and give you a drink.' And with that I took a swing at him."

"And then what, Joe?"

"Well, cap'n, he must have hit me. I didn't remember nothin' till I woke up in the emergency hospital with one of the sawbones bathin' me face. When I went back to the corridor, this guy wasn't there. They had him out, I guess. But, honest, cap'n, you got me wrong. There was no party in my place Saturday night, only them two fellers for a quart and this guy around eleven o'clock for one drink. He's a Federal dick, I tell you."

4

A SLY THIEF

BRADY PUSHED A button and the desk man appeared.

"Take him back up," said the captain. Joe's loud protestations were shut off by the closing of the door, and Brady again reached for the telephone.

"Gimme the jail. This is Brady talking, Forbes. How about that fight up there? Who beat up Joe Loeb and gave him the shiner? Smith, eh, the guy that Riordan brought in? That's funny. Well, keep them two apart. Good-by."

Detective Captain Brady leaned back in his chair and scratched the thinning hair on the top of his head, holding his uniform cap between thumb and finger as he did so. Then he placed the cap carefully on the top of his desk, dived into his report basket and searched until he found the typewritten statement of Moffett and Lewis on the Wolff store "job." This he perused attentively for some time, then placed it aside and went downstairs to the chief's office, to which he was at once admitted.

The head of the police department looked up, then pointed to a chair. "Tell daddy all about it," he said. "You look worried."

"I got a right to be worried, chief, between one thing and another. In the first place Wolff's place has been touched off, and it's a dinger. And in the second place I got your pet stool pigeon upstairs with a black eye."

"Joe Loeb?"

"You guessed it."

"What did you bring him in for? I thought it was understood Joe was to be left alone."

"I know, chief. We've had that out before. The understanding was that I was to leave your friends alone as long as they didn't interfere with me, regardless of what I think of stools."

"Well?"

"Well, chief, Riordan was going out Saturday night when a guy set on him and tried to beat him up. He was drunk and he said he got drunk at a party at Joe's. Now I can't have my men beaten up by any drunks from Joe's place, so I brought him in."

"Where does the black eye come in?"

"That's the funny part of it. Joe pegged this guy in the jail corridor and rushes him, says he's a liar and there wasn't any party. And the two mixed. Joe got the shiner. I haven't seen the other fellow yet."

"Well, Brady, you can lay to it, then, there was no party. Joe may be a bootlegger, but he's honest. I never caught him in a lie yet—outside of his business—you understand. Selling hootch he regards as one of his personal liberties—same as you think voting the Democratic ticket is all right. Outside of politics I never found you a liar, either.

"And, on top of that, if Joe crowned this guy for lying about him, you can bet Joe was righteously indignant at having his place blackballed. If Joe says there was no party there, then there was no party. As a matter of fact, I've told

Joe I won't stand for parties; only bottle trade, with maybe once in a while one drink, if he's got to save a man's life. You better turn him out again."

"Not me, chief. You can turn him out if you want to— you're my superior officer."

The chief reached for his desk phone.

"Forbes," he said. And after a moment: "Forbes? This is the chief. You got Joe Loeb up there. Turn him out."

He hung up and looked at Brady. "Joe 'll tell you anything you want to know, if he knows it; and if he says he doesn't know it, you can believe him," he said. "Now you leave him alone—he's my man, see?"

"You'll bank on him, will you, chief?"

"Just like I'd bank on you, Brady."

"All right, that's what I wanted to know. But at that I'm glad I pulled him. I'll be going now, with the rest of my troubles."

It was ten minutes after four when Sergeant Riordan arrived at Brady's office.

"I was up and eating when the phone rang," he said. "Made it down here from the house in eight minutes. Some driving. What's doing?"

"Read this and soak it up," said Brady, passing him the report on the Wolff robbery.

Riordan read the report as attentively as his chief had done. When he laid the papers down he not only knew all that Moffett and Lewis knew about the case, but he had practically memorized the list of missing property in all its detail. And being more or less familiar with the jeweler's shop—as he was with most of the more important stores in the city—he had a good working idea of the case in his mind.

"Now listen to me," said Brady. "I was over there this morning, and this is what I found out," and he detailed rapidly but exactly his conversation with Wolff, his inspection of the place, and what he had seen and not seen. Completing his account, he added:

"We're going over there. I want you to look around the same as I did, and see what you see. Then we'll get together and match up. Come on, let's go."

At Wolff's, Sergeant Riordan followed very much the procedure that had occupied Brady in the morning, while the captain and the jeweler sat in the office beside the safe, saying little. His inspection completed, Riordan came back to the office.

"That fellow in the workshop nearly through for the day?" he asked.

As if in answer to the question, the repair man came out of the door, nodded good night to Wolff and went out.

"I'm going in there," said Riordan, "and have a look. That's the only place I haven't been yet. Be out pretty soon."

He entered the workshop and pulled the door shut behind him. Brady, a smile flitting over his face, got up and slipped the heavy bar that locked the door at night into its place.

"Maybe he won't be out as soon as he expects," he said. "Nothing like a little play with your work, Wolff. Keeps the wrinkles out of the face."

"It is easy for you to talk of play, captain," said the jeweler, "but for me there will be no play, no fun, till this is cleared up. You think you will find something?"

Brady nodded his head. "Sure—but I don't know how soon. In a day or two, maybe. The pawnshops ought to show some of the stuff by that time. I've had a description of the stuff wired north and south."

The two sat there, Anthony Wolff, with his none-too-pleasant thoughts, and Brady waiting for Riordan to pound on the workshop door and demand release.

"I cannot see how the man—the robber—got in," said the jeweler, after a few moments. "The Protective Association man was here since you were and tested all the wires. Everything was perfect. And there is no mark of entry."

"I'm not worrying about how he got in," said Brady. "What worries me is how he got out."

"How did he get in, then, captain?"

"Through the front door. Slipped in when the girl came in for wrist watches, or when Hemmingway came in, or this Trelawney man. That is easy. A good sneak can come in any door with another person and only one in a hundred would notice.

"Take it from me, Wolff, you were tired after a long day. This fellow evidently had been watching the place. He picked his chance, slipped in and hid—maybe over under that settee to the right of the door. He hid there till you went out. But what gets me is how he got out again."

"It is possible, captain. But I usually watch the door very closely."

"Sure you do. But you don't know sneaks—and you weren't expecting one. You've been lucky a long time, Wolff—the boys have laid off your—"

Brady stopped with his mouth open. Sergeant Riordan

was standing in the doorway of the office, his face blank, but a twinkle in his eyes.

Captain Brady turned about, the bar was still across the workshop door. He stepped over and lifted it from its heavy fastenings, opened the door, and entered the little room. In this he trotted nervously about, looked at the window, opened it, looked out into the narrow airshaft, closed it again. Then he stepped back into Wolff's office.

"Well," he said, "we'll be going, Mr. Wolff. "We'll be around to-morrow, most likely. Keep your heart up; I can see by Riordan's eyes that he's got an idea. Come on, Riordan, we got business to do."

5

THE MEMORY OF MR. SMITH

WITHOUT WAITING FOR Wolff to voice his surprise, the two sleuths hurried downstairs, through the shop, and into Brady's waiting automobile. The captain started it with a jerk, and, dodging the streets on which was the heaviest traffic, drove out to the entrance of the park. There he shot to the curb, jammed on his brakes and then turned to his aide.

"Now come through," he said.

Riordan laughed.

"It was a pipe, chief. I heard you slip that bar into place. So I figured I'd put one over on you. Any good, limber youngster could make that airshaft. It's just like climbing a ladder—window ledges on each side, and the thing just wide enough to give you a chance to brace your back. I went up it to the third floor, where there was a window of a public washroom open, and into that. Luckily there was nobody inside. I could have gone clear to the top of the building if I'd wanted to. Of course, an old, fat stiff like you couldn't have made it."

"You said it, Riordan. I'm getting old. I looked that shaft over and it never even occurred to me. That's the way the bird got out—went up to some washroom and then down

the elevator, like any late tenant or caller in the building—
it's open all night because there's a lot of twenty-four-
hour-a-day offices in the Empire. Of course I thought of
that airshaft first thing, but it looked too small and steep
for anybody but a blame fool to try."

"This guy was no fool, chief. He wore gloves. No finger-
prints, but you could see the marks of a gloved hand on
the window sash where he shut it after him. The one in
the workshop, I mean. The way I've got it doped, this guy
sneaked into the place along with one of the customers, hid
out until this card writer came in. You know Wolff had the
stuff in the safe then, but hadn't shut the door.

"While Wolff was looking at the show card, this guy
reached into the safe, got what he got, and then slipped
into the workshop and shut the door. He probably stood
behind the door, so if Wolff opened it and looked in, he
wouldn't have seen him. If he had have seen him he'd probably have sapped the old bird. When Wolff put that bar on
the door he was just covering the guy's escape, that was all."

"You got a head on you, boy."

"Besides that he wore rubber soled and heeled shoes.
There's a mark where he stepped on a cabinet in climbing
to the gallery down there in the front of the store. He came
in the door, hid under that settee, watched his chance while
the old boy was reading, swung up onto the gallery and
waited. Luck was with him and he didn't have to blow the
safe—he probably would have tried it after shorting the
alarm wires. I'll bet he was a right smart hand at his work."

"Boy, you're all right. I saw that footprint myself. That
was why I wanted you to look around, too. I wanted to

see if you'd make it. I didn't know about the gloves, but I suspected 'em. You're sure that he had gloves?"

"Saw the mark of the seam below the thumb on the sash of that window. Chances are the guy went out the third floor washroom, the same as I did—there's no catch on the window. Might be a good plan to talk to the night elevator operators."

"Let Moffett and Lewis do that—it's a bum chance. Probably a hundred people went out or in between eleven and midnight Saturday."

"That's so. Well, now what? You said we had something to do."

"We've done it. I wanted to know how you got out of there and didn't want you to show me up before Wolff. He thinks I'm still good."

Riordan laughed.

For a few moments both men sat silent, then Brady laughed in his turn.

"At that I got one on you," he said. "Your drunk friend that you went to court about beat up Joe Loeb in the jail. It seems he wasn't so drunk as he might have been. At least, the chief says Joe doesn't lie, and Joe swears the fellow only had one drink and spilled most of that. The chief was kind o' sore when I told him I'd pulled Joe. He let him out."

"The guy smelled like a distillery," said Riordan.

"Joe says he spilled most of the liquor on his shirt— naturally he would smell."

"Well, he got his ten days, anyway. He was planning to make a journey, he said. I reckon he'll more than miss one train."

Brady jerked erect in his seat, started the engine, and

threw the car into gear. Driving a few blocks, he pulled up beside a police call box and took down the telephone within.

"Gimme the property clerk," he demanded, while Riordan listened, puzzled by his chief's new turn. "That you, Duke? This is Brady. Say, look in the envelope of that guy, B. Smith, that Riordan brought in Saturday night and see what railroad tickets or letters he's got. I'll hold the line. Huh, what's that? Well, I'll be jiggered. All right, much obliged."

He hung up, closed the box, and stepped back into the car.

"He didn't have a thing on him but twenty dollars, sixteen cents, a penknife, and a bunch of keys," Brady said to Riordan. "I want to talk to that guy right now. You sit in on the talk, see, but be dumb. And don't glare at him— leave him to me."

They drove rapidly to headquarters, and presently B. Smith was ushered into Brady's office. He was a tall man, but lithe, and walked like a cat.

"Sit down, Mr. Smith," began Captain Brady. "I want to ask you a few questions about this party you staged down at Joe Loeb's. We're going to prosecute him. Maybe if you show you can be a good witness, we'll get the judge to reconsider the little matter of the ten days."

Smith made no suggestion.

"How many of you were at the party?"

"Three, besides myself, captain."

"Who were they?"

"Really, captain, I can't drag my friends into the matter."

"How many drinks did you have?"

"Oh, maybe eight or ten. We all bought a round once—maybe more than that. My friends were going to the train with me, and somebody suggested we have a farewell drink—you know how it is."

"What train were you going to take?"

"The Owl—it leaves at midnight. I was going to Central City."

"What for?"

"To visit my sister."

"What broke up the party?"

"Joe put us out, he said we were getting too noisy."

"How'd you happen to lose your friends?"

"They wanted to go to another place. I had to make the train. We argued about it on the corner, and I left them."

"How come you headed down to the police station when the depot is the other way from Joe's place?"

"I don't know, captain—only that I was drunk, I guess."

"Want to send a telegram to your sister that you've been detained?"

"No, thanks. It was a surprise visit. She wasn't expecting me."

"What's your business?"

"I'm an expert machinist—trouble man, they call me. Fix up complicated machines, like printing presses, bottling machines, can-makers, and things like that."

"What do they pay you?"

"Eleven dollars a day—sometimes more."

"Where do you live?"

"At a hotel."

"How long were you going to stay at your sister's place?"

"Oh, I don't know. Till I got a call to a job somewhere."

"Keep extra clothes at your sister's, do you? You didn't have a grip with you, did you?"

"I had already checked my suit case before I went out with the boys."

"Where's the check?"

Smith shrugged his shoulders. "I suppose it's with the rest of my stuff, in the property room. They frisked me when I was locked up."

"Got a good memory for a drunken man, haven't you?"

"I don't know. Booze never went to my head very much—that is, in some ways."

"Yet you were crazy enough to want to lick a cop?"

"Freak of intoxication, captain."

"Will you testify against Joe Loeb?"

"I suppose you can hold me till I do."

"Where'd you meet these four friends of yours that were at the party?"

"There were only three, captain,"

"Oh, that's right. I forgot. Where did you meet them?"

"Up at the club."

"What club?"

"The Athletic Club."

"You're a member?"

"Yes, captain."

"Well, Smith, I think you're a liar. I'm going to call up the club and ask the secretary. I know him pretty well myself."

Brady reached for the telephone, but Smith extended a hand to stop him.

"Smith isn't my name, captain. I gave an assumed name when I found I was arrested. Let me call up De Graves, the club secretary, and you'll be convinced that I'm a member from the way I talk to him."

"No, I won't do that. But I tell you what I will do. I'll drive you out to the Athletic Club myself. I'll take off my uniform and we'll go like we were friends. If you're a member, you can introduce me as your guest. We'll shoot a game of pool, and then come back. You convince me you're on the level, and in the morning I'll speak to the judge."

"That will be very good of you, captain. I'll convince you."

"All right. Riordan, take Smith upstairs so he can wash up, and then bring him down to the garage. I'll get off my uniform and put on regular clothes and be waiting for you in my car."

6

AFTER THE GAME

RIORDAN, HIS FACE immobile, got up and motioned the prisoner to follow him. Brady pushed a button and to the responding deskman said:

"Moffett or Lewis out there?"

"Both of them just come in, captain."

"Send 'em in here."

Brady was slipping from his uniform as they entered, and while he was donning citizen's dress he gave them their orders.

"You two go out to the Athletic Club and stick around outside. I'll be driving up there with a fellow pretty soon and go in. When I come out, you two happen along and hail me, and ask if there's a chance to ride down to head-quarters. Get me? I'll say, 'Sure.'

"Climb in the back seat of my car, and if the fellow with me starts anything, one of you stick a gun in his back and the other of you get him by the throat. I think maybe he'll be a bad hombre."

A few minutes later Brady and the prisoner who had given the name of B. Smith were driving uptown in the captain's car, chatting casually enough about traffic jams, the nuisance of flivvers, and such topics. In the midst of this the prisoner broke in.

"I wonder, captain," he said, "if you'd take a chance and drive me to my hotel before we go to the club. I'd like to change my shoes and socks, they're not altogether comfortable after all this time. And this shirt is pretty dirty."

"Sure," agreed Brady. "But I'm going to your room with you. And you want to remember that I'm heeled. Don't try anything."

"Assuredly not, captain. I give you my word. It's the Essex Hotel."

Brady turned down the proper street and parked in front of one of the city's more modest hostelries, and followed Smith closely as he alighted from the car. Together they walked to the desk, where the clerk nodded to Smith, reached in the key rack and handed him a key and a letter.

Then they entered the elevator, rode to the second floor, and went to room 206. Smith thrust the letter into his coat pocket, tossed his coat and vest on the bed, found another shirt in one of the bureau drawers, changed; got fresh socks and another pair of shoes, and in a few minutes announced himself as ready to proceed. He had made no move that was in any way suspicious.

The ride to the Athletic Club was uneventful. They stepped up to the desk together, and "Smith" twirled the register around and wrote:

"Albert Bassett and guest, Captain Brady."

De Graves, the club secretary, looked at the register, and smiled.

"That's good, Brady," he said, "you being listed as a guest.

You're a life member, aren't you? Why don't you come round oftener?"

"Too busy," grunted Brady. "Fact is, I haven't been here for a coon's age. What's my friend's special line?"

"Why, you must have heard of 'Blondie' Bassett, captain. He's one of our stars in the gymnasium. And a good amateur wrestler and boxer, too."

"Oh, so you're 'Blondie' Bassett, eh?" exclaimed Brady with apparent surprise. "And you telling me all the time he was your brother! Some kidder, you are. Well, let's go shoot that game of pool."

"Let's have supper first, captain. I guess the grille will stand for one of my tabs. I lost all my money in the poker game."

"Yes," cut in De Graves, "Bassett's a rotten poker player."

"No," said Brady. "We'll get supper where we're going after the pool game. One game of pool was the bargain, remember."

They went to the billiard room and shot a game of pool, Bassett winning easily, and Brady paying the bill and bets with a laugh. Then they went out to the captain's car, apparently the best of friends. Brady had just switched on the lights, and was stepping on the starter when Moffett and Lewis stepped up.

"Beg pardon, cap," said the former, "but me and Lewis been on a case up here a coupla blocks, and it's quitting time. Any chance to get a ride down town, so we can report off quicker?"

"Sure, pile in the back seat."

The car rolled along a way, with all four silent. Finally Brady turned to his companion on the front seat.

"Better give me that letter, Bassett. Save you being frisked again when you go in. I'll give it to you in the morning."

"I think I'll keep it, captain."

"Better give it to me."

"That would be a violation of the postal laws, captain. It wouldn't be your mail."

"Postal laws, my eye! The letter has been delivered to you, and it's out of Uncle Sam's jurisdiction now. You're a prisoner and can't have personal property on your person. Fork it over."

"Not a chance in the world, captain." The voice was level and even.

Brady took one hand from the steering wheel, as if he was about to attempt to take the letter himself. As he raised his hand, the man beside him shot out his left palm and closed it about the wheel, to wrench the car into the curb; but Brady's upraised hand fell on top of his, and the man suddenly stiffened in his seat, while Moffett's voice came from the rear:

"One more try, feller, and I'll let daylight through your ribs."

At the same time Lewis dexterously reached inside the prisoner's coat and obtained the letter—the only thing in his pocket. The rest of the drive to the headquarters garage was uneventful.

As the car came to a halt, however, the prisoner leaped from his seat and slid over the front door without opening it, but Brady snapped a viselike grip onto the man's feet and he fell head first to the garage's cement floor. While he was squirming in an effort to get free, Moffett and Lewis wrapped themselves about him, assisted by a couple of motor cycle men who had run forward on the instant the struggle started.

"Take him up to the Bertillon room and mug him, finger-print him, and find out who he is," said Brady. "Then lock him in solitary. He's probably in the picture books. Look back about three years or more. Let me know what you get on him; I'll be in my office."

7

WHO CAUGHT HIM?

RIORDAN ROSE TO give his chief the desk chair and asked no questions. Brady took the telephone, flung the prisoner's letter down before him on the desk, and read the address. Then he turned to Riordan.

"Go outside and get one of the other phones. Get hold of Byrnes, of the Protective Association, and tell him to run right over and be ready to take me to dinner—and you, too. We'll make him pay double. Then come back here."

Riordan gone, Brady called for the manager of the Essex Hotel.

"This is Captain of Detectives Brady speaking, Mr. Wamsley. You have a tenant named John H. Lurch in room two hundred and six—how long has he been with you, please?"

He waited a few minutes for his answer, while the records were being consulted, then expressed his thanks for the information obtained. Riordan, returning as he hung up, announced that Byrnes would be right over. And showed his training by asking no questions.

Byrnes, ushered in shortly, was eager to know what it was all about. Brady tossed him the letter bearing the name of Lurch, addressed to the Essex Hotel.

"It's all there, Byrnes—or I lose the bet," he said. "Open it and see."

Byrnes ripped the envelope open. A telegraph blank, void of writing, dropped out, and with it a claim check from the parcel room at the depot. He looked at the enclosures, bewildered.

"I don't get you, Brady," he said.

"Didn't suppose you would. Go over to the depot—one of the motor cycle men will whisk you over there—and claim that suit case, or whatever the check is for. Then bring it back here, and you'll see who wins the bet."

Byrnes grasped the idea then, and hurried out.

"Riordan," said Brady, "hop into your car and shoot over to Wolff's. He's probably there yet. Bring him here. If he isn't there, it will spoil the evening. Try and beat Byrnes back."

Left alone, Brady drew a cigar from his pocket and fired up. He looked extremely happy, and sprawled back in his chair. Thus Byrnes found him when he came back, entering the room just as Riordan and Anthony Wolff, the latter plainly bewildered, came through the outer office. When they had all gathered about the desk, and the door had closed behind them, Brady turned to Byrnes.

"What did you find?" he asked.

"The check was for this small bag of brief cases."

"Well, open it."

"I can't—it's locked."

"Riordan, hop upstairs and bring down the keys in your drunken friend's envelope in the property room."

Riordan vanished.

"You have found something, captain," asked Anthony Wolff piteously.

"I'm betting I have, Wolff. I'm betting dinner for all of us. But we won't know till the bag's opened."

They waited in tense silence till Riordan returned, the bunch of keys in his hand. He gave them to Byrnes at a sign from Brady, and the special agent of the Protective Association fumbled with them some seconds before he found the one that would unlock the small bag. When he opened it a shower of jeweled rings fell out onto the desk, followed by a gray, soft leather packet, which, on being opened, gave forth a tiny cascade of unmounted diamonds.

Anthony Wolff started forward, then sank into a chair.

"Oh, Captain Brady, I am so glad!" he said.

Byrnes straightened up.

"It's good work, cap," he said, "but it doesn't prove that I was wrong. You know our bet—it was that you show me this wasn't an in—"

Brady, touched by the look of pain on Anthony Wolff's face, held up his finger. Swinging to the phone, he lifted the receiver, then dropped it back and pushed one of his desk buttons. To the man who responded he said curtly:

"Go up to the Bertillon room and tell Moffett and Lewis to bring that man down here. They'll know who. And put irons on him."

The aid saluted and closed the door.

"Byrnes," said Brady, "you can begin thinking up an apology to Mr. Wolff for your hasty remarks. I've always told you that you went off at half cock. That's why you're not on a real force, only playing round with insurance companies."

Byrnes blushed and turned toward the jeweler.

"It is all right, Mr. Byrnes," said Wolff. "I do not blame you. It still looks bad, I admit. Captain Brady has not yet explained everything. But you will see that he knows."

The door opened again, and Moffett and Lewis entered with B. Smith, or Bassett, or Lurch, manacled between them. Anthony Wolff rose, his face paling.

"Why, Mr. Trelawney!" he gasped.

"What does this mean?"

"It means, Wolff," spoke up Brady, "that Trelawney isn't a novelty salesman or a card writer. He's a prowl, or worse. He didn't go out of your store Saturday night. He started out, dropped down, shut the door, dodged into the dark corner by the settee, and as you went back to look at his work, he stepped on that cabinet that holds fancy handled umbrellas and parasols, swung onto the gallery, ran with his rubber-soled shoes back to the half open safe, reached in and grabbed what he could, slipped the stuff into his bag, dodged into the workshop and waited for you to lock him *out* of the store.

"Then he opened the window, shinnied up that narrow airshaft the way Riordan did this afternoon, went into the washroom on the third floor, came down the elevator, went to the depot and checked that bag, tore off a telegram blank, wrapped the check in it and mailed it to his hotel—or to one of his hotels, at least—went to Joe Loeb's and spilled booze on his shirt, and then came down here and insulted Riordan, who happened to be the first cop he saw—so he'd be locked up Saturday night and so have an alibi for a robbery that gave every indication of being committed Sunday.

"Isn't that about it, Smith, or Lurch, or Bassett?"

The prisoner merely snarled.

Brady turned to Moffett. "You boys make him yet?" he asked.

"The Bertillon man thinks he's Blondie Anderson, an escapee from Deer Lodge and a parole breaker out of Stillwater, cap'n," said Moffett. But he ain't sure yet. He's got to check up on him."

"I hope he is," said Brady. "It will save us a lot of trouble. Well, Byrnes, do you buy the dinners and cigars?"

"I sure do, cap'n, and I want to apologize to Mr. Wolff—"

"Never mind, Mr. Byrnes. It is all right. And you do not buy the dinners nor the cigars, either," said the jeweler. "Captain Brady, have you a good safe where you can lock those things up? I will be the host, gentlemen. But right now I want to say this. If it was not for my friend, Captain Brady, I do not know what I should do to-night. It was getting so I could not bear it."

"Ah, go on," said Brady, uncomfortably. "It wasn't me. I was all at sea, honest, I was. It was Riordan here who did it."

THREADS OF EVIDENCE

*Brady's Best Man Works With
Phenomenal Cleverness In Penetrating
The Roles Of Two Bad Actors*

1

AS A LAST RESORT

CAPTAIN OF DETECTIVES Brady, just about to go home for the evening and turn the management of his department over to Sergeant Riordan of the first night relief, frowned as the telephone on his desk jingled, hesitated a moment as if to turn the call over to his aide, and then picked the receiver from the hook.

"This is Brady—yes, chief—right away."

He hung up, turned to Riordan, and shrugged his shoulders.

"Put somebody on the desk and come on downstairs with me," he said. "The old man wants me and 'my best man,' as he said. I guess that means you. Wilson's out there in the front room, put him on till you get back."

While Riordan was attending to the detail of office discipline, Brady slipped out of his street clothes and into his uniform, and donning his gold-braided cap, was ready as Wilson came into the office to temporarily assume charge. Then with Riordan he went down to the main floor of headquarters in answer to the summons of a moment before.

The chief nodded to the two officers, and then waved his hand at an elderly man sitting beside his desk.

"Captain Brady, this is Mr. Ralston—of the railroad. He's got a little matter that I think will interest you. It's got me beat, anyway."

"What seems to be the difficulty, Mr. Ralston?" asked the head of the detective bureau.

"We're being robbed blind, captain," said the railroad man. "And it's got to be stopped, that's all."

"Office job," queried Brady.

"Nothing so simple as that, captain. As a matter of fact, the railroad is not being robbed—it's our passengers. However, in a great many of the cases we have to make good a part of the loss at least—tickets in almost every case, and quite frequently cash. Sometimes considerable sums. You can't let your best patrons be robbed, you know, and then shrug your shoulders."

"Mr. Ralston is vice-president in charge of the western division, you know, Brady," put in the chief. "The matter has become so serious that he has come down here from his headquarters in the north to enlist our help."

Brady nodded. "Tell us about it, sir," he said.

The railroad executive leaned forward. "There isn't much to tell, captain, I'm sorry to say. Somebody is robbing our passengers. That's all. The seat of the trouble seems to be in your city. About two-thirds of the robberies are reported as taking place in the depot here. The rest of them occur on the trains leaving here or arriving here. None of them have been reported from farther north than Mountainview, which is about one hundred and fifty miles up the line."

"What sort of robberies, Mr. Ralston?"

"All sorts. Pocketbooks, wallets, jewelry, suit cases, ladies'

He launched himself like a catapult below
the level of the automatic.

bags. Whoever it is mixes with the passengers, and then robs them."

"Your special agents haven't got anything, then?"

Ralston laughed. "We've had half the special agents of the whole road working on it. The only thing they got was that one of them was touched for his wallet. He thinks it happened in the dining car on No. 5, between Mountainview and here, but he isn't sure."

"How long has this been going on," asked Brady.

"About ten months, captain, and it's getting worse."

"You should have reported it to us sooner," put in the chief.

"I realize that," replied the railroad man. "But, you know we're naturally a bit touchy. And then we hoped every day our special agents would turn up something. But they haven't made any headway, nor have they found any of the stuff that's been taken, though they've visited all the pawnshops within a radius of five hundred miles, I think. As a last resort we've come to you."

"All this stuff gone from passenger cars and the depot only, eh?"

"That's the idea. Suit cases and hand bags and personal property of passengers, taken in the depot waiting room, in the coaches or in the Pullmans."

"Steady worker, is it," asked Brady, "or only on certain days? Any special trains?"

"I'd say it was a steady worker. We get about three cases a week reported to us. They come quite irregularly—sometimes three or four from the trains; then a half dozen from the depot and none on the trains. Whoever it is doesn't seem to be partial to any one train—it's a local to-day and one of the overlands to-morrow."

"I didn't know the overlands stopped at Mountainview," said Riordan, speaking up for the first time.

"They stop there on flag to let off passengers from points on the central division, or further east," replied Ralston. "All the thefts on the overlands have been on inbound trains that have stopped there. Our special agents, of course, thought that a very good clew; that the thief must live in Mountainview, but a check on the tickets didn't bear it out.

"There were no robberies reported on overlands that had picked up passengers there—but on several incoming trains that didn't stop, passengers were relieved of valuables. But it so happened that in every case the passenger robbed was able to fix the robbery as having occurred between Mountainview and this city."

"You checked on the trainmen?" asked Brady.

"That was one of the first things we did, when this thing got defined to definite territory, captain. Our special agents say none of the trainmen could have done it. Of course we don't believe our men are crooks, anyway; but we've checked on them just the same."

"This special agent who was touched—what'd he have to say?"

"He hasn't any more idea than you have how it happened. He was coming here to work on the case. Came from our eastern division—one of the best men we have. He went into the diner just before the train got to Mountainview— probably twenty miles the other side. Before he went in he took out his wallet to get a deadhead slip—to charge his lunch, you know. So he knows he had his wallet then.

"Just as he was finishing lunch the dining car steward, who knew him, asked him if he could change a twenty-dollar bill. He had a lot of small bills in his wallet. When he reached in his pocket for the wallet, it wasn't there. He had been sitting alone at one of the small side tables. He doesn't recall that anybody brushed against him or came near him.

"As soon as the train got in here he searched all the negro waiters and the cook, but there wasn't a sign of his wallet, nor of any money that he had. It happens he had drawn an expense account before he came here, and all the money he had was in new reserve notes. There wasn't one to be found on the dining car crew nor in the dining car till."

"Sounds like a fairy story," said Captain Brady, after considering the case awhile. "Well, Riordan and I will see what we can see. Will you be in the city long, Mr. Ralston?"

"I'm going to stay here until it is cleared up, captain. I'll be at the Belmont Grand Hotel when I'm not in the company offices at the depot. I want you to call me up the moment you get anything, and if any of our special agents can help you, just let me know. I need hardly say that any expense to which you are put will be taken care of by the company."

"Very well, sir, we'll do our best. But it will likely be several days before we get anywhere at all. Call me up, Mr. Ralston, if you think of anything else. Ask for me, personally—or for Riordan, here."

2

MRS. REYNOLDS REPORTS

BACK IN HIS own office, after banishing Wilson to the outer room, Captain Brady slipped back into his civilian clothes, lighted a cigar, and then sat down at his desk, swinging round in his chair to face Riordan, who was pacing back and forth the length of the office.

"Nice little job, isn't it, son?"

"Simple case of a good 'dip,' I'd say," answered Riordan.

"That's what makes it so blamed hard," said Brady. "I don't wonder these here special agents all got buffaloed. Lot o' strangers, they are. Don't know much plain police work. Why, while some of those birds are smart enough, they wouldn't know you nor me was cops if we got on their trains in plain clothes. They're specialists on baggage lifters and ticket scalpers, and box car men. They ought to have let us have this long ago."

"Bet you it's a local party, chief. Works out of the city just as a blind. I'll take a mosey round to-night and see if I can see anything in the pool halls. Might recognize one of the good workers."

"Uh-uh," answered Brady, screwing his cigar into a corner of his mouth, but apparently not very enthusiastically backing Riordan's idea. He sat silent a long time, and then suddenly bounced to his feet and put on his soft hat and driving gloves, in preparation for going home.

"I'll tell you what you'll do," he said. "You got to do most of the work on this. I got the bureau to run. We'll call Willis in from the hotels run and put him in here nights, and you, beginning to-morrow, will be a plain harnessed bull for awhile. I'll speak to Captain Edwards and have him lay Foster off the depot beat. You go on down there and take over his trick, and loaf about the waiting room and answer fool questions o' tourists and help fussy women with their cryin' babies. You're more apt to see something down there.

"Looks to me like you ought to be able to get an idea in a week of watchin' the depot. Keep in touch with Coffin-berry down there—he's the super—and have him send for you any time a passenger reports being robbed. All the reports 'll go to him. You go off early to-night, and report to Captain Edwards at eight o'clock to-morrow morning. I'll see him or phone him to-night and fix it up. Good night to you, and pleasant dreams."

The next day saw Captain Brady's program carried out, to the joy of Patrolman Foster, who was glad, indeed, to be relieved from the depot beat, with its ceaseless torrent of foolish questions and over-burdened passengers seeking assistance, all the way from having their grips carried to having strayed children hunted up. In the afternoon Captain Brady was just preparing to drive down to the depot to see how Riordan was getting along, when the outer office man came in and announced:

"Lady wants to see you, sir—won't talk to me. Looks like she was some quality, too."

"Show her in," snapped Brady, wondering what had broken loose.

She looked like "quality" all right. Tall, supple, faultlessly gowned, composed, and beautiful, she entered Captain Brady's office, sank into a chair, and leaned forward.

"I want to report a robbery, captain," she said.

"That's what we're here for, madam."

"What makes you think I'm married, captain?" She smiled at the question.

"See the sign on the door? 'Captain of Detectives.' That means I'm supposed to know something, anyhow. You are married?"

"I have been, captain. I'm a widow. Mrs. Amanda Reynolds is the name. I live at the Court Apartments, Washington and Main Streets, Mountainview. I want to report a robbery. While I was coming in to town this afternoon to do some shopping my purse was taken on the train."

Brady turned to his desk and picked up a pad, writing the information down.

"What was in the purse, madam?"

"There was sixteen dollars and some small change, probably a couple of dollars. An address book, some samples of silk I was trying to match, and a gold compact with my initials on it. It was octagonally shaped and chased, save for a circle in the middle, which bore my monogram."

"Have you any idea where it was stolen?"

"Why, yes. You see I rode in the parlor car. I paid the parlor car fare almost immediately after boarding the train. Then the conductor came through just after we had stopped at Bellevale, and I paid my railroad fare then—I hadn't bought a ticket. So it must have been after the train passed Bellevale."

"What makes you think you weren't robbed after you left the train, madam?"

"Because, captain, as we neared the city I started to take my compact from my purse—you know we women like to look fresh when we leave the train—and it was then I missed it. So it must have been taken on the train before it got here."

"Quite correct, madam. You have reasoned it out perfectly. I'm sorry we can't do anything for you—you see it was outside the city limits, and we have no jurisdiction beyond the city line. My advice is for you to report the matter to Superintendent Coffinberry at the depot. I am sorry we cannot help you.

"I'll keep a description of the compact, however, and if it turns up in any stolen property we recover I will notify you. Coffinberry is the man you want to see—second floor of the depot building."

She thanked him and left, the office. Brady sat at his desk, looking at the notes he had taken, and shaking his head. Then he reached for the telephone.

"Get me the manager of the Court Apartments at Mountainview," he said.

Presently the connection was made.

"This the manager of the Court Apartments?" he asked. "This is Captain of Detectives Brady, down at the city, speaking. Have you a Mrs. Amanda Reynolds as a tenant? You have, eh. Do you know if she is at home? Went to the city shopping, you say? No, nothing's the matter. Got a party in here who sort of gave her as a reference, that's all.

Just wanted to be sure the reference wasn't an imaginary person. Much obliged. No, I wouldn't say anything to her about the call, might embarrass her to know the police had called up. Good-by."

He hung up, left the office, and drove to the depot. He nodded casually to Riordan as he passed through the waiting room and went upstairs to the superintendent's office. Coffinberry was out, a clerk told him.

"Any robberies been reported?" he asked.

"Not to-day, captain," the clerk answered. "This is hardly the day, you know. Had one yesterday, though—drummer's sample case, out of the waiting room. Ought to have another to-morrow or the next day."

"It's tough luck. Tell Coffinberry I was just dropping in—nothing important."

Down in the waiting room he walked up to Riordan. "Can you tell me when the eight o'clock train goes to Yonkers," he asked.

"At nine o'clock, on track four, sir," answered his aide. "Try a new one, chief, that one isn't funny any more."

"What's doing, anything?"

"Haven't seen a thing that interests me. Heard anything?"

"Yeah—swell dame from Mountainview relieved of her purse on the way in. I sent her to Coffinberry. Sixteen dollars and some change and one of these gold powder cans."

"Tall jane, green dress, hat with feathers on it, pretty as sin, was she?"

"Yeah."

"I noticed her when she came through. She seemed lit

up about something. I figured she was going to meet 'him,' most likely."

"She said she was a widow, maybe she was. Said she was touched in the parlor car."

"There was a whole flock of people got off that train. Wished she'd come through first—but them parlor cars are on the rear end. I didn't notice anybody special from that train—except her. I'd have had to be blind not to have seen her. Say, chief, this is an awful job; they ask the darnedest questions!"

"Well, stay with it. You ought to make something before a week is out. And don't hesitate to get rough, if you think you got somebody. I'll drop round to-morrow."

3

"HE IS A THIEF!"

THERE WAS NOTHING the next day, nor the next day after that. The third day following promised to be as futile in the chase as the preceding ones until late in the afternoon. Brady was closing up his detailed reports for the day, when his phone rang. Taking the receiver down he answered, to hear Riordan's voice.

"Shoot a harnessed bull down here quick," he said. "I'm going off shift. And come on down yourself—in plain clothes. Don't speak to me, but stick around and jump in if you think you ought to. I'm going to play a hunch. Don't tell the bull anything, just tell him to take the depot beat."

Things buzzed at headquarters for a moment, and presently Captain Brady, in plain clothes, was driving his car to the depot at the best speed he could make through the traffic.

Once in the big waiting room or concourse, which he had entered casually enough, apparently from the baggage room, Captain Brady sauntered over to the news-stand and picked out a couple of cigars from the case. Paying for them, he lighted one, and turning sideways, leaned upon the counter and talked to the clerk, the while he looked over the rows of benches in the big chamber.

His inspection revealed nothing of special interest visible from that vantage point, so presently he leisurely made his way around the concourse to the opposite side, where he entered one of the public telephone booths, and from the semigloom within again surveyed the room through the glass door of the little cupboard. From there he saw nothing that in the remotest way resembled that for which he was looking.

Leaving the booth, he walked down to the farther end of the chamber, and beside one of the doors leading to the train shed he met Coffinberry. The superintendent asked Brady what brought him to the depot, and for answer Brady said:

"Step over here by the gate and talk to me. Keep your back to the waiting room—I want to look over your shoulder and see what I can see. I sort o' expect to see something."

The depot superintendent obliged, and the two men stood in a little nook between two of the train gates, the one apparently talking and the other listening. As a matter of fact Coffinberry was reciting a considerable portion of "The Lady of the Lake," which he had been forced to memorize when a boy, and which he had never forgotten. Brady, unconscious of the mumbling of the other's voice, was looking at a couple seated on one of the short benches facing the gate, perhaps twenty feet away, and a little to one side.

They were a strangely assorted pair. The man was bareheaded, his black, curly hair having a somewhat tousled appearance. He wore bib overalls, turned up at the bottom; a faded flannel shirt open at the throat, white socks, and broken russet Oxfords, which seemed too large for his feet. He was counting a roll of greenbacks which he held in his hands.

Beside him, and watching him with not too close interest, was a tall, thin woman, poorly but neatly garbed in black of some cheap material, with an untrimmed straw "sailor" hat upon her head. Her hair was drab, streaked with gray, and was pulled down flat over her ears and done up in a small, unkempt knot at the back.

The man, having counted his money, shoved it in one of the front pockets of his overalls and addressed a remark to the woman. She answered him, and presently they were in a desultory conversation, the man smiling often and waving his hands in foreignlike gestures as he talked. He pulled out the roll of bills again and displayed them to the woman, laughed gleefully, and then put them back in his pocket. The woman shifted her position slightly, and Brady noted that she was then much nearer to the man, half facing him.

A train arrived just then, and a score or so of passengers passed through the gate, obstructing Brady's view, and when they had passed it was very evident that there was trouble between the man and woman he had been watching. They were apparently arguing excitedly, the man waving his hands, and the woman beating a tattoo upon the floor with her foot. The man was shaking his head violently as he talked, and the woman's mouth had a firm and set expression.

The man rose from his seat, the woman reached up and took hold of the front of his overalls as if to drag him down again. Their voices became raised, and people on near-by benches turned to look. Foster, who had been sent back to his old beat to relieve Riordan, heard the loud voices where he stood near the smoking room door, and hurriedly walked over to see what was the trouble.

As he approached the man jerked free of the woman and rose to his full height, pointing one of his fingers accusingly at her; while she, also rising, cried out:

"Help, somebody! Help, this man is a thief!"

At the words Coffinberry stopped his recitation of poetry and darted in the direction of the cry; but Foster was quicker and was there first, grasping the man by the arm and holding him with a strong grip. Brady followed Coffinberry over and joined the group, about which a crowd was already gathering.

"What's the matter here?" demanded Foster.

"This man has stolen my pocketbook," said the woman.

Everybody looked at the man.

"Not so, Mr. Policeman," he said, breathing quickly. "I very much hate to say it, but this lady, she steal my money."

"Bring them both upstairs to my office, officer," said Coffinberry, "and we'll find out about this. Move back, there, please, and let us pass."

The crowd parted, the patrolman and his prisoner moved forward, Coffinberry and the woman following, with Brady in the rear. As the man stepped forward the woman pointed down to the floor.

"There's your dirty money," she said, "where you dropped it. Give me my pocketbook."

Brady bent over and swept up the pile of crumpled currency from the floor.

"Just step upstairs, lady," he said, "and we'll get this all straightened out."

She made no further remonstrance, and the little group forced its way through the crowd and ascended to Superintendent Coffinberry's office.

"Vice-President Ralston happen to be in the building?" asked Brady.

"I think he's in Mr. Shear's office," answered Coffinberry.

"Well, step out and ask him in here. I'd like to have him hear this."

While Coffinberry was gone, the woman sat down in a chair near the superintendent's desk, while Foster and his prisoner stood near the door. Brady dropped into a seat on the opposite side of the room. They waited in silence for Mr. Ralston, who came in quickly with Coffinberry and took the superintendent's chair, while the latter stood leaning, with his elbow on the top of his desk, beside his chief.

"This woman," said Brady, "says the man there robbed her. The man said the woman robbed him. Here's his money—it was lying on the floor. You'd better question them, Mr. Ralston."

The vice-president looked the two of them over, and then turned to the woman.

"Will you tell me what happened, please?" he said.

"I was waiting for my train, sir. This man came and sat down beside me and counted his money. Then he spoke to me. He said he had just been paid off and was going home to his wife. He showed me his money. I think he said there was a hundred and forty dollars in his hand. He seemed very happy, and I asked him about his family. Then suddenly I felt his hand at my side and he wrenched my pocketbook away.

"I told him to give it back. Instead, he accused me of

taking his money. I did not want to make a scene, and we argued about it. Finally he swore at me and started to go away, and I called for help."

"Yes, and then?"

"Then the policeman came, and these two gentlemen, and that gentleman there picked up the money from the floor. Then we all came up here."

"What have you got to say about it?" asked Ralston, turning to the man.

"Not very much, sir. I was waiting for my train, and I count my money. I think maybe the ticket agent, he make the mistake. It has happen. My money is all right. This woman, she was sitting some way off, but she slide up close to me and begin to talk. Pretty soon I feel her hand in my pocket, but I let her get the money. I want to catch her. I do catch her. Then I accuse her, and she say no, that I have stole her money. I tell her I go call the policeman, and she cry out. When the policeman come, she drop my money on the floor."

Ralston stroked his chin.

"Have you got the woman's purse?" he asked.

The man laughed.

"Of course not. You may search me."

"Search him, officer."

Foster ran rapid fingers over the man in overalls, hesitated a moment, reached down under the bib of his outer garb, and pulled out a worn, black leather pocketbook, which he handed to Brady. The detective captain passed it to Coffinberry, who placed it on the desk beside the vice-president.

4

RIORDAN GETS SHELL SHOCK

"I TOLD YOU he was the thief," said the woman. "That is my pocketbook."

Ralston looked puzzled.

"If that's your pocketbook, suppose you tell us what is in it," said Brady.

The woman bridled. "Are you insinuating—" she began.

"I ain't insinuating nothing, madam," said Brady. "I happen to be a detective. This whole thing looks fishy to me, and I want to give you both an even break. What's in that purse?"

The woman shrugged her shoulders. "Sixteen cents and my ticket," she said.

"What kind of a ticket?"

"Railroad ticket, of course."

"Where's the ticket to?"

"Southdown Junction."

"Open it up, Ralston, and see what you find."

The vice-president picked up the pocketbook and emptied it on the desk. A dime, a nickel, and a penny rolled out, and also a little pasteboard slip—the ticket.

"It's to Southdown Junction," he said.

"When did you buy the ticket?" asked Brady.

The woman looked at him sharply.

"The other day," she answered.

"What day?"

"If you are a detective I don't like your manner," she answered, and then, turning to Ralston, she added: "If you are in charge here, will you not relieve me from this man's insulting questions? I have proved my case, I think. All I ask is to be permitted to go home."

Ralston looked at Brady, but the latter shook his head.

"When did you buy that ticket," he repeated.

"I suppose the date is on the back of it," she answered, after a pause.

Ralston turned the pasteboard over, and his eyebrows arched.

"It's two months old," he said. "Madam, don't you know that these tickets are good only for the twenty-four hours following the date of their issue?"

She grew indignant. "I don't see what this is all about," she protested. "I said this man stole my pocketbook. The officer here found it on his person. I identified the pocketbook by its contents. I didn't say I was going to use the ticket. I demand to be permitted to go."

"You said you were waiting for your train, madam," said Ralston. "If you weren't going to use this ticket, what train were you going to take—with only sixteen cents in your purse?"

"Did you never hear of a woman carrying money in her— in some other place than her purse? However, I will admit I was going to attempt to use that ticket. I bought it from an agency down town. I have used those tickets before. I have not much money, and if I can save on carfare, I do it."

Ralston pursed his lips. "May I ask your occupation, madam?"

"I am unemployed, sir."

"He didn't ask you what you did," snapped Brady, "he asked you what your occupation was."

She flashed him a look of fire.

"Must I be humiliated by that person," she demanded of Ralston.

"I am afraid you must, madam. But permit me to explain the circumstances. We have been seeking a thief in—in this building for some time. This detective has been working on the case, as have others. It will greatly aid us, and possibly yourself, if you answer his questions and mine fully. I am a vice-president of this railroad, and if it develops that we have done you any injustice or wrong, I give you my word we will do our utmost to make things right."

She sank back in her chair resignedly.

"I will tell you," she said at length. "I am a performer— you would say an actress. I have been at liberty—that is how we express the condition of being idle—for several months. I have very little money left. I have been looking for work—any kind of work—all day, but have been unsuccessful. You can have no idea, sir, the things men say to a woman who is poor and looking for employment. This, coming on top of a futile day, is really about all I can bear."

"Good," said Brady. "You're talking sense now. Now I want to tell you something, to save your time and ours. This man didn't steal your purse, because he isn't that kind of a man. He's the best detective in this city. And if he says you stole his money, and then dropped it when he caught you at it, I'm inclined to believe him."

The woman turned and looked earnestly at the man she had accused, then faced Brady again.

"The officer here found my pocketbook in his possession, didn't he?"

"He did. But what would you say if I told you that I was standing twenty feet away from you, looking at you, when you slipped it—"

"I'd say you were a liar," she said, emphatically.

"How about it, Riordan?"

The man smiled. "You were twenty feet away, all right, chief," he answered. "And you were watching us over Mr. Cooper's shoulder."

"Did you know when she took your money?" asked Ralston.

"Sure. I planted it for her. I wanted to get her right."

"Did you know when this pocketbook was placed in your possession?"

"No, sir, she's got me there. She's good, I'll say. But it was her pocketbook all right—I saw it in her hand when she edged over to get closer to me. I had been fishing for her for quite awhile."

Ralston turned to the woman. "Now what have you to say," he asked.

Tears welled in her eyes, and she dabbed at them with a handkerchief. Two or three sobs shook her, and then she pulled herself together.

"I cannot understand it all," she said. "I don't know why this man should have picked me out. To 'make a case,' perhaps. I came into the depot so tired I could hardly walk another step. I had been looking for work, as I told you. This man came and sat down beside me, and began counting this money—ostentatiously. Then he began to talk to me. Then he showed me the money again.

"I was tempted. I took it. The moment I had done so, however, I realized that I had committed a grievous sin, and I dropped it on the floor. He accused me of taking it, and I told him I had done it to teach him a lesson, not to show his money in public, not to show it to tempt women. I said I had dropped it at his feet—and he cursed me, and snatched my pocketbook away and said he would keep it until I gave him his money.

"I told him it was on the floor. He got up and started away with my pocketbook. Then I called for help. That sixteen cents will buy my supper. I am sorry I have been the victim of this entanglement, sir—won't you let me go now?"

"That's a swell sob story," said Brady. "See if you can tell another one. What's your name?"

"Hazel Parrott."

"Where do you live?"

"I'm boarding at Southdown, with a family named Emerson."

"What are you boarding there for—when you have to come to the city to look for work?"

"My trunk is there—the show I was with broke up there. They are kind enough to let me stay at very cheap board."

"What was your act with the show?"

"I was with a troupe of prestidigitators—sleight-of-hand act, you know."

"What was the name of the show?"

"Adamson's Frolic."

"When did it bust up?"

"Three months ago."

"Do you expect me to believe all that?"

"I think I can prove it."

"Well, I'll give you a chance."

The woman brushed her eyes again with her handkerchief, and reached over to Coffinberry's desk and picked up the empty purse. Then she turned to Brady.

"Shut your eyes," she said, "and keep them shut while you count ten. I will slip this purse in your pocket and you won't know it."

"I'm from Butte, I'll do anything once," laughed Brady, and shut his eyes. The woman rose, walked over to him, bent over him, and in a flash turned around, Brady's automatic pistol in her hand, its barrel leveled at Vice-President Ralston's chest.

"One of you make one move," she said, "and I'll shoot."

"Oh, please, lady," whined Riordan, "don't start any rough stuff. I got a weak heart."

"Shut up!"

She walked like a cat to the center of the room, keeping the gun pointed at the railroad executive, then sidled over to the wall by the door, where she had all five of the men within her range of vision.

"Please, lady," whined Riordan, "listen. I may be a bull an' all that, but I got shell shock in the war, and any gun—even the sight of one—makes me go nutty. Please put that gat out o' my sight."

She looked at him appraisingly, and he began to swallow violently.

"I won't bother you very long," she said. "Try and buck up for a few minutes. Keep still, you, there by the desk or this thing will go off."

Coffinberry, who had moved one foot stealthily, froze stiff.

Mr. Ralston regarded the steady barrel of the automatic with interest.

"You're nervy," he said.

"Shut up!"

Riordan, swallowing violently, began to sway. "Please, lady," he said, "I can't stand it, I'm going to faint."

She shot a glance at him, but made no move. His legs began to tremble violently, and he swayed back until he leaned against the wall.

"Listen, all of you," said the woman. "I'm going out of here. I'm going to be out in the hall for a minute, while I make a change of my costume. I'm going to shut the door behind me. If any of you open that door before the minute is up, I'll shoot—right through the panel the minute the door moves. Understand? You sit here for one minute, or there'll be an ambulance case, and it won't be me."

"Please, lady, can I sit down—right here on the floor?" whined Riordan. "Honest to Gawd, I'm all in. That gun's got my goat—oh, I'm going to faint."

He began to slump down. The woman bored him with a glance, and then looked at Coffinberry. "Just one more wiggle out of that foot of yours," she said, "and—"

Riordan pitched forward, but halfway to the floor launched himself like a catapult, below the level of the automatic's barrel. One hand flew up and gripped the gun, the other encircled the woman's waist, and they went to the floor together. It was all over in a jiffy. Brady slipped a pair of handcuffs upon her wrists and dragged her into a chair.

5

"TAKE ME TO JAIL!"

"THAT SHELL SHOCK stuff had me going for a minute," said Ralston, drawing a deep breath. "But I guess you were exaggerating a bit." He laughed nervously.

"That's the trouble with Riordan," said Brady. "He's an awful liar. If you knew his war record you'd understand."

The woman glared at her captors, but said nothing.

"Well, captain, this has been very entertaining," Ralston spoke up. "But what's it all about. I confess I'm rather in the dark."

"Ask Riordan," answered Brady.

"Take a look at her hat, chief."

Brady reached over and picked up the "sailor," which had rolled to one side of the room in the scuffle. It was of good Milan straw, but devoid of any trimming. Above its brim a few black threads showed where a ribbon or flowers had been removed. Brady turned it over; aside from the lining there was nothing in it.

"I don't get you," he said.

Riordan blushed, then took a deep breath. "I told you I was going to play a hunch, chief. Here's this dame. Since I've been down here I've seen her hanging round the depot—always like she was waiting for something. She'd come in, sit round an hour, maybe, and then go out. Three hours later, maybe, she'd be back again, sit around another hour, and go out. Not every day, you understand, but often enough to make me curious about her. So I got to studying her.

"Her clothes were modest and neat, and she was quiet and seemed like she'd been refined when she'd seen better days—all but her hat. Them threads. They got my goat. I couldn't see how a woman who had a neatly ironed waist, even if it was old; a skirt that was always brushed clean, even if it was cheap; cotton stockings with no holes in them, and shoes that had been blacked—not polished, mind you—could wear a hat with them threads sticking out that way.

"A neat woman would have pulled the threads out. Her hat didn't jibe with the rest of her. And it didn't jibe with any woman that I know anything about, for it showed the trimming had been taken off. I've seen dames with untrimmed hats, chief, but I've never seen one that wouldn't put something on her hat if she had a chance. I've seen dames pick up old, cheap, flimsy ribbon off candy boxes and put them on their hats. Fact, I have.

"And so this dame's hat got my goat. I knew she was wearing it for a purpose. And knowing what you and me was after, I thought I'd test her out. So this afternoon, when I saw her come in, I slipped out to the baggage room and telephoned you, ditched my uniform, borrowed a pair of overalls and a pair of shoes out o' the lost-and-found room—and here we all are. I don't know as I've got the party we're looking for, but I betcha I got something."

Captain Brady looked at the Milan "sailor" again, and

passed it to Ralston. "Riordan's got a head, ain't he," he said. "Now that he mentions it, that hat is out of keeping with the rest of it."

Ralston looked at the woman. "Maybe you'd like to explain the hat, and the—er—er—what you might call 'threads of evidence' upon it?"

She shook her head.

"I have nothing to explain. You'd better send me to jail."

Captain Brady began to show a new interest. Ralston was surprised at the gleam that came into the detective's eyes. As for Riordan, who had been rather the star of the affair so far, his face showed frank amazement. Brady leaned forward toward the woman.

"You want to go to jail, do you? What for?"

"Can't you think of any charge?"

"Yes," answered Brady, "I can think of several. Larceny from the person—you stole my gun. Assault with a dangerous weapon—you pointed that gun at Mr. Ralston and threatened his life if he moved; that is technical assault. Vagrancy—by your own admission you have no occupation. Any of those charges appeal to you?"

"I do not care what you charge me with—take me to jail. You've won."

"You admit you're a crook?"

"Of course, if you say so."

"Well, I'm going to fool you. I know what you want to go to jail for. You want to beat this case before we get any more on you. The minute you get into jail you'll send for your attorney and he'll prove by all of us here that no money was found on you, that Riordan here had your purse, and that it was evident that there was an attempt made to 'frame up.' He'll make a squawk to the papers and stir up public interest; he'll picture you as a poor woman out of work persecuted by the police—and the judge, who's elected to office, will throw you out on your preliminary hearing and roast us bulls to a fare-you-well. That's your idea, isn't it?"

"No—I hadn't thought of that. I'm not as clever as you are. But I'm obliged for the tip, it may come in handy at that."

Brady laughed. "You're a cool one, I'll say. How old are you?"

The woman, in reply to the question so suddenly shot at her, opened her lips as if to speak, and then closed them. After a moment's hesitation she said: "I am thirty-nine."

"You're getting rattled, buck up," replied Brady. "You begin to think maybe it isn't as simple as it looked, don't you? If you're thirty-nine I'm a grasshopper. Take that wig off."

"I have no wig—besides that, I'm handcuffed."

At a glance from Brady, Riordan swept his hand forward quickly and the prisoner's gray hair vanished. Coiled flat upon her head was a wealth of mouse-colored locks.

"I had a hunch all the time," said Brady "Now how do you feel, Mrs. Amanda Reynolds, of the Court Apartments, Mountain view? "

"I don't know what you're talking about. My name is Hazel Parrott."

"Yes, when you wear the old clothes and this hat with the threads sticking out. But when you're all dolled up like a million dollars it's Mrs. Amanda Reynolds. You came into my office a few days ago and reported that your purse had been stolen on the train. You were faking then.

"You came in because you saw a new cop in the depot waiting room, and you wanted to find out if the police were next to you. When I didn't act as if I was interested in your story, and sent you to Coffinberry you figured you were safe. And you never reported the alleged robbery to Coffinberry."

"You can't prove anything like that at all."

"Can't I," asked Brady. "Well, you made another poor guess. Nobody talks to me in my office alone—there's always a man stationed behind that picture over my desk, watching and listening."

This was, of course, pure moonshine, but Brady noted that it seemed to impress the woman, as her lips tightened and her eyes narrowed.

"Now," he continued, "how are you going to explain overlooking a loss of sixteen dollars, when a little while ago you squawked about losing sixteen cents? How are you going to explain the swell apartments in Mountainview, and this rig you're wearing here?"

"I don't know that I shall have to explain it," the woman answered coldly. "I suppose you'll search this place you're talking about in Mountainview—but you won't find anything there."

"I won't even search it," said Brady. "I know there's nothing there. You, as Mrs. Amanda Reynolds, don't interest me at all. But I tell you what I'm going to do—I'm going to uncover you at this end, as Hazel Parrott."

She sneered.

"You don't believe it?"

"There's nothing to uncover, as you call it. Take me to jail and let's get it over with."

"Maybe to-morrow, girlie." Brady turned to Ralston.

"Mr. Ralston, I'm going to ask you to help me a bit. This woman, of course, has got a partner. I don't figure the partner works the trains or the depot—I figure she does that. But the partner takes care of the stuff she gets. I want to uncover the partner—probably a man. That's why she wants to go to jail—so he'll see that she's been arrested and then act according to a prearranged plan. She's too anxious to be locked up—after the fight she put up here.

"Can you get a couple of your special agents and give her a ride in private? I'd like to have her kept missing overnight at least. Lock her up in a compartment on a sleeper, and give her a nice long trip—say until to-morrow night."

"Why, certainly, captain. My private car is here. I'll send a matron with her, and fill the car with special agents, and have it hauled up to River Junction and back again. That ought to do."

"I don't want to be hauled around the country—that's kidnaping," protested the woman. "If I'm guilty send me to jail. I'm all alone, I tell you. If you think you've got a case, lock me up. You can't drag me around that way."

"What'll you bet we can't," asked Brady as Ralston turned to the telephone on Coffinberry's desk and gave some orders in a low voice.

"I'll scream, I'll make a terrible scene," said the woman. "I'll fight you all. Take me to jail, and lock me up, if you're so sure you've got a case."

"Go ahead and scream your head off, Hazel," said Brady. "We'll put you on a stretcher and have a couple of men in white suits carry you out, and tell everybody you're crazy.

You've got as much chance as a rabbit now—and you know it."

"The car will be ready in fifteen minutes, captain," said Ralston. "The man whose wallet she took on the train will be in charge. He'll enjoy looking over her—maybe it will refresh his mind."

"That's good, Mr. Ralston. Well, I've got to get back to my office. Riordan and Foster can hold her here till your men come. If you have nothing to do this evening you might drop down to my office—I think I'll have news for you."

As Brady rose to go the woman raised her manacled hands. "Captain," she pleaded, "for God's sake take me to jail. I'll confess everything."

"Not a chance, Hazel—I'm playing this hand."

6

HIS UNBALANCED DAUGHTER

SERGEANT RIORDAN AND Captain Brady were contentedly smoking cigars in the latter's office when Vice President Ralston was ushered in about half past nine that evening. Their expressions were almost gleeful.

"You seem quite happy," said the railroad executive. "Something happened?"

"Just like clockwork, Mr. Ralston," said Captain Brady. "I don't think you'll have any more robberies for awhile. After Riordan, here, played the hunch that hat gave him this afternoon the rest was all according to Hoyle. But you've got to thank Riordan for starting things."

"I intend to thank him. Sergeant, I am so greatly impressed with your work that I want you to be my chief special agent. The job pays probably considerably more than you're getting at present. Will you take it?"

"Go ahead, boy—it's your chance," put in Brady.

Riordan shook his head. "I'm very much obliged, Mr. Ralston. But it was just luck—that's all. And—and I like it here, sir. Thank you, sir, a hundred times. But I can't quit the force—not now."

Ralston saw that he meant it. "Well," he said, "you know your own affairs best. But if at any time you change your mind, let me know. We can use men who have your kind of luck. You said you wanted to see me to-night, captain— what was it?"

"Sit still and listen, sir, if you don't mind."

So saying the captain pushed a button on his desk, and to the responding officer he made a sign. The man withdrew, and returned presently, ushering in a small, middle-aged man, who gave every appearance of being both highly nervous and highly indignant.

"Pray sit down, sir," said Captain Brady. "You wanted to see me?"

"I want to see the chief of police."

"I'm sorry, sir, but the chief is out. I am the head of the detective bureau, and am in charge during his absence. I have just come in myself, and received your rather unusual message. What is it all about?"

The stranger waxed eloquent. "That's what I want to know, sir. I am a reputable citizen and a taxpayer. I came down here on personal business, and without any warning or charge being placed against me I was forcibly detained, searched, locked up, and held without being permitted to send for my counsel. I demanded to see the chief and was refused. Finally I sent the note—which I presume has been given to you. I want to know what it means."

Brady fingered a note on his desk. "If what you write here is true, sir, I want to know what it means, too. I have just come in, as I said, and sent for you at once. Will you tell me just what happened, please?"

"I shall be very glad to do so, sir. I came down here after supper to inquire for a missing person. Instead of being treated courteously I was at once locked up and subjected to search and other indignities. I shall sue the city, sir."

"I hope not," said Brady, in a conciliating tone. "I hope we shall be able to explain this and to make a satisfactory settlement. I am Captain Brady, sir."

"The only settlement you can make is to release me at once."

"Your name, please?"

"I am Thomas Parrott. My residence is at 681 First Street. I run a small jewelry shop at 457 Jefferson Street. I have papers in my pocket to prove—"

"Not at all necessary, Mr. Parrott," said Captain Brady, kindly. "I know you by reputation. This is a very strange matter—what was it brought you to headquarters, may I ask?"

"I came to inquire about my daughter, captain. She did not come home to supper. She is somewhat unbalanced, mentally, and I feared she might have met with some mishap. I was terribly worried—it is the first time she has not come home in the evening. As soon as I told my business to the sergeant downstairs I was seized and thrown into a cell, despite my protests, and despite the fact that I told him my daughter's life might be in danger."

"My, my! That is too bad, Mr. Parrott." Brady's voice was tragic in its sadness. "What was your daughter's name, and how old was she?"

"Her name, captain, was Hazel. She is twenty-six years old, but because of her mental condition she looks much older at times. Have you any word of her?"

"Yes, she is my prisoner."

"Your prisoner?" The elder Parrott was thunderstruck. A moment later he exploded wrathfully:

"What does this mean, sir? Where is my daughter? I demand to see her at once. I demand that my physician, Dr. Talmadge, be summoned. You shall pay for this, sir, and pay dearly."

"Cut it out and keep your shirt on, Parrott," replied Brady, dryly. "The jig's up. We got the girl this afternoon. I figured you'd come in, and gave orders to have you pulled. I figured you'd have papers on you showing who you were and all that, and I figured right. We got your address out of you, and the store address, and while we held you we searched them both.

"Got all the stuff in the property room—except the money, of course. From the books you kept you apparently deposited that in the bank, in the name of Mrs. Amanda Reynolds. She was your best customer at the store, wasn't she? And as a matter of fact she's your wife and not your daughter, eh?"

Parrott had lost all his bluster, had paled and wilted.

"You figured you had a perfect get-away, didn't you? Half-witted daughter. If she was caught it was to be her first offense. Your apparent standing would clear her. If you were caught, everything was in the wife's name, and you'd do what the court gave you and then get out. When she worked it was out of your place, and if she didn't get back at a certain time it was your cue to come here and start to holler. Pretty work—but it blew up."

The man had slumped down in his chair, dejection on every feature and in his very attitude.

"Where is she, captain?" he asked.

The telephone jangled. Brady turned and lifted the receiver.

"Yes, this is Brady—who?—oh, yes—she did, eh? Too bad. Yes, I'll look after things at this end."

He hung up slowly and turning back rose and walked over to Parrott's side. Putting his hand on the man's shoulder he said:

"I'm sorry Parrott. She's dead. She was a prisoner on a train and took a chance and jumped out of the window. They just telephoned. But it's better that way, Parrott, and you'll realize it later. She was too fine a woman, in lots of ways, to go to prison. And we had her—just as tight as we've got you."

The prisoner sobbed softly.

"You said it, captain, she was too fine a woman to go to prison. She was too fine a woman for me, captain. I dragged her into it."

Brady squeezed the man's shoulder.

"Tell you what we'll do, Parrott," he said. "We'll give it out that it was Mrs. Amanda Reynolds who died—fell from the train. We'll spare her memory—if you'll help."

The prisoner pulled himself together and looked up, a wan smile on his face.

"I'll help, captain—I'll plead guilty."

WHAT THE CIPHER TOLD

Though The Telegrams Were Never Delivered,
Their Treacherous Messages Were Read,
Until Sergeant Riordan Got Busy

1

THE UNDELIVERED MESSAGES

"THEN, AS I get you, chief," said Sergeant Riordan, "you calculate a plain bull who uses his head is worth as much, if not more, than a dick who's been trained—"

"I didn't say that at all," interrupted Captain Brady, of the Detective Bureau. He and his chief aide had been having one of their late afternoon arguments—merely to pass away the time before the captain went off shift and his right-hand man went on duty for the first night relief.

"What I said," the captain continued, "was that the trouble with most dicks—and professional detectives, too, including Sherlock Holmes and all those guys—is that they're too apt to jump at conclusions; whereas a plain, 'harnessed' bull, by the very nature of things, has got to think out his problems one step at a time. That's why, when I got the run of this department, I brought in a lot of you fellows who had been pounding the pavement.

"You'd been in the habit of using your heads as well as your feet, and that was the kind of men I wanted. As you know, my men have got to prove their cases to me before I'll go to the district attorney and make any reports—I don't want any theorizing that'll go back on me when some good lawyer starts to try and tear my cases to pieces."

"Well, whatever your system is, I guess it's right," said Riordan, moving over toward the desk.

The door to the outer office opened and the man on duty outside ushered in a caller. Both Brady and Riordan nodded to him and smiled.

"Hello, you two birds," said the newcomer. "Fighting again, are you? It's a funny thing, but the only time you two agree on anything is when you have somebody dead to rights—all the rest of the time you scrap like a couple of old maids."

Brady grinned. "You said it, Stanley. But you got to admit we agree when we're right, and disagree only when we're wrong. That's the system, isn't it? What you in for?"

Stanley smiled in return. "I'm not in, thanks. Just dropped up to show you some curiosities. Thought maybe they might fit in somewhere with your work. They don't mean anything to me."

Stanley, local superintendent for the telegraph company, laid a number of flimsy sheets upon Brady's desk.

"Copies of messages we can't deliver," he said. "Addressee not to be found. The messages don't say anything, either—lot of gibberish."

Brady picked them up and glanced at them in order, then passed them to Riordan.

"Code," he said.

"Code, your grandmother. We got a code man down at our place and he says there isn't anything that looks like a code in them. And he ought to know. He's been handling code messages all his life, and was with Intelligence during the war."

*He produced an apparent duplicate of the first
bag, which he placed before Stanley.*

"They're not addressed here—how did you get hold of them?" Brady asked.

"They're all to small towns around here, you'll notice," said Stanley. "They come to us on the direct wires from the north and east, to be relayed on the local loops. Of course we copy them as they go through—have to. And on every one, we've sent a report back that we couldn't deliver them. They're all prepaid, though—we should worry."

Brady took up the copies as Riordan laid them down and scanned them again. They were dated over varying periods for the past three or four months, and were addressed to suburbs and near-by communities of the city, which was his territory. The telegrams were sent to people with such nondescript names as "John Smith," "Peter Brown," "Willie Green," and so forth, and, save for the name of the town, bore no specific address. Each message contained merely a jumble of letters. They came from Chicago, St. Louis, the Twin Cities, and other centers in the Middle West. They were all signed the same: "T B C."

"You people tried to locate old 'Tuberculosis,'" asked Brady.

"Yes, we've tried. But locating 'T B C' in a city like Chicago to tell him his message wasn't delivered isn't as easy as you might think, especially when he doesn't seem to care whether they're delivered or not. Our people have figured out 'T B C' is just a plain nut."

"Then why bring 'em to me?" asked Brady.

"General orders, old scout. Western headquarters notified all district managers to turn copies over to the local police 'for general information.' You can toss 'em in the wastebasket—I've followed instructions and cleared my skirts."

"I'll keep 'em and dream on 'em—much obliged," said Brady. Then there was some small talk, and the telegraph man went out. Brady picked up the messages again and looked them over. As he placed each one on his desk Riordan took it up and read it—but when the series had been perused neither man was any less mystified.

"Don't it beat the dickens what some nuts will do," said Riordan.

No nut is going to spend a dollar or so every couple of weeks telegraphing half the alphabet out to the wild and woolly West. Nuts haven't that much imagination, boy," Brady replied. "Maybe we got something here that will interest us, and maybe we haven't. Let me get at that phone."

Riordan shoved the instrument over, and Brady called the Protective Association, which, in response to his inquiry, assured him everything was peaceful in financial circles—just the usual run of petty forgeries and check-kiting. So Brady, after a moment's thought, tried another tack. He called the local office of the express company and asked for Stacey, the chief special agent.

"Hello—Stacey? This is Brady, down at headquarters. You look worried, anything the matter? How did I know you were worried? Why, I got one of these new-fangled phones that you can see the movies through! That so? Well, come on over."

He hung up and turned to his aide. "Stacey is one of the best boys outside the police bureau that I know, Riordan," he said. "But he's like all the rest. Afraid to call in the department, because he thinks if we know anything we'll give it right out to the papers. Stacey says he's worried to death, and he wants to know what I've got that I should call him up. He's coming right over. I thought things were too quiet to be as peaceful as they looked. We haven't had a good job for five months."

Stacey arrived in less than ten minutes. The moment he entered the office both Brady and Riordan knew that it had been cruelty to ask him if he was worried—his face was pale, there were black blotches under his eyes that told of sleepless nights, and his whole manner was nervous. He was no more like the usual, jolly Stacey they knew than a sick man would be like Samson.

"Sit down, Stacey, and tell papa all about it," said Brady, dragging forward a chair and holding out a cigar at the same time. "Why the devil didn't you call me up long ago?"

"Brady, I've wanted to, but the old man wouldn't stand for it," answered Stacey, lighting the cigar and puffing at it nervously. "You know how he is—afraid of publicity. Thinks everything the police know gets in the papers. I've told him repeatedly that you're all right—but you know how it is. The public mustn't know—might lose confidence. I'm glad you called—I can tell him you had something, and that will give me the excuse for letting you in on this thing."

"Sure—tell him anything. Tell him I stole the jewels, if you want to. What's it all about?"

"It's no joking matter, Brady. We're being robbed blind, right and left. Of course we're insured, but that isn't the point. And it's so bad even the insurance men are howling now."

"What's gone?"

"Everything—bonds, money shipments, furs. Anything that can be handled quickly. Take it right out of our hands."

"Inside jobs?"

"No. It looked like it at first. There may be somebody on the inside at the other end, but not at this end. We've watched every man, we've had guards on every truck. But the stuff goes."

"Yeah," said Brady, drawling the word. "How come?"

"Well, here's an instance. Eggers & Company had a shipment of ermine coming down from the north. We posted men all along the line. Even had a guard on the train. The shipment got here and a truck backed up to the car, one of our trucks with two men on it, one wearing one of our caps. The other wore a star. They said they'd been sent special to get the Eggers shipment and take it up to the office under guard. Of course they got it. That's all. It never got to our doors. It wasn't given to our men. And though the truck was painted like ours, it wasn't our truck.

"That was one trick. Another was with a package of bonds for Elwell, Epstein Brothers. We'd lost several packages before that, and this one was specially guarded. Apparently one of our messengers, with good credentials, got on the train at Mountainview, explained he'd been sent to take the bonds personally so there'd be no chance of funny business at the depot. Got the bonds, gave a receipt for them—and vanished. Receipt was a forgery of our forms."

"Like taking candy from a kid," said Brady. "Why didn't you come to me? How long's this been going on?"

2

BRADY GETS BUSY

"I TOLD YOU why we didn't come to you. But it wasn't altogether that. Every case looked like an inside job. Time we checked on it, it was cold. And every job was different. It's been going on for four or five months. We don't know what to expect next. One time they forced their way into the express car on the Overland and blew the safe, after tying up the two men in the car—and nobody knew anything about it till the train got to Southdown Junction.

"Another time a couple of men came down to the main office after a telephone call from the People's Bank and presented an order for a package of bonds. Two minutes after they'd gone the real messengers came in. There's been a job every three or four weeks, and every one's different."

"Gimme a list of them," snapped Brady.

Stacey reached in his pocket and drew out memorandum, which he handed over.

"You go and tell the old man I've got this stuff, Stacey. Then you go home and sleep round the clock. I can't give you what I've got till to-morrow night anyway. Maybe what I've got isn't any good—maybe it is. But you do as I tell you. And if the old man makes a holler you send him down to see me. I'll tell him something about the police business and about his business that will surprise him. Now go on home and sleep."

"I'll do that, old horse. It helps a lot to know you're working with me. And I'm just about all in."

As Stacey went out, Brady handed the memorandum and the copies of the telegrams to Riordan.

"Play with 'em," he said. "I'm going out to eat and then take the air. I'll be back by and by, and then we'll see what we've got. Maybe I'll call on the old man while I'm out and save him from coming down here."

Which he did, for when he returned to the detective bureau at nine o'clock Riordan noted the light of battle in his eye.

"You saw the old man, then?"

"I did that, me boy. I went to his house. I told him the police department and the detective bureau was responsible for the suppression of crime in this city, and that I didn't take it kindly of him to have the insurance companies hear that a bunch of crooks was stealing thousands of dollars' worth of stuff here and us not turning a hand. I told him some more, too. When I left he said he was glad we had the case. The old turnip! Well, have you made anything out of that mess yet?"

"Not much, chief. But there seems to have been one of these fool telegrams two or three days before each of those jobs. But the telegrams weren't sent here."

"Maybe the gang was lying out in the rhubarbs between jobs."

"That's a bright idea—but you forget none of the messages were delivered. They were all dead."

Brady pursed his lips. My gosh, boy, you are using your

bean," he said, and dived in his pocket for a cigar, upon which he began to chew.

"Them messages," he said at length, "were all relayed through here. Somebody copied them, or somebody listened in on the through wires. These fake addresses were just blinds. Somebody here got the messages—that is, if they had anything to do with the jobs. Let's get Stanley down here again—you locate him and call him, while I take a look-see at this crazy stuff."

While Riordan was using the telephone Brady pored over the copies of telegrams and the memorandum that Stacey had left. He made pencil notes on the back of an envelope, then lighted his cigar, closed his eyes, and lay back in his chair, scowling as he thought. Riordan, through with calling, did not disturb his chief, but slipped into a chair at his own desk and busied himself with routine affairs, which had to be attended to no matter what other matters might be before the bureau.

Brady was still turning things over in his mind, though the scowl had left his face, when Stanley came in. He paid no attention to his entrance, and it was necessary for Riordan to speak before he opened his eyes and sat up.

"Bless me, I was dreaming—having them nightmares you spoke about," he said. "Say, Stanley, that was a nice kettle of fish you brought me in those crazy messages. Listen, who copies them down at your place?"

"They copy themselves, captain—on a machine. Do they interest you?"

"Everything that's crazy interests me, Stanley. Now don't kid me. Remember I'm not as smart as you—tell me all you know about those messages."

"I'm not kidding you, Brady. They are copied mechanically in the office on one of the machines—'mokrum' we call them. They work automatically. We have girls watch 'em and put in paper, that's all. After the messages are copied that way girls distribute them. The local ones go to the delivery department—two copies, one for the customer and one for the files. Those we have to relay on to local loops are sent to the operators to send out. They file their copies with the sending time on them. Then we have a couple of copies for office files. I gave you one of those files."

"Same girl handle them all the time?"

"No—we have a whole harem of girls working on that stuff. They come and go. The work isn't very interesting or attractive. It doesn't require much brains or training."

"I can believe that—after some messages of yours I've read," said Brady, with a grim laugh. "Well, listen, is the same girl apt to have been on those machines when all these messages came through?"

"It's possible. Some of the girls stay with us a long time."

"Could you find out for me?"

"Yes—but not to-night. I'll have to get the timekeeper's checks."

"Can you do it to-morrow—to-morrow morning?"

"Yes—I guess so. What's doing?"

"I don't know as anything is doing. I'm just naturally curious and nosey—that's why I'm a dick, I suppose. Listen, I want you to find out if the same girl might have been at the machines when all those messages came in; and if the same girl might have been there, I want her name and address and anything else you happen to know about her.

But don't let her know you're making any inquiries. And whatever you do, don't fire her or let her quit. If she wants to quit, marry her if you have to; only hang onto her till I can get there."

Stanley, who had seemed somewhat amused at Brady's interest, grew serious. "Then there is something doing, eh. Well, I'll get right after the timekeeper in the morning. Anything else I can do?"

"Yes, be deaf, dumb, and blind if you hear anything."

After Stanley had departed Brady turned to his aide.

"Some of them messages have an even number of letters in them, and some don't," he said. "Have the night clerk run off duplicate sets of copies of them. I want to take one home with me. You take the other set. And don't crack anything about these robberies. And don't get the idea in your head that a general round-up would be a good thing. We've got to step easy until we know where we're stepping—then we've got to jump."

Riordan took the flimsy sheets out to the night clerk, and presently the clicking of a typewriter in the outer room told Brady his orders were being carried out. When Riordan returned with the copies Brady put one set in his pocket, placed the originals in his safe, and gave the duplicate to Riordan.

"I'm going home now," he said. "There's not a word of this to be given the papers. If the papers get a smell of it I'll break your neck and fire every man in the bureau. Get that? Keep those messages out of sight, except when you're alone. If anything cracks, or you get an idea, call me up."

3

KELLY PAYS A CALL

CAPTAIN BRADY AND Sergeant Riordan were not exactly the two best-natured men in the city when they sat down to conference the following afternoon. Both had been working hard, and neither had slept very well. Nor had either of them made very much progress on the matter in hand.

"I'm frank to confess I'm no puzzle-guesser," said Brady. "I've read those messages till I don't know the proper order of the alphabet. But I can't get a thing out of them."

"Get anything out of Stanley, chief?" asked Riordan.

"Not a whole lot. There's two girls, sisters, been working on those machines for the past year. He says neither one of them has any brains, not even enough brains to flag some fellow and marry him. That's why they're there. They come of a decent local family, and while I've got a man working on that end, it don't look now as if he'd turn up anything. What did you get?"

"Not a whole lot, chief," admitted Riordan. "I sat up with those messages most of last night. There's three of them that I got an idea about. But only three."

"That's three more'n I've got," grunted Brady. "Shoot your stuff."

Riordan spread out a piece of paper, upon which he had typed the following.

> Shipment of furs for Eggers stolen June 4. On June 2 the following message, addressed to John Jones, Mountainview, was received by wire from Winnipeg:
>
> Rgukhoikuvdx Sluvrodneosl Urmr Bb Di Mp.
>
> People's Bank was robbed of shipment of bonds July 20. On July 17 following message, addressed to Sam Brown, Southdown, was received by wire from Chicago:
>
> Utefboswhtdjmv Bbrceodp Eous Ix I Eep.
>
> Elwell, Epstein Brothers were robbed of package of bonds August 2. On July 29 following message, addressed to George Smith, East Everleigh, was received by wire from St. Louis:
>
> Rgenicmhdqmo Efutrusauibihv Mqmr Uv SE.

Brady looked the paper over carefully, and then gazed sadly at his aide.

"You sit up all night getting that much?" he asked.

"Don't be so snappy, chief," retorted Riordan. "I haven't told you what I got yet. This is just 'Exhibit A.' I could have written down a lot more of those messages if I'd wanted to, but I didn't find anything in the others. I admit I haven't found much in these. But that first word in the first one, you'll note, has twelve letters. Eggers—who lost the fur—has six letters in his name.

"In the second message the first word has fourteen letters and the second eight—which is just double the number of letters in 'People's Bank.' In the third message the first word has twelve letters and the second fourteen, which again is just double the letters in 'Elwell, Epstein.'

Each of the messages came just before the place with the corresponding group of letters in the name was bumped off. Now I may be crazy, but I think those cipher words refer to the names of the firms that were touched."

Brady counted out the letters with his fingers, looked closely at the messages, and nodded his head.

"But the heck of it is," continued Riordan, "that if my guess is right, this is a dickens of a cipher to solve, for the same sign isn't used for the same letter each time. I've plotted it out a hundred times, but I don't get very far."

"Have you found the letter e yet?" asked Brady. "You know they say e is the most used letter in the alphabet, and solves most ciphers."

"I found nothing but e, chief," answered Brady. Look at those names, they're full of e—'Eggers,' 'Elwell, Epstein Brothers,' 'People's Bank.' Yet, if I'm right, and this cipher says what it looks like it said, the guy that uses it puts down ef for e twice, uses rg for e a couple of other times uses dj or ik or some other fool combination. So maybe I haven't got the right idea at all."

Brady studied the sheet Riordan had prepared anew. He scowled over it and shook his head.

"You got more out of it than I did, boy," he said at length. "And I've always found your hunches good. Maybe this guy uses different signs for the different times—one sign for the first time e is used, another sign for the second e, and so on."

"I got that same idea, but it doesn't work out, chief."

"Here's a funny thing," said Brady, pointing to the second message. Down at the end, there, he uses one letter and then three. That looks bad for your two-letter sign idea."

"I knew there was a catch in it somewhere," laughed Riordan bitterly.

"Probably them one and three-letter signs are numbers," said Brady. "I think you've got the right idea—only we haven't got brains enough to solve it. I wish we could get hold of Mike Kelly."

"Who's Mike Kelly?"

Brady smiled. "Mike is a human fairy story," he answered. "As near as I know, he's a Treasury detective. However, most of the time he don't work at it, but is on detached service for the President or the Secretary of War or some big bug who wants a man who knows everything. The tales I've heard of Mike Kelly you wouldn't believe—but I believe 'em. I was in just a little bit on a case with him once, and, oh, boy, what that man did! By gosh, I'm going to try."

He reached for the telephone, and in a voice so low that even Riordan could not distinguish the words, called a number. He waited a long time, but finally got the party he sought.

"This is Brady—Detective Captain Brady, at headquarters—talking," he said. "You don't happen to know where Mike Kelly is, do you? I didn't suppose you did. Well, listen; if you happen to see him in the next few days, tell him Captain Brady wants to see him; that it is very important, will you?"

He hung up slowly, and pushed the telephone back on his desk.

"You can never tell," he said to Riordan. "Kelly may be in Timbuctoo, or he may be here. If he's here, I think he'll come. It's just a matter of luck."

"Any reason to think he is here?" asked the sergeant.

"None—except that this is his territory when he works at his Treasury job."

They both turned back to Riordan's notes again, and pored over them. But they got nowhere, and were soon simply arguing about the possibilities of solving the supposed cipher. They were doing this heatedly when the desk man outside knocked sharply on the door. Brady rose and unlocked it, looked over the desk man's shoulder, and beckoned to somebody beyond to enter.

A tall, lean, but powerfully framed man came into the room.

"This is Sergeant Riordan, my second," he said to the newcomer. "Riordan, this is Mr. Kelly, whom I was speaking to you about."

Riordan gripped the extended hand, and was surprised at the strength in the thin fingers that rested within his own. He decided at once that Kelly was a man of sorts.

"You phoned just in time, Brady," said the Federal agent. "I was just going away—little hunting trip. What's the matter?"

Brady picked up Riordan's set of notes and thrust it into Kelly's hand.

"We got this thing," he said, "and I thought maybe you could give us a hunch as to how to go at it."

Kelly swept his eyes over the paper rapidly, and then looked more intently at the notes Brady and Riordan had jotted on the margin in attempting to solve the hidden meaning of the groups of letters.

"I'm sorry, Brady," he said; "but it can't be done."

"What do you mean, can't be done?"

"Just that," said Kelly. "This thing is either a nine-line cipher or a thirteen line cipher. And it can't be solved."

Brady was dejected. "Then we're sunk," he said.

Kelly laughed. Riordan sat up with a start, for the laugh was a great, bullish bellow of abandoned mirth, yet Kelly's face hardly wore a smile. Brady, more familiar with his man, gave no sign of surprise.

As quickly as the laugh had burst forth it stopped. "Pardon me," said Kelly. "I didn't mean to hurt your feelings." His voice was soft and low as a Southern woman's. "But you're just wasting time if you are trying to solve that thing. There are at least nine possible signs for every letter of the alphabet in it—possibly there are thirteen signs. Possibly there are even more. I have seen them with more than thirteen; but then there are complications. The diplomatic service uses a cipher something like that, only more complicated. But the principle is the same."

"But if you know all that," burst in Riordan, "why can't—"

Brady silenced him with a look, but Kelly smiled gently.

"It isn't the cipher that's important," he said, turning to Riordan, "it's the key word. The cipher is mechanical. The person who uses it only has to remember the keyword. We use one in our department like that, with a different keyword for every month—twelve words a year to memorize; and twelve new ones the next year. With the key word you can read that stuff, after a little practice, almost as easily as you can read ordinary English. But without the key word—"

He waved his hands.

"Riordan thinks these combinations mean e—will that help?" asked Brady.

"Not very much. You might get seven or eight of the combinations for e, and lacking the other two, were it a nine-line cipher, you'd be little better off," said Kelly. "What's it all about—these express robberies?"

4

RIORDAN GOES FISHING

BRADY TURNED TO his aide.

"I told you Kelly was a human fairy tale," he said. "Now you'll believe me. Yes, Kelly, we think it is."

"Forget the cipher, then. All you'd get from them, if you were lucky enough to solve them, would be past history. They hardly come far enough in advance to give you much warning of a coming job. If I were you, Brady, I'd run down the person who's transmitting these ciphers; trail his or her companions, and get your men that way."

"But nobody seems to be getting them."

"Stuff—they're sent for a purpose, aren't they? Of course somebody is getting them. Go bore into the telegraph company force."

"I got a man tracking down a couple of girls," said Brady.

Kelly shook his head. "Crooks like these don't play with girls," he said. "A crook who's got brains enough and experience enough, to use these things, and get away with the jobs this gang has, knows too much to trust girls. Put a man in the telegraph company—don't bother fussing round outside."

"Are you working on this case, too," shot out Brady, after a moment.

Kelly shook his head. "No—but some of the boys are. I've heard them talking about it. The last package of bonds stolen happened to contain some government stuff. I wish I was on it—it would be a pleasure to coöperate with you. Sorry I can't give you any more help, but I've got to toddle along. Only forget that cipher, and put a man in the telegraph office."

They shook hands all round, and Kelly departed.

"I'm going to solve that cipher anyway," said Riordan.

"All right, son—amuse yourself with it. Me, I'm going to follow Kelly's advice. I know that bird. I'm going out right now and frame me a nice plant down at Stanley's place without his knowing anything at all about it."

Sergeant Riordan surprised Captain Brady by appearing at the office at one o'clock the next afternoon, instead of at four, when he was due.

"You getting on all right, chief?" he asked.

"I sure am, son. I've got a friend of mine who's an operator working down there at the telegraph office, and he's wising me up to a lot of things. I've got six men running down his stuff already. Next one of those messages that comes in, everybody who reads it is going to be run down and watched, if it takes every man in the bureau to do it."

"Well, then, chief, since you're so well set, I guess I'll lay off for two or three days."

"Huh?"

"Yes, I've lost a lot of sleep, and I want to make it up. I think maybe three days lay off, now—"

Brady's eyes narrowed. Then he smiled.

"You got an idea, haven't you? Want to work on it alone? I know you, lad. And at that you're just as liable to be right as I am. Go on, lay off—only we won't call it a lay off on the report. I'll put you down for special duty. Can I get you if I want you real bad?"

"Sure, chief, I'll be on call. Phone the house, they'll know how to reach me. I just want to try out a hunch I've got."

"Go to it, and may you have luck," said Brady seriously enough.

He would have been more surprised, however, had he followed Riordan, for the sergeant walked leisurely out of headquarters, met a girl palpably by appointment at a corner a few blocks away, and then climbed with her into a taxi and sped away. There was nothing in his demeanor— or the girl's, either—that indicated either of them were on anything but pleasure bent.

Brady had nearly spoken the truth when he declared he would put every man in the bureau on the tips his operator friend gave him, were such a course to be necessary. Within the two days following Riordan's departure from duty on the first night relief, an even dozen of the bureau's sixteen sleuths were running themselves ragged after employees of the telegraph company and their acquaintances, for still another mysterious cipher message had been received.

This one was from Omaha, and was addressed to "Joe Rivers" at a local hotel, and like all the rest, was reported back "undeliverable, no such person known at address." Four sleuths combed all the hotels and lodging houses in the city, seeking Joe Rivers, but found him not. The message which had caused all this excitement read:

Rdmodkio Eyhtmuis Uqem I.B.U.

Stanley brought a copy of it to Brady on the afternoon of September 3rd, and remarked that he hoped it would prove of at least as much interest to the captain as the former messages had.

"It will interest me a whole lot more; it's fresher," answered Brady. "The other ones were ancient history, and if they meant anything at all, we had slim chance to find it out. We'll try and see if this means anything."

Stanley wished him luck and departed. After he had gone, Brady, who already had been informed of the receipt of the message earlier in the day by his operator at the telegraph company, put in a call for Riordan's home. Much to his disgust he was informed that Riordan had gone out on a fishing trip, and there was no certainty when he would be back.

"Leave word, then, for him to call me the moment he returns," said Brady.

But Riordan apparently did not return that day, which was Wednesday, nor did he call Thursday or Friday morning. And in the meantime Brady was driving his men frantic with directions to follow this person or that, or to investigate as quickly as possible, the business of the people living at such and such a place. He had, of course, communicated the receipt of the message immediately to Stacey, of the express company, and that worthy had not only placed extra guards upon all the wagons, but had appealed to the sheriff's office for special deputies to guard the express office and to virtually surround the depot when express cars came in.

There was so much excitement, in fact, around the detective bureau, that the chief heard of it, and Friday afternoon he stepped up to Brady's office and inquired, in his slow, drawling way, what was doing.

"Doing?" snapped Brady. "What's doing? I'm waiting for a robbery to break. I've got all the places where it could break covered, and I'm just waiting for the lead to fly."

"I think you're overworked," said the chief. "They don't usually advertise robberies in advance. From what I hear, you've got the jimmies, or something, and you're running your men ragged. Snap out of it. If you think something's going to be pulled, go out and get the guys you suspect."

Brady reddened. "I don't know who to suspect, sir," he answered. "Fact is, I'm up against it. I'm doing the best I can—"

The door opened and the deskman in the outer room announced:

"Mr. Stanley, of the telegraph company, sir—says it's important."

"Show him in."

The chief withdrew to a corner of the room and sat down. Stanley, very much excited, hurried in.

"I've been robbed, Brady—right on the street," he said. "I don't know how much, yet, but it's several thousand—maybe ten thousand."

"Where'd it happen—tell me quick," snapped Brady, reaching for the telephone.

"At Tenth and Main Streets—I was carrying a valise with the money in it, and a man slipped up, snatched it from my hand, leaped into an automobile, and drove off."

"Get the number of the car?"

"I was so startled I couldn't."

"Give me any description of the car and the man you can."

"I—I don't think I can give you any, captain. The man came from behind, you see, snatched the bag, and ducked away behind me. I naturally turned to the right—the bag was in my right hand; that was next the building line, for I was going north on the east side of the street. When I finally got turned all the way around I saw a car—a big red one, pulling away from the curb. The whole thing was just like that," and he snapped his fingers.

"Where'd you get the bag—at the bank?"

"No, captain. I got it at the express office. Got a wire this morning saying the company was sending some money for pay roll and extension uses, and for me to personally receipt for it. They offered, at the express office, to send a guard with me, for the bag was insured; but I told them I only had a couple of blocks to go, and thought a guard would attract more attention than to be alone."

Brady took the telephone off the hook and demanded to be connected with the desk sergeant.

"Got any report of any excitement at Tenth and Main Streets just now? This is Brady speaking. No? Well, if you get anything, call me at once. Buzz up the man on that beat, it's important."

As he hung up Sergeant Riordan entered without knocking. He nodded casually to Stanley, saluted the chief in the corner, and also his immediate superior.

"Something doing?" he asked. "I just got home, and got your message."

"I'll say," answered Brady. Another one of those things we were working on."

"Where?" said Riordan, showing keen interest.

"Tenth and Main. Stanley, here. Ask him, he'll tell you about it."

"Had some trouble, did you, Mr. Stanley?" asked Riordan, turning to the telegraph company man.

"You'd think it was trouble, sergeant. Man snatched a satchel out of my hand. Had several thousand dollars in it. Jumped into an automobile and whizzed away."

"Do tell!"

Captain Brady stiffened in his chair at the burlesque exclamation from his aide's lips, but he said nothing. The chief, too, rose from his chair in the corner and took one nearer the desk.

"It may sound fishy," said Stanley, "but it really happened."

"What kind of a satchel was it?" asked Riordan.

"It was a flat, leather valise, dark brown, two straps and two locks. It had a tag on the handle, addressing it to me. It came from the company's branch office at Omaha, and contained pay roll and extension money."

"I didn't know you got your pay rolls from Omaha," said Riordan casually.

"We don't, usually. We pay by check. But we've been doing a lot of extension work lately in this district, and our local deposits were running low. Omaha happened to have a surplus of funds, so they made a transfer."

"Would you know the bag if you saw it?" asked Riordan.

"Why, it's got my name on the tag."

"Yes—but suppose the tag was torn off, would you know the bag?"

"I think so."

5

"A GIRL OF MY OWN"

RIORDAN ROSE, OPENED the door, reached outside, and came back with a valise much like the one Stanley had described.

"That look like it?" he asked.

Stanley did not immediately answer. He looked at the bag in a startled sort of way, then at Riordan, whose face was bland and expressionless; then at the head of the detective bureau, and last of all at the chief. Finally he looked at the bag again.

"I'd say that was the bag—or one exactly like it, sergeant," he said.

"Well, let's open it and see," suggested the sergeant.

"I—I—haven't the keys with me. They are in the office. In the safe."

Riordan smiled.

"Try another one, Stanley," he said. "I think you've let your foot slip. Get your keys out and open that bag—or I will, for you."

Stanley turned to Captain Brady. "Is your man crazy? What's he intimating? That I framed this thing, and was trying to steal the company money? I came here to report a robbery. If he's got the stolen bag there, bring it over to my office and we'll get the keys and open it, and see if the money is all there."

Brady twisted up one eye. "Riordan may be crazy—that's always possible, Stanley. But if he is, I'd sort of humor him. Try any keys you've got on that bag."

Stanley looked at the chief.

"Go on, get your keys out and try," said that worthy. "If this isn't a framed case, the quickest way to prove it is by showing up Riordan."

Stanley hesitated a moment, then drew a bunch of keys from his pocket and tried several of them in the locks on the bag. None of them would open it.

"You see," he said, "the real keys are at my office."

"Tell you what you do," suggested Riordan. "Take the phone there and call your bookkeeper, and tell him to get those keys and bring them over here."

"What's the idea?"

"You do it, that's the idea. It will save you a lot of trouble later on."

"I don't understand this at all—and I don't like it," protested Stanley.

None of the three answered him, or moved, so presently he rose, took up the telephone and did as Riordan had suggested. They all waited in silence until the bookkeeper arrived with the keys. After he had delivered them to Stanley he was deftly thrust from the room by Riordan and told to wait in the outer office.

"Now you try those keys on the bag," said Riordan.

Stanley tried, but the bag refused to open. The two keys on the ring the bookkeeper had brought failed utterly to even fit the keyholes.

"I guess it isn't my bag," said Stanley. "Now will you explain all this witty work of yours?"

"Sure, I'll explain it—in a minute. But first I want you to try those keys on another bag I've got."

He opened the door, reached outside again, and produced an apparent duplicate of the first bag, which he placed on the floor before Stanley.

"Try your keys again," he said. "Not your own keys, I mean, but the office keys."

Stanley, his fingers trembling, bent over the bag. The keys slipped into the slots as if they had been greased, and in a moment the bag was unlocked. Stanley then undid the straps and opened it. Within was a neatly but tightly packed pile of gold-backs and silver certificates.

"Well," said Stanley, "I guess I've got to apologize. I congratulate you. You've recovered the stolen bag."

"Looks like I had," said Riordan, smiling dryly. Then he turned to Brady.

Cap, you get a couple of your tired out men and send them with the bookkeeper and this money up to the telegraph office, will you? Then us three are going to have a little talk."

"I'll take the bag," said Stanley, rising.

"You sit down," exploded the chief. "We'll deliver that money to the telegraph company and take the bookkeeper's receipt for it. It looks to me like you've got a lot of explaining to do."

"But, chief, I'm the manager of the tel—"

"Shut up and sit down."

Brady pressed a button and in a few seconds the valise, locked by the bookkeeper in the presence of all of them, and escorted by two husky detectives, was on its way to its destination, and the three officers and Stanley were once more alone.

"Now," said the chief, "let's hear all about it, Riordan."

"Well, sir, it's a funny sort of a proposition. I can't tell you all of it till we get rid of him," said the sergeant, pointing to Stanley, who was looking from one to the other of the officers. "But I can tell you this much now. You see, I knew this money was coming. I'll tell you how I knew it later. When it got here me and Stacey, of the express company, carried it over to the express office, and Stacey called up Stanley here, and told him he had a package for him.

"We agreed, Stacey and I did, for reasons, that we wouldn't offer to send any guard along with Stanley. But we had a string of men posted all along the route from the express office to the telegraph office. Stanley, in answering the telephone, said he'd be right over for the bag, so I sloped up the street, along the route we had guarded, to see what I could see.

"Up at Tenth and Main Streets, which is a pretty busy corner, I had an automobile all staked out, because I sort of figured I'd need it. The engine was running and there was a driver in it—in fact, it was my own car. Tenth and Main, you know, is a pretty crowded corner.

"Well, when I got there what should I see but a guy stalling along with this here first bag in his hands. He was looking for somebody, but he wasn't going anywhere. Of course I'd seen the real bag down at the express office, and I knew the one this party had was a duplicate—so I signalled one of Stacey's men, and we just naturally made this first fellow disappear.

"Then I waited, and pretty soon along comes Stanley, carrying the real valise out from him like it was full of dynamite—or as if he was waiting for somebody to grab it. And I grabbed it, ducked into my car, and brought it down here. Thought it would be a lesson to Stanley, maybe, not to carry money round loose that way."

"You've surely done a fine job, sergeant," spoke up Stanley, seemingly with relief. "You must have spotted the man who had planned to rob me—exchange bags in a shuffle, or something like that, in the crowd. I owe you a great deal."

"You want to remember that you owe me a great deal, Stanley," said Riordan, seriously. "And I'm going to make you pay, too."

"I'll be very glad to."

"Well, we'll get to that later. In the meantime Stacey's man gets this fellow with the other bag up to a certain place, and there Stacey comes in and tells him the game is all off, that he's been doublecrossed, and that the other guy has the money. Stacey tells him how the other guy has squealed that this first fellow was going to switch bags, and with that the man naturally gets sore and he spills most all of what he knows."

"Are you trying to say that I framed to have myself robbed?" shouted Stanley.

"That's the idea exactly, Stanley, and this fellow will turn State's evidence and bawl you out to save his own skin."

"Why, you're crazy. In the first place, you robbed me, not this other man you're talking about. And my word's as good as this other man's. What's the matter with all you, anyway?"

"Listen, Stanley, you just said you owed me something, and you'd be glad to pay me, didn't you?"

"Ye-es. But that was before you started this crazy talk."

"Well now, listen. The money that was going to be stolen is in your office safe now. The fellow that was going to steal it and one of his pals, whom he blames for his mishap, are locked up. That's two of them. Now you come clean and give us the names of the rest of the gang and where we can get 'em, and we'll forget your end of this case and say nothing about it—as long as you keep straight."

"You're out of your head, Riordan," protested Stanley.

Captain Brady pressed a button. To the man that responded he said:

"Take this fellow out of here and lock him up in solitary till you hear more from me," and he pointed at Stanley.

With Stanley gone the chief hitched forward in his chair.

"I suppose you two Wisenheimers know what you've done," he said. "You've locked up the manager of the telegraph company, and, as far as I can see, you ain't got a thing on him. He ought to sue for about seventy thousand dollars."

"He'll not sue," returned Brady. "I don't know any more about it than you do, chief, but I'll bet on Riordan here. I'm all balled up on this case, but now I feel better. All I knew, as I told you, was that there was a job slated to be pulled off. Well, it seems Riordan's gone and spoiled it. If he's done that much he must be on the right track."

The chief turned to Riordan. "Sergeant, if you can explain this thing to me so I can understand it, I'll—damn if I don't fire Brady or something and put you in charge."

Riordan grinned. "I'm not good at explaining, sir, but I'll try. You see, sir, it was this way. Some time ago Stanley brought in some telegrams here that he said he couldn't deliver, and that his company had ordered him to turn over to the police. Capt'n Brady here, he dopes out that they are ciphers, and the two of us, putting one thing an' another together, we found out that a couple of days after each of the messages had been received there'd been a big job pulled. Capt'n Brady here, he—"

"Suppose you leave me out of it, son," interrupted Brady. "Fact of the matter is, chief, that I was stumped—plain stumped. If this case is jake now, it's Riordan who did all the work. I don't want any credit. Now, Riordan, you talk to the chief and leave me out of it."

Riordan grew red and shook his head.

"Don't you believe him, chief," he said. "He's just tryin' to give me a boost before you. We worked together on this case, him and me, like we always do. But to get back to the dope; we asked a Federal dick named Kelly about these here ciphers and he gave us a tip to never mind the ciphers, but to watch the telegraph office. Well, we done that—that is, sir, Capt'n Brady did that, and he detailed me on other work.

"Now it so happens that my younger brother is soft on one of the girls down at the telegraph office and they're always kidding me about not having any girl of my own and always promising to get me one of the telegraph girls. So I tells 'em to get me one, and who d'you think they got me? Stanley's own office clerk, Marie Partout. She's a French girl and lives up the hill with her widowed mother—"

"Say, what is all this, a family history," shouted the chief.

"I want to know what you got Stanley locked up for, not what you and Brady's been doing."

"Leave him alone, chief; he'll tell you," said Brady quietly. "Here, have another cigar and let him talk."

6

THE MYSTERIOUS JOE RIVERS

"**WELL, AS I** was saying, they got me this Marie Partout," went on Riordan. "I was only with her, you understand, when I was off duty, chief. After we'd got acquainted she tells me she's a nut on cross-word puzzles, and that her mother has second-sight and can solve 'em with her eyes shut. So I says to her, 'Have you tried to solve them puzzles that's worrying your boss and that he's turned over to the police?' You see, I thought I might get a lead.

" 'What puzzles?' she comes back with. 'Has he got any puzzles? It's the first I've heard of it.' Well, that kind o' floored me for awhile, so I talked about something else, and found out she was Stanley's very special private clerk and knew all his affairs, and then I edged back to these queer messages.

"I had a copy and showed 'em to her, and told her Stanley said the company told him to turn 'em over to the police. She says she's seen every message that came to Stanley, but that he hadn't been told to turn nothing over to us; but she's all lit up over the messages, and says her mother can read 'em.

"Well, to make a long story short, next day I asked the capt'n here to let me go up and see the old lady and have a talk with her and he says to go, as it looks like it might be a lead. So I went up and Marie was there, and the old lady—that is, her mother, and she ain't so old either, about forty-five, maybe. Her mother says she can't read 'em because they're in English, but maybe she could if they was translated to French.

"Come to find out, her husband was something or other in the French army and he used to write things like this. I told her Kelly had said they were nine or thirteen-line ciphers, and that you had to know the keyword to read 'em, and asked her did she know how those things worked. And she said she did, and asked me did I think I knew any of the words. I said I did, that I thought 'Rgukhoikuvdx' meant 'Eggers,' and that—"

"Here, chief," interrupted Brady, "is a copy of the messages he's talking about. That's the word there that he's talking about."

The chief looked at the cipher messages and Riordan pointed out several of the cryptic groups of letters to him.

"I told her," he said, "that I thought this one was 'Elwell' and this one 'Epstein,' and that these two meant 'People's Bank,' and asked her if she could show me how to work 'em out. She said she could, and she got some paper and drew a diagram on it, all letters—ten lines of them, and then she explained how the top line was half the key, and how the keyword would be written on the side, and by designating two letters, one from the keyword and one from the top line in the corresponding column, you could designate any letter you wanted to—here, I'll show you."

And Riordan took up a piece of ruled paper from Brady's desk and rapidly filled in the following:

	A	B	C	D	E	F	G	H	I	J	K	L	M	N	O	P	Q	R	S	T	U	V	W	X	Y	Z
1	a	b	c	d	e	f	g	h	i	j	k	l	m	n	o	p	q	r	s	t	u	v	w	x	y	z
2	b	c	d	e	f	g	h	i	j	k	l	m	n	o	p	q	r	s	t	u	v	w	x	y	z	a
3	c	d	e	f	g	h	i	j	k	l	m	n	o	p	q	r	s	t	u	v	w	x	y	z	a	b
4	d	e	f	g	h	i	j	k	l	m	n	o	p	q	r	s	t	u	v	w	x	y	z	a	b	c
5	e	f	g	h	i	j	k	l	m	n	o	p	q	r	s	t	u	v	w	x	y	z	a	b	c	d
6	f	g	h	i	j	k	l	m	n	o	p	q	r	s	t	u	v	w	x	y	z	a	b	c	d	e
7	g	h	i	j	k	l	m	n	o	p	q	r	s	t	u	v	w	x	y	z	a	b	c	d	e	f
8	h	i	j	k	l	m	n	o	p	q	r	s	t	u	v	w	x	y	z	a	b	c	d	e	f	g
9	i	j	k	l	m	n	o	p	q	r	s	t	u	v	w	x	y	z	a	b	c	d	e	f	g	h

"You see, chief, it works like this," he went on, pointing with his finger. "The keyword goes where I've put the numbers. It can be any word you agree upon. She showed me how it worked—if you wanted to put the letter 'e' in a message, you'd look in the top line for 'E' and then take one of the letters below it, say the 'g' in the third line. Then you'd put before that the third letter of the keyboard in place of the '3'—so your 'e' would appear as '3g,' only instead of a '3' you'd have some letter. Well, we took the word I thought was 'Eggers' and, working it backwards, we got five letters of the keyword—putting them in-place of the numbers, it looked like this:"

And Riordan wrote down, in place of the first column:

1

R

4

U

D

I

8

H

"Well, chief, to make a long story short, we found out in time that the key word was *'Bermudish'* if we were on the right track, and it seems we were, for we got so we could read all the messages. Look now, this first message translated was like this:"

And Riordan wrote down:

Rgukhoikuvdx Sluvrodneosl Urmr Bb Di Mp

e g g e r s   e r m i n e   N o   b   d   m

Continuing, he went on: "That 'No b d m' stuck us for awhile, till I happened to think that 'No' stood for 'Number,' and the old lady, Miss Marie's mother, said that in this cipher you used the nine letters in their order for numbers, and if you had to have a 'O' you used the letter 'o.' That made it mean 'Number 1 6 4.' That was still Greek, till I looked up the case and found that the ermine that Eggers was robbed of came in on Number One from the north on June 4—sixth month, fourth day. After that it was easy.

"Well, we made out the other messages. These two here on the list read 'People's Bank, No. 3, July 20,' and 'Elwell, Epstein, No. 3, August 2.' Some of the other messages before them said bonds was coming, or whatever the swag was, with tips on the shape it would be in. You see I was getting the hang of the thing good. But Miss Marie still insisted that her boss hadn't received any orders to turn the messages over to the police.

"That got me thinking. And the more I thought the more I figured, like Capt'n Brady did, that somebody in the telegraph office was getting the messages. Capt'n Brady, he'd been having the different clerks watched and followed, and it was evident to him and to me that in the rush of work they had up there nobody could copy those messages down without it being noticed, and it was a cinch nobody could memorize 'em as they come clicking in off the wire.

"So we got to looking for the one man who'd have a chance to copy them at leisure, and there were only two of 'em—Stanley, who got copies of them in his regular reports on undelivered messages, and the delivery clerk. Well, chief, Capt'n Brady laid over the delivery clerks and found they wasn't botherin' their heads about these things, and me—I just laid over Stanley.

"And Wednesday morning Marie—I mean Miss Partout—called me up and said Stanley had another of those messages and that she'd made a copy of it, unknown to him. That was the morning of the day he brought it in to you, captain. So I run up to the telegraph office and got a copy and then out to Mrs. Partout's house, and we figured it out to read:

" 'Your coin, Number Three, September 5.' That left us two days to work on. I got hold of Marie that afternoon and asked her what coin was coming, and she said Stanley was expecting some money from the Omaha office. 'That will be on a draft or a bank transfer,' I said, but she said not—that it was coming in money: that Stanley had written several letters to Omaha about it, saying there had been a bunch of robberies here and to send the money by express in currency to him, and he would be personally responsible for it. He'd had to argue quite a bit to get Omaha to do it, but they finally agreed to send it in an insured valise, and the keys by airplane mail.

"Well, that looked pretty soft. I knew Stanley didn't

know a thing about these robberies—or wasn't supposed to, unless these messages had been for him, and he was head of the gang here, or one of them. So I made it my business Friday—to-day—to have Stanley pretty well covered. And because Tenth and Main Street is a good place for a mix-up, on account of the traffic jam, I was up there with my car and my kid brother driving it, and with the engine running.

"And, as I've told you, there was a guy there with a bag just like the one Stanley was going to get, and we put him away. And then up the street comes Stanley, just dying for somebody to jostle him and switch bags with him—holding it way out from him, he was, just like bait. And I grabbed the bag, ran around behind him, and come right down here, and waited outside there by Barton's desk for him to come in and make his holler."

"Plain as the city ordinances about spittin' on the sidewalk," said Captain Brady. "He gave us those messages, figuring we'd work them out in connection with the other robberies, which he figured we were working on; and the whole thing would make an alibi for him. He'd claim to have been robbed, too; and in the inquiry it would have looked like it. Then he and the gang would have cut it up. And he figured we'd always be two or three days behind him, so it would all look natural, and that we'd never suspect him, because he'd given us the tip. But you fooled him, didn't you, Riordan?"

"You did a good job all right," said the chief, "but I don't see yet that you got anything on Stanley."

"Don't you worry about that, sir," Riordan explained, with a wave of his hand. "We've told those two we grabbed that Stanley turned them in, and that he'd got tired of splittin' with them. They've both belched already, and implicated him a-plenty; besides which we've got these messages; and the two bags, and the fellow with the other bag; and the letters he wrote the Omaha office to send cash—oh, we can make the case.

"But at that, sir, I think the best thing is to hold Stanley till he squeals and we round up any others who may be in it—and then we'll grab Mister Stanley for State's evidence, and that will queer him with the company and he'll lose his job. The express people will help us, too."

"I guess you're right," said the chief. "Here, let me have that key thing there for this cipher, and those messages; I want to take them down to my office and work 'em out for myself."

He picked up the papers and went out, and Brady looked at Riordan.

"Son," said the captain, "I've got to hand it to you. You sure saved me on this case, and then covered me up fine before the old man. Anything I've got is yours."

Riordan laughed. "I'll tell you something you want to remember a lot more than that, chief."

"What's that?"

"That last cipher message. It's a dinger. The old lady and I spent damn near the whole day on it. It didn't read. Finally she said—she's French, I told you—finally she said: 'Zees Joe Ree-vairs I can not understand at all '—and then I nearly knocked her over as I slapped her on the back. 'You got it, old girl,' I said. 'Ree-vairs—Reverse is what you mean.' Then we worked it from the other end, just reversed it, see, and it came out all right. The chief will be up here in a minute, and you want to remember that. I got to go out and take Marie home. See you later."

Brady was still chuckling when the door of his office was slammed open and a very wild and angry Chief of Police burst in.

"See here," he shouted, "I knew' you were crazy and Riordan an idiot. This key doesn't work out at all. And we've got that man locked up. He'll sue for false arrest an'—"

"Here, sit down, sir, and I'll explain that to you," said Brady, pulling him into a chair. "That puzzled me at first. Trouble with you, sir, if I do say it, is that you haven't got a trained mind. Now look. See this 'Joe Rivers' here. Well, that means—"

And Brady explained it all.

THE HONEST THIEF

*The Millionaire's Daughter Lost Her
Bracelet, And She Learned More Than
She Expected Before It Was Found*

1

THE MISSING BRACELET

"YOUNG LADY OUTSIDE to see you, chief," said Sergeant Riordan as he entered the inner office of the detective bureau just before four o'clock in the afternoon, when his shift on duty began, "She looks like real people, but won't give her name to the desk man."

"I've told him to let anybody in who wants to see me, but he's always fussy," exclaimed Captain Brady. "Stick your head out and give him the office, son."

Riordan did, and the young lady entered. She looked inquiringly from one to the other of the officers and then addressed herself to the superior, as indicated by the legend and the amount of gold braid on his cap.

"Has Mr. Laird—Bartholomew Laird, I mean—been in to see you to report a robbery, captain?" she asked.

Captain Brady showed no surprise at the mention of the name, though Bartholomew Laird was one of the city's big merchants—the proprietor of "Laird's, the Store that Saves you Money," as its ads proclaimed.

"What sort of a robbery, miss?" he inquired.

"A bracelet, captain—an emerald bracelet."

Brady smiled. "Well, now," he answered, "I can't answer

that question, miss, without asking another. Whom might you be?"

She cast a questioning glance at Riordan.

"He's my twin, miss," reassured Brady. "He's my right hand. You may as well tell both of us, for if you don't I shall tell him when you go out. I have no secrets from Sergeant Riordan, miss.

She smiled and took a seat in a chair near the desk, against the corner of which Riordan was leaning.

"I am Miss Laird, captain, Miss Grace Laird—Mr. Laird's daughter. You see, it was my bracelet."

"Oh, yes, Miss Laird, I see. And when was it stolen?"

"That's just what I want to see you about, captain. It wasn't stolen at all. I lost it. I had it on Thursday afternoon and Thursday evening it wasn't there. It was quite loose, and I must have lost it somewhere. I've looked everywhere for it, but can't find it. Father noticed I wasn't wearing it, and I put him off. Friday morning he asked me about it again and I told him then that I had lost it. Er—do you know my father?"

Captain Brady made a wry face. "Slightly, miss."

She laughed. "Well, then, you know how he is. He doesn't believe I've lost it. He thinks it was stolen from me and that I know who stole it, and that I am shielding a thief. Father doesn't approve of the interest I have in working people; doesn't approve of my charities at all, in fact. He's had his store detectives looking for it ever since, and he told me that if they didn't find it this week he was going to report the theft to you. That's why I came here."

"And what do you want me to do, Miss Laird?"

"Why, I hardly know. But I don't want you to look for

*The turnkeys presently turned up with a
violently protesting individual.*

the thief. And don't tell father I have spoken to you—he
would be furious. I think the bracelet will turn up shortly;
somebody will find it."

"What makes you think it wasn't stolen, Miss Laird?"

"Oh, I just *know* it wasn't. In the first place, I wasn't
where anybody *could* steal it."

Captain Brady looked at her quizzically. "Suppose you
tell me all about it," he said.

She hesitated a moment and then gave a helpless little
gesture with her hands.

"There isn't much to tell, captain. The bracelet is an heirloom in the family. I suppose it is quite valuable, just for
the emeralds. I was going to a masquerade at the Prindles's
Thursday evening and decided I'd wear it. I was having
dinner with them just before the party, and about four
I called the car and left the house to drive out there. My
costume was already there ahead of me—I'd sent it over by
my maid earlier in the day. As I entered the car I—there
was a rough edge on the running board where some flivver
had run into the car and I tore my stocking on it.

"So I told Joseph, that's the chauffeur, to drive to the store on the way out. At the store I bought another pair of stockings. Then I happened to think of the little cripple girl whom the Prindles are caring for—she's one of my charity cases, you know—and I went over to the candy counter and bought her some peanut brittle. Then I went out to the car and Joseph drove me straight to the Prindles. When I was getting ready for dinner I missed the bracelet. You see, it must have dropped from my wrist in the store somewhere."

"Why don't you think it could have been stolen in the store, Miss Laird?"

"Oh, it *couldn't* have been. In the first place, all the girls at the store are honest, I know—and then I wasn't in a jam anywhere. Nobody pushed against me or anything like that."

"I see."

"And when I told father about it—that is, when he made me tell him, of course he went right into one of his tantrums. You know he does not think very highly of— well, of working people. He was sure one of the clerks had stolen it, and said he would have them searched. At that I refused to tell him what counters I'd visited. So he has had the store detectives accusing all the girls of stealing it, and one of them admitted I was at the candy counter, and he had her rooms searched. The poor girl nearly had hysterics. She—"

The deskman discreetly opened the door and poked his head within.

"Mr. Laird to see you, captain," he said.

Brady motioned him out.

"Oh, gracious, captain, my father musn't find me here," exclaimed the merchant's daughter. "He'd murder me!"

Brady motioned to Riordan and he beckoned Miss Laird to follow him through an inner door. Captain Brady reached into his desk and drew out a cigar, which he lighted, and then, pacing about the room, he blew clouds of smoke into the air in all directions. Riordan returned alone presently and Brady thrust another cigar into his hand.

"Fog up and blow it all around," he said. "The old boy mustn't smell that perfume. You let her out the side entrance?"

"Took her down through the inspection room and out through the alley," answered Riordan between puffs. "She had her car parked round the corner."

"Well, I guess the smoke screen is thick enough now," said Brady, and he pushed a button on his desk.

Bartholomew Laird was ushered in. The tobacco-laden air was evidently not to his liking, for his expression became at once hostile. He was a man of patrician mold, and the smoke seemed to drive him still further within himself.

"Captain Brady," he inquired stiffly.

"At your service, Mr. Laird. This is my aide, Sergeant Riordan."

Laird gave a barely perceptible nod and plunged at once into his business.

"I wish to report a robbery, captain. My daughter's emerald bracelet, stolen, I regret to say, in my store. I should like to turn the case over to you."

"Why, may I ask?"

Laird looked surprised. "You are the executive officer of the city detective bureau, are you not?"

"I am, Mr. Laird. But it was only last Monday, at the annual banquet of the Merchants' Association, that you referred to me as 'the Sitting Bull down at headquarters.' After what you said in your speech I am surprised that you come to me with—with this robbery."

The store owner gave a short laugh. "I—er—the fact of the matter is, captain, that I was trying to be clever in that speech. I am sorry if it offended you. I meant no reflection. I realize that as an executive you have to remain in your office and direct the work of others. I dare say you are a very capable man, in your way."

"That is good of you, Mr. Laird. Probably the police commissioners shared your view when they appointed me to this office, after some thirty years running around at the work you now say I direct. But I've been 'Sitting Bulled' so much this week I'm still sore about it. However, what about the robbery?"

"The robbery occurred Thursday afternoon in my store, captain. I have had our own men working on it. They have found that my daughter was at the hosiery counter and in the candy department. They have made diligent investigation of all the employees at these two counters, but because my daughter foolishly refuses to assist them have made but little progress. I warned her that if she did not help us I would place the matter in the hands of the police, with all the unpleasantness that might entail. And I am now doing so."

"Why won't your daughter help you?"

"She's a—a foolish girl, in some ways, captain. She is given quite largely to charity work, and she thinks all the poor are honest. She would rather lose the bracelet altogether than see one of my employees sent to jail as a thief. She cannot see the moral side of it at all—that the girl who stole that bracelet must be punished for the good of society."

2

AMONG THE "PERSONALS"

"WHAT MAKES YOU think the bracelet was stolen?"

"Because my daughter would not willingly talk about it. If she had lost it, as she says, she would have voluntarily come and told me. Because she is trying, mistakenly, to shield the thief, she insists that she lost it. It is ridiculous for a woman to talk about losing a bracelet of that value. If she had lost it she would have wept."

"Of what value?"

"Probably twenty-five thousand dollars, captain. It is very old. My great-great-grandmother received it as a gift from court when she was a lady-in-waiting on the queen. It has been in the family ever since. It was foolish of my daughter to wear it. It was an invitation to thievery. The stones composing it—"

"Could be all cut up by this time and disposed of," interrupted Brady. "Why didn't you report this thing to me when it happened? What's the idea of letting your fool store detectives fuss around with it and spread the alarm? You get up at the Merchants' Association dinner and roast the police for their slowness in solving crime, and for their negligence, but it's just tricks like this that hinder the police. Why, your store detectives can't even catch a shoplifter in your own store—they always follow them to another store, so the arrest won't be printed in the papers as being in your store. And if the shoplifter doesn't work another store they let 'em go! When did this thing happen?"

"Thursday afternoon, captain, between the hours of four and five."

"And here it is Saturday, and you come and drag it to me!"

"I don't like your manner, captain."

"And I don't like a cold case, Mr. Laird. If this bracelet was stolen and the thief or thieves have a two-day start on me, and I can't find them, you'll get up at some other banquet and damn the police and say some more about 'Sitting Bull.' As a matter of fact you are the man at fault.

"If a twenty-five thousand dollar robbery in your store isn't worth reporting to the police the moment you discover it, what in blazes would you report to the police? In my opinion I got a license to be sore about it, haven't I?"

"I see your point of view, I think, captain. But let us not discuss it. I have reported the case to you now. My man Tompkins, head of our special agents, can give you any information that you may require. He has the names of all the suspected employees—"

Captain Brady slammed his fist down on his desk. "Tompkins be eternally damned," he shouted. "Tompkins was fired off the police force for a muttonhead. I won't touch the case unless you keep Tompkins and all his stool pigeons off it. I start on it clean or I don't start at all—and you can go to the commissioners and tell 'em I said so, if you want. Now listen to me and answer my questions: What was the description of the bracelet?"

Mr. Laird grew frigid, but he answered bluntly. "Sixteen large emeralds joined by a silver, hand-wrought chain. The royal coat of arms surmounted the buckle that joined the bracelet. The emeralds are of the finest quality."

"What time was it stolen?"

"I have already told you—Thursday afternoon between four and five."

"What makes you think so—Tompkins?"

"I have investigated myself. My daughter came to the store about a quarter after four. She was there probably twenty minutes. The store closed at five."

"Where was she during that time?"

"At the hosiery counter and the candy counter, both on the main floor."

"Any new employees at either counter?"

"No, it happens that they are all old employees."

"Any of 'em admit seeing the bracelet?"

"No—and they have all been questioned."

"Got a technical description of the stones?"

"Yes, here it is."

Laird reached in his pocket and drew forth a sheet of paper and placed is on Brady's desk.

All right, Mr. Laird, I'll do what I can. But mind you this: until I give up, you keep off this case and keep that man Tompkins off it. Understand?"

Laird nodded his head, rose, and walked out without the courtesy of a good-by.

Brady took a deep breath and turned to Riordan.

"I guess I gave him something to think about, son," he said. " 'Sitting Bull' me, will he. I'd like to punch his head. However, that isn't business. What you think of it?"

"Me? I think the girl got in a jam and pawned the thing. That's why she's trying to cover it up. Lot of these society dames get in jams, you know."

Brady shook his head. "Nope," he said with finality.

"Then a moll-buzzer got to her in the crowd," suggested Riordan.

"That might be—and she, not knowing, would think she lost it. Well, we got something to do. Of course we can't do much till next week, but put this thing here on the board and have the pawnshop squad wised up."

He pointed to the memorandum Laird had left.

"Women's all fools," remarked Riordan, glancing over the description of the jewels. "The idea of wearin' a thing like that on a shopping trip. Might as well put on a sign saying 'Come and get me; I'm easy.' Twenty-five thousand—twenty-five grand—and all yuh got to do is to reach for it."

"I was just thinking," said Brady, "whether it would be wise to put a 'personal' ad in Sunday's paper. No, I guess not—yet. No use tipping our hand. If it was stolen, let 'em think only Tompkins is working on it. That will make 'em careless. It gets my goat, though, to have to wait over Sunday—but I don't see anything else to do. Well, boy, I'm going home; maybe I'll go fishing to-morrow. You better have Daly or somebody round in the morning if I don't get here. Give that stuff to the pawnshop men—some cheap guy might have 'em at that, and try to unload 'em here. And put it on the wire north and south. Good night to you."

Brady's route home, however, was not direct. He dropped in at "Frenchy" Chaumond's little jewelry store on his way. It was a mere cubby hole in the wall down in the market district, but Frenchy was a man of parts. As far as Brady knew he was honest, but he had a world of information. After a few commonplaces Brady asked:

"If sixteen emeralds was worth twenty thousand bucks, Frenchy, what would they be worth cut up?"

Chaumond's eyes grew big and his hands animated. "Now, my captaine," he said, "why zee fairy story. What is zee ansair; I gif up?"

"It's no joke, Frenchy. I got a case on. What would they be worth cut up?"

"Well, if zee cutting was vaire good, maybe nine t'ousan'; not much more."

"Anybody round here able to do it?"

"No, captaine—no, nobody—but me!"

"Well, if you get the job call me up first."

The Frenchman laughed. "Captaine mine, if I get zee job I would retire."

Then Brady went home—and Sunday went fishing. But he caught nothing, not because the fish didn't bite, but because he was not thinking of fishing at all. He was reviewing, over and over in his head, the things Miss Laird had said to him. Of what her father said he gave not a thought.

One of the first things Captain Brady did every morning, after he had scanned the overnight reports and attended to such detail as was most pressing, was to read the "personal" ads in the daily papers. Monday morning he found one in the *Chronicle* that interested him. It ran:

EMERALD:

Important. Where can I communicate with you confidentially? Answer this paper.

He called up the advertising office of the *Chronicle* at once and made inquiries. After consulting the books the clerk replied that the ad had come in about three o'clock Sunday afternoon, being sent in by messenger boy in a sealed envelope with a dollar bill included. No, he didn't notice whether it was a telegraph messenger or whether the boy wore the cap of one of the local messenger agencies.

Inquiries at the messenger offices by two detectives assigned to the matter failed to turn up anything. There was no record of any call at that time to deliver an envelope to the *Chronicle* office. All the managers agreed, however, that boys were often stopped on the street and given messages to deliver and tipped for the service. That was the boys' graft. Such inquiries as could be made among the boys failed to elicit anything definite.

Of course the "personal" might have nothing to do with the case. But it was a chance not to be missed. Captain Brady went to the *Chronicle* office himself and left a personal to be inserted in the next day's paper. It read:

EMERALD:
   Be at southwest corner Tenth and Main at ten o'clock. Will
   recognize you.   B.

The pawnshop detail turned up nothing, though the "combing" had been unusually thorough. Nor did the wires sent north and south Saturday night produce any hopeful replies. And Monday night was Riordan's regular night off.

3

ARRESTING A MASHER

THE PERSONAL COLUMN of Tuesday morning's *Chronicle* was by way of being a richly jeweled affair. At the head of the column was Brady's advertisement, setting a rendezvous for Tenth and Main Streets at ten o'clock. Scattered, down the column were others, all of which Brady cut out and pasted upon a sheet of paper. When he got through the list, aside from his own composition, was like this:

Emerald:

Will meet you waiting room Union Station at noon sharp. Wear picture hat and roses. I will carry black walking stick.

Tom.

Gentleman wearing light tweeds will meet Emerald at ten o'clock Tuesday morning at Interurban depot. Strictly confidential.

B.L.

Emerald:

Pabst Café, Tuesday afternoon. Will be at corner table.

Diamond.

Miss Greenstone entrance Franklin Park, south side, at noon.

Old Gold.

Will be glad to meet Emerald corner Broadway and Fifth.
Wear green.

YOUR FRIEND.

Captain Brady looked them over and then decided he
needed Riordan's help. He called his aide, but was surprised
to hear that the sergeant had risen early and gone out, leaving no word. Looking over the personals again he quickly
decided the first one had been inserted by Tompkins,
Laird's store detective; and the second one he credited to
Laird himself. The other three he was somewhat uncer-
tain about. The third one, he was reasonably sure, was just
the effort of a masher. The fourth and fifth might be real
replies to the original personal. And any of them might
apply to the stolen Laird bracelet, or none of them might.
The whole thing might just be a coincidence. However, he
decided to be protected on all of them.

Pushing a button, he gave the responding deskman
certain orders and there followed a stream of "pairs" of
his detectives to his office. To Collins and Cone, the first
two, he handed the first personal on his list.

"You two know Tompkins, of Laird's," he said. "Get
down to the station before noon and look for him. I think
he's the guy that put this ad in the *Chronicle*. If he's got a
black walking stick he is. In any event, I want either Tompkins or the fellow with the black walking stick brought in
here and any jane they may speak to—if it looks like they
met for a date. Get me? Be nice, but bring him in."

Collins and Cole remarked that it was as good as done
and departed, to be followed by Harrahan and Boyle, the
detective bureau's prize bruisers and "rough stuff" men.

Most of their time was spent in the lower end of the city, where muscle as well as brains were needed. To them Brady gave the personal signed "B.L."

"I want you two birds to go up to the Women's Protective Division," he said, "and borrow that new female dick they got—the one that brought in sixteen mashers last week. You take her down to the interurban depot and put her in plain sight. Tell her to act like she was expecting somebody and to be real nervous about it. If a 'gentleman wearing light tweeds' comes up to her and speaks to her I want you to rough him up and bring him in, and lock him up for violating the mashers' law. Then report to me. You see the time in that thing—ten o'clock."

Harrahan and Boyle smiled knowingly and went about their business. To three other groups of two he gave orders, along with copies of the remaining personals, and then, feeling that he had done all he could for the time being, turned to his routine duties. Shortly before ten o'clock, however, he doffed his uniform, slipped into citizen's attire, and, putting the day sergeant in charge, went down to the police garage, climbed into his own car, and drove down to the southeast corner of Tenth and Main Streets, where he parked just at the cross-walk. Settling back in his seat he watched the passing throng, and particularly those of its members who dallied at the corner.

Once or twice he moved as if about to leave his seat, but each time refrained. He parked there until a quarter of eleven, then decided his errand was futile, and returned to his office. The day sergeant told him Harrahan and Boyle had somebody for him. He smiled grimly, changed into his uniform, and sent for the two official bruisers.

"Well," he asked them.

"Yis, sor," said Boyle, speaking for the two of them. "We did as ye told us, sor. We got Miss Wilkins and planted her. About tin minutes after tin a guy in a light tweed outin' suit steps up to her, sor. Harrahan, here, goes over and gives him a shove and grabs him by the shoulder. The guy swings at Harrahan wid a little bamboo cane which he has, an' I clouted him over the face wid me open hand. Then we dragged him out, sor, and called the wagin. He made a bit of a fuss, and, as you said, sor, we roughed him up to quiet him—and brang him in. He's booked to Miss Wilkins for the mashers' law. He's ravin' up in the jail to see his attorney."

"Good," said Brady. "Leave him rave till I get ready for him. Now go on, boys, about your regular stuff. You've done fine."

As they went out Brady produced a cigar and seemed to be enjoying life as he lighted it. He hummed a little tune as he busied himself over reports and other work, and was still apparently contented with the world when Collins and Cole entered a little after noon with Tompkins, the store detective at Laird's.

"Good morning, captain," said Tompkins at once. "The boys said you wanted to see me."

He ignored the way the "boys" had said it, and did not dwell upon the persuasion they had used to overcome his objections. It was apparent, however, that there had been no great difficulty.

"Yes, Tommy," answered Brady pleasantly enough. "I want to know what you're putting personals in the papers for and walking 'round with a black stick in your hands. Can't you keep busy at the store?"

"That was in reference to a case, captain."

"Did Laird tell you to do it?"

"Not exactly, sir."

"Did he tell you not to?"

"Well, captain, he said to me Saturday night to lay off that case for a few days."

"Why didn't you do it, then?"

"Well, it looked to me like I had a chance to get something. But after I see the paper this morning it didn't look so good. Still, I figured I'd better have a try at it."

"Well, Tommy," said Brady emphatically. "Get this in your head. Laird has turned that case over to me. Until I tell you, you keep off it, see? I don't want the works gummed up by any of your ideas—you had it from Thursday to Saturday and didn't turn up anything but dust. Now you go back to the store and stay there, and if I find you horning in on this thing again I'll just naturally take you apart and see what makes you tick. Understand?"

"Yes, captain."

At a nod from Brady the three went out, Collins and Cole rather amused, but Tompkins not at all in a jovial mood.

Left alone again, the captain reached for the telephone.

"Tell the jailer to send down that fellow Harrahan and Boyle brought in," he said.

Two turnkeys presently turned up with a violently protesting individual in a light tweed outing suit. He had one excellent black eye, his collar was torn and ragged, his suit quite dirty, and there was a smear of dried blood on his chin. His language was shocking.

"Shut up," roared Brady, and then, in apparent surprise, he added in a gentler voice: "Why, bless my stars! What has happened, Mr. Laird?"

More violent and shocking language followed and the turnkeys had some difficulty restraining their prisoner.

"Take him up to the emergency hospital and clean him up," said Brady. "Let him send for his friends, if he wants. Then I want to see him."

The turnkeys dragged their still violent prisoner out of the office, and Brady chuckled. He was still chuckling when the door opened and Sergeant Riordan entered.

" 'Phoned the house a little while ago," he said, "and they told me you'd called up early and wanted to see me. Sorry, chief, but I was out keeping a date. Something doing?"

"There was—a moment ago," answered Brady dryly. "Sit down over there—second show starts in ten minutes."

It did. Bartholomew Laird, in somewhat better order physically and sartorially, and accompanied by the Hon. Peter Nesbitt, his personal attorney, returned to Brady's office escorted by the two turnkeys. Brady dismissed them with a nod and looked blandly at his callers. Nesbitt took the lead.

4

A SOCIAL WORKER'S SIN

"**THERE SEEMS TO** have been either an unfortunate mistake, captain," he said, "or else something a great deal more serious. I trust you will be able to explain it. Mr. Laird here was set upon without reason in the Interurban depot by two of your detectives, beaten, knocked down, dragged to the patrol wagon, brought here, and held *incommunicado* in jail for several hours and denied the advice of his counsel."

"Really, Mr. Nesbitt," said Brady, "I can hardly believe that—or I could hardly believe it, if I hadn't seen Mr. Laird a few moments ago."

"I demand the names of those two brutes," shouted Laird.

Brady swung round to his telephone. "Send me the report on that Interurban depot case," he said snappily.

Laird glared at him during the brief interval that followed. Then the deskman in the outer office laid a paper on Brady's desk and withdrew. Brady passed it to Nesbitt.

"You read it," he said.

The attorney put on his glasses and read aloud:

"To Captain Brady—Following orders, we went with Miss Wilkins of the Women's Protective Bureau to the

Interurban station this morning. Shortly after we arrived there a man came up and spoke to her and she signaled us. Harrahan went up and told the man he was under arrest for violation of the mashers' ordinance, and the man struck at Harrahan with a cane he carried and used vile language. I then went to Harrahan's assistance. The man put up a stiff fight, but we overpowered him, called the wagon and brought him in, charged with violation of the mashers' ordinance, using vile and indecent language in a public place, and resisting an officer. The prisoner refused to be booked, and we locked him up to cool off. Boyle and Harrahan."

Laird sputtered.

"You know Miss Wilkins, do you," asked Brady in a conciliatory tone.

"Dammit, no; never heard of her," said Laird.

Brady waved his hands.

"Don't see as I can blame the officers much, then. We've been trying to stop this mashing business. It's something awful the way young girls are being insulted—and worse."

"Mr. Laird must have gone to the station to meet somebody else," said Nesbitt. "I've hardly had a chance to talk with him, captain. He telephoned me to come right over, and we just had a few words in the hospital while he was—while he was cleaning up. He must have mistaken this operative of the women's bureau for somebody else."

"You went to the depot to meet somebody, did you?" asked Brady. "Somebody you knew?"

Laird started to answer, but remained silent. For some minutes he regarded the captain of detectives closely, and then he suddenly smiled wryly.

"I think I have made a fool of myself, captain," he said. "I'm willing to drop it if you are."

Brady drummed on the desk with his fingers.

"It's a funny thing, Mr. Laird, but there was a personal in this morning's *Chronicle* about a man in a tweed suit going to meet somebody called 'Emerald' at the depot at ten o'clock. Was that your business there?"

"It was, captain."

"And why, may I ask?"

"You know why, captain."

"I thought I told you to keep off that case—you and Tompkins? I got Tompkins, too, down at the Union Station. Now if you don't think I can handle this case, Mr. Laird, why I'll drop it."

"I told Tompkins to keep off—but I thought—"

"The case is yours, Mr. Laird. I'm through. This fight you put up at the depot probably gummed up all chance my men down there had to get a line on this thing—if the line was there. I can't work if you are working against me like that."

"Then you have a 'line' on the—on the case?"

"I have several, Mr. Laird. But there's no use of two of us crossing each other up. I told you that Saturday when you came to see me."

Laird pulled at his collar and then turned toward the door.

"Come along, Nesbitt," he said. "It's all been a mistake. Captain Brady, I am leaving the case with you. I give you my word neither I nor Tompkins will attempt to make any further moves. Good day."

After the merchant and his attorney had departed Brady turned to Riordan.

"Well, boy," he said. "I reckon I'm square now for all that 'Sitting Bull' stuff. I sure framed him. But all this isn't getting us anywhere. You see that personal in yesterday's *Chronicle?*"

"Yeah."

"What you think of it?"

"Might be a lead. Did you follow it up?"

"That's what I'm doing nothing else but to-day. I put in that one about Tenth and Main Streets myself, but it flivvered. That was why I called you. I wanted you to watch one of the others. But I guess I've got 'em all covered."

"You had one of 'em covered anyway—Franklin Park. I was up there. Found Ralston and Brown there and shooed 'em off; told 'em you'd sent me out later."

"So that was it, eh," said Brady. "I figured maybe you had put one of those personals in. So you're 'Old Gold,' eh. Did you get anything?"

"Not much," said Riordan, "only this."

He reached in his pocket and threw something upon Brady's desk—something that gleamed with green light and silvery fires. It was the missing Laird heirloom.

"You see, chief," he said, sheepishly, " 'Old Gold' sounds sort of honest. That is, it would to a woman. And I figured this 'Emerald' party was a woman. She was."

Brady picked up the bauble, worth a small fortune, and examined it. While he was looking at it the telephone jangled and Riordan picked up the receiver.

"It's Hinkman and Ebberley calling up from Broadway and Fifth," he said. "They say the only party wearing green around there is Laird's daughter, and that she's looking for somebody—"

"Tell 'em to tell her to come in here," said Brady without looking up. Riordan followed instructions and grinned as he watched his chief turn the emerald bracelet over and over in his hands. Finally the older man looked up.

" 'D you make any pinch, son?" he asked.

"Nary a pinch, chief. I'm going to put that up to you— later. But I got a party where I can get at 'em if I have to."

Captain Brady put the bracelet in a drawer in his desk and locked the drawer.

"I'm going out to lunch," he said. "You sit in. If Miss Laird comes in before I get back you entertain her. But don't tell her anything till I get here. I want to hear it. I think it's going to be good."

Riordan was glad when his chief returned, for Miss Laird had been difficult to entertain. She wanted to know why she had been summoned and what developments had occurred. She freely admitted to the sergeant that she had inserted an answering personal to the original "Emerald" message, but "I was so excited," she said, "that I forgot to specify any time. And after I saw all those other messages I was distracted. But I determined to spend the best part of the day at the rendezvous I had set."

"You don't want to be excited, miss," Riordan replied. "I think the captain must have some definite news or he wouldn't have sent for you. We had all those meeting places covered, you know. Maybe the boys at one of them turned something up."

"I'm sure they must have," she said. "And I know you know about it. Won't you, please tell me?"

Riordan, however, kept his own counsel, and, to his relief, Captain Brady soon returned from lunch. Miss Laird greeted him with an expectant countenance.

"I sent for you, miss," the captain said, "to save you from walking round and round till you dropped dead. No use trying to be an amateur detective. There've been too many of those on this case already."

She refused to give any indication of downheartedness.

"That was very kind of you, captain. And what news have you?" she chirped.

"I have your bracelet, miss," he replied bluntly. "But you don't get it. Your father put the case into my hands and I must return it to him."

"Let me telephone him to come right over," she said, but Brady shook his head.

"No—for two reasons. First, he's not quite ready to hear from me, and, secondly, I don't think you'd better be around when he comes."

"You have a prisoner, then?" she asked, her face suddenly growing serious.

Brady pointed to Riordan. "Ask him," he said.

"I have no prisoner, Miss Laird. But I ought to arrest you."

"Me?"

"Exactly. Let me tell you something, Miss Laird. You play around at what you fancy is charity. You give away money. But you don't do very much good. If you devoted half the energy to the rich that you do to the poor you'd be doing a lot more good."

Her eyes fell for a moment and her cheeks flushed. "I'm afraid I don't understand you, sergeant," she said.

Brady began to look interested.

"Well, I'll be plain about it, Miss Laird," continued Riordan. "You've been responsible for a whole lot of grief for a whole lot of people, and by rights you ought to be made to pay for it. I don't mean pay in cash—that wouldn't make any impression on you. Money is the cheapest thing you have—unless maybe you value your jewels less."

"It may seem so to you, sergeant," the girl replied seriously. "But it really isn't so. I have no limitless fund of money: I have to keep within my allowance."

Riordan laughed. "Allowance! I don't know what it is, but I'll bet it's more than the captain and I make in five years. Now look here, Miss Laird, I'm going to talk rough to you, and you've got to stand for it. Here's what you've done:

"You went out of the house with let's say twenty thousand dollars' worth of emeralds hanging loose on your wrist, a bait for every hungry man and woman you passed or might meet. You had enough work wrapped up in those emeralds to keep the whole police force busy for a year—if somebody had wanted to go after 'em. But they didn't mean anything to you—"

"Pardon me, sergeant, they are—"

"Don't interrupt. The emeralds meant so little to you that when you went into your father's store to get a pair of stockings you pulled a silk hose over your hand while you looked for flaws and pulled the bracelet off with it. And you didn't know you'd lost it. It was late in the afternoon.

"The girl who waited on you was tired and flustered—flustered because she was going to be married the next day, and it was her last day in the store. She was working on the day before she was going to get married because she needed the money—you see money meant something to her; even the miserable fourteen dollars a week your father pays her.

"Now don't interrupt me, I tell you—I want you to get this. Next day this slimy dick your father's got up at the store traced to her the sale of a pair of stockings to you, and what do you think he did? Because she'd quit the store he figured she was a thief—in spite of the fact that all the other girls at the counter told him she was going to get married and had given notice of quitting a week before—and he busts out to her house without a warrant or anything and searches her rooms and puts her into hysterics so she can't get married that day at all. Your carelessness with these twenty thousand dollars worth of emeralds damned near wrecked that girl's life. And then you say you value money!

"Now that girl didn't have the emeralds. She didn't know you'd lost them. She swears she didn't even notice them on your wrist. When you pulled that stocking that you'd been examining off, with the emeralds inside of it, she just threw it back in the box and put it back in the case; and the emeralds would have been there yet if something else hadn't happened."

5

THE HONEST THIEF

RIORDAN STOPPED, A bit abashed, for tears were cours-
ing down Miss Laird's cheeks. "Oh, the poor child," she
said in a moaning voice. "Tell me who she is, so I can make
it up to her."

"What with? Money? Money's no good. Money won't
wipe out the stain your father's man Tompkins cast on that
girl's wedding day."

"I can see that," said Laird's daughter. "But I must know
who she is—I can find some way to show her I'm sorry."

"Well, we'll come to that later, miss. I want to tell you
the rest of it. Your father employs a lot of women and girls
to clean up his store at night. And he's as liberal with them
as he is with the rest of his help. While you're giving away
twenty-dollar gold pieces to the pet charities you have he
pays these women and girls six dollars a week for scrubbing
away at floors and dusting showcases half the night. You
never thought it would be charity to ask your father to pay
his help more, did you?

"Now one of these girls had, by saving and skimping
and going without enough food, bought her a party dress.
Neither you nor me would call it much of a dress, but
she thought it was grand. The only thing lacking was that

she didn't have any silk stockings to go with it, nor even imitation silk. So what do you suppose happened? While you were giving away money to a lot of panhandlers who work you for an easy mark the devil tempted this girl like he's tempted a lot of other girls who get six dollars a week.

"She cleaned on the main floor. She'd spotted the boxes containing the size stockings she wore, and she'd made up her mind she was going to steal some. She knew it was stealing—but she wanted silk stockings.

" 'Old Laird only pays me six dollars a week,' she said to me, 'and what I do is worth more than that. Why, he pays the boys who run the elevators ten dollars a week, and they don't work half as hard as I do. So I got a right to swipe some stockings—he'll never miss 'em.' That's the kind of logic it's hard to beat—when you're poor.

"Well, the night of the day you carelessly lost your twenty thousand dollar bracelet she swiped the box of number nine stockings on the top of the case, shoved it under her dress and took it home. She was the happiest girl in the city. Miss Laird—even if she was a thief. For she had silk stockings to go with her first party dress.

"She got home about one o'clock in the morning, after sweeping and scrubbing in your father's store all night; and first thing she did was to open up that box of stockings. And out tumbled two stockings—all that were left in the box—and something hard in one of them. She reached into it—into the stocking—to see what it was, and drew out twenty thousand dollars' worth of emeralds.

"That was the end of the dream for her. She'd only steeled herself to swipe some stockings—maybe eighteen dollars' worth, six pairs to the box, if she was lucky enough to get a full box. And she found she'd stolen one pair and more jewels than she'd imagined were outside of Russia. She hid the emeralds in the old mattress on her bed and lay awake all that night.

"By next day she was sick—crazy. She couldn't go to work—though she knew your father would dock her for not showing up. She didn't eat, she didn't do anything. Finally she decided to commit suicide. Then some bit of reason came into her head and she realized that if she did that maybe the emeralds never would be returned. Or that some real thief would find them.

"Finally, somewhere, she scraped up enough money to put a personal in the *Chronicle*, in an effort to get in touch with the owner of those emeralds. She was going to ask mercy—not any reward. And Captain Brady, here, and I found her—and the captain's got your emeralds. And you—you've got two tragedies to answer for, just because you don't know the value of money or how to take care of enough jewels to lead men to murder. Now, what are you going to do about it?"

Grace Laird, her face sober and her eyes brimming with tears, shook her head. "What can I do?" she asked faintly.

"I want you to see this little girl who got your emeralds," said Riordan. "You sit here a minute—I've got her upstairs in the matron's quarters. The emergency hospital doctor is taking care of her, but I guess she can toddle down here. I want you to see an honest thief; one who realized she was wrong and spent her own money to turn back the swag."

Riordan left the room. Miss Laird turned to Captain Brady.

"Your sergeant is a fine man, captain. He made me see

things I've never seen before. He won't believe it—but after I've gone, will you tell him that—that I'm very grateful?"

"You tell him, miss; he's not as hard-boiled as he looks."

Riordan returned just then, carrying what at first seemed to be a roll of blankets. He placed it carefully on the old couch in Brady's office, and beckoned Miss Laird over. Under the glare of the electric lights she saw a thin, childish face, with deep black shadows under the eyes and about the mouth. But the blue eyes that looked out over the shadows were unafraid.

"This is the lady who owned the bracelet, Jennie," Riordan said softly.

Grace Laird dropped to her knees beside the old couch and took the frail figure in her arms, kissed the sunken cheeks, and smoothed the hair back.

"Oh, my dear," she said, "it's going to be all right now. You're a brave and fine little girl, and I'm going to look after you. I'm going to take you to the country—down to my summer home, and nurse you back to health. And then we'll see if we can't find something better than scrubbing out the store for you to do. I need a girlie just like you to help me do some work I've just found out I have to do."

She kissed the girl again and then turned to Riordan.

"Take her back to the hospital again, sergeant, until I can make arrangements for an ambulance to move her. Thank you for bringing her down."

Riordan picked the blankets and the sufferer up in his big arms and strode from the room. Miss Laird stepped over to Brady's desk and picking up the telephone, called a number.

"Mr. Booth, please," she said on getting the connection.

"Dick? This is Grace speaking. Will you please drop every-thing and come right down to the office of the captain of detectives at police headquarters? No, I'm all right, but hurry."

Riordan, returning, waited with Brady in silence for some time. Grace Laird wiped her eyes dry of tears, calmly powdered her nose and cheeks, and then presented to them a face that showed she had a new purpose. When Booth arrived she introduced him to the two police officers as "my personal attorney." Then, turning to the newcomer, she said:

"Dick, if you and I were to be married to-day and if, while I was dressing for the wedding, an officer entered my room without a search warrant and accused me of being a thief, and searched my trunks and things—wouldn't that be grounds for action, as you say?"

Booth looked belligerently at the two sleuths and clenched his fists.

"I'll say it would be grounds," he answered levelly.

"Well, Dick, in such a case, what would you sue for?" she asked.

"Five hundred thousand dollars damages, to start with," he said.

"Well, Dick—Dick—will you sue my father for that amount? Captain Brady, here, and Sergeant Riordan will give you the particulars—it's all about one of the girls who used to work in my father's store. And if you'll do it, Dick, I'll—I'll go right over to the City Hall with you now and the Mayor can marry us right away, can't he? And we'll go down to my cottage at Northport for our honeymoon, and take with us a little sick girl who's done me a great favor."

Captain Brady reached in the drawer of his desk and took out the bracelet, which he slipped quickly into his pocket.

"You folks stay right here and talk it over," he said, smiling broadly. "Sergeant Riordan and I have got to take this thing back to the man who gave us the case. When we come back we'll give you all the evidence you need for that damage suit. Come on, Riordan, we've got to hurry."

Riordan paused at the door. Grace Laird and Booth were plainly waiting for him to close it behind him.

"There's just one thing the matter with that damage suit," he said. "The idea's fine, miss, and I admire you for it. But the girl recovered from her hysterics and was married the next day."

"Hysterics? Good, sergeant," said Booth. "We can add that to the complaint. Be sure and hurry back and give me the particulars."

"I'll hurry all right," said Riordan. "But I think the cap'n and I may be gone some time."

ANOTHER USE FOR WATER

Riordan Becomes An Expert On
Listening Dinguses, But Brady
Furnishes The Final Technical Point

1

THE DOORMAN, AFTER knocking, poked his head in Captain Brady's office and said: "One of the uniformed men wants to see you, sir."

Brady nodded and jerked his head to signify that the caller was to be admitted. Sergeant of Detectives Riordan, who was in a corner of the office, donning his uniform as a sign that he was about to go on duty to relieve his chief, hurriedly buttoned his coat so that the visitor would not find him apparently disregarding discipline.

But the uniformed patrolman who entered was too flustered to notice Riordan at all. He saluted Captain Brady, then, as if deeming it necessary to accord him still higher honors, removed his helmet.

"Please sir, captain," he said, "there's a matter I'd like to be so bold as to speak to you about, sir."

Brady scowled at the newcomer, then asked gruffly:

"What's your name?"

"Upton, sir, of the second night relief."

The captain's manner softened. "Well, Upton, put your hat back on again if you feel more comfortable that way. Harnessed bulls don't have to uncover in here unless they want to. We ain't the United States flag. In fact, Sergeant Riordan here, and I, were harnessed bulls ourselves once. What's on your mind?"

The caller showed that he was much relieved. "Thank you, captain," he said, replacing his helmet, and then shoving it upon the back of his head, as he scratched his hair to stir his thoughts. "Fact of the matter is, captain, I come here to knock one of your cases, and to give you another you don't know nothing at all about. May seem sort of impertinent, sir, but it's a sort of a trade."

Brady looked puzzled in his turn. "Trade?" he asked.

"Yes, sir; it's like this. You see you got a breakin' and enterin' case up at the Tudor Arms, an' I want to get you to call it off. That's a favor, sir? And in return I'm goin' to tip you to something."

"Sit down, Upton," said Brady. "We got to get this straight. Oh, Riordan, come over here and listen to this. Now, say it all over again, Upton."

The uniformed man had drawn one of the chairs forward from its place by the wall and sat down, leaning close to Brady's desk. Riordan, answering his chief's summons, leaned over the top of the desk.

"I said, sir," repeated Upton, "that you got a breakin' and enterin' case at the Tudor Arms. Only it ain't. And I want you to forget it. A favor to me, see? And in return I'm goin' to give you a real tip."

"How'd you know I got a case at the Tudor Arms?" snapped Brady, reaching for his reports at the same time.

Upton smiled. "I'll tell you, captain. I got a friend—"

Brady interrupted him with a sign and drew a report sheet from his files, reading it out aloud:

"Mrs. A.N. Gerlinger, Apartment 5, The Tudor Arms, reports an attempt to enter her flat some time last night. We investigated and found the dumb-waiter door forced

*"You can tell what's going on in any room
he cuts in on," he explained.*

from the inside, indicating that a prowler must have pulled
himself up in the dumb-waiter from the basement and
tried to break open the door. The door was splintered and
the latch broken, but it had jammed and wouldn't open.

"The prowler was evidently scared by the noise and got
away. Mrs. Gerlinger says she was out last evening, coming
home about midnight and going right to bed. When she
got up about nine o'clock this morning she found the
bursted door and notified the police. Nothing was stolen.
Respectfully submitted, Smith and O'Malley."

"That's the case you're talking about, Upton?"

"Yes, sir, that's the one. Only it ain't a case, sir. It was this
way, sir. Mrs. Gerlinger is a widow lady with one son, Bob.
He's a good boy, sir, and tries to help his mother. I know
him pretty well, sir; you see I live only two doors from
the Tudor Arms, sir, and Bobby is usually going to school
about the time I get home mornings from going off shift.
Him and my boy, sir, is in the same school, and they're what
you might call chums.

"Well, Bobby went home to lunch today and his mother

told him how burglars had tried to bust into the flat last night while they was both asleep, and shows him the busted dumb-waiter door, and tells him she's had a coupla dicks up there—and he gets scared and comes to me and asks me to square it for him. Woke me up, he did.

"It was funny, in a way, too, captain. This Gerlinger kid, he tells me, woke up at the usual time this morning and, knowing his mother was out late the night before, he decides not to waken her before he goes to school. So he dresses and gets his own breakfast, and then he washes what dishes he used, and puts 'em away.

"He'd cut a canteloupe for breakfast and eaten half of it, and when he was cleaning up he throws the rind and the seeds in the garbage can. And then he remembers his mother maybe won't wake up in time to put the garbage can on the dumb-waiter for the janitor to empty, so he puts the can on the dumb-waiter himself.

"But he don't shove it in far enough, and in slamming the door shut it catches on the can and jams and splinters some. He opens the door again, pushes the garbage can back on the dumb-waiter, where it should have been in the first place, and sends the thing down to the basement. Then he tries to shut the door to the shaft, but can't do it, it being broke.

"His mother ain't awake yet, so he goes to school, intending to tell her about it when he comes home to lunch. But as soon as he gets home his mother tells him about the dicks being there, and then he's scared to tell. So he come to me. I told him I'd fix it, and not to be afraid his mother would find out.

"So if you can have them two dicks next time they're up that way tell Mrs. Gerlinger they caught this here imaginary prowler of hers somewhere else it will satisfy her and save the kid from a licking."

Brady grinned. "I always thought Smith and O'Malley was a couple of mutton heads, but I didn't think they were that bad! Tell you what I'll do, Upton. I'll drive up that way on my way home and take a look at the door, and if it at all looks regular, like you say, I'll fix the Gerlinger party with a story that'll make her think we're all heroes, and that will cover up the kid, too."

"Much obliged to you, captain."

"That's all right, Upton. But you said you were going to give me a tip, too?"

"Yes, sir. You know old Juillard, the Frenchman that has that show-place up on the Heights?"

"Yes."

"Well, he's being robbed right along."

The smile that had hovered in Brady's eyes disappeared instantly.

"Robbed of what?" he snapped.

Upton shook his head. "I don't know, captain. He's a nut and won't talk—won't talk much. But his place is on my beat, and I see him prowling around at all hours, some nights. I've asked him what was the trouble, but he won't say nothin' definite. Tells me he's looking for something.

"The other night one of the maids come home late from a party and I buzzed her. 'The master's crazy,' she says, 'and if it wasn't for the extra money he's givin' me I wouldn't stay a day longer.'

"She says the old fool has got all the outside doors and windows wired and fitted with home-made alarms, and that he's got some kind of a dingus in his room that he won't let anybody touch, and that he monkeys with all night. She says he sleeps all morning, but sits up all night when it's dark, and forbids the servants to move above the basement except by the back stairs.

"They threatened to quit on him, but he says he's had 'em so long he knows he can trust 'em, and he gives 'em more money to stay—a lot more. This maid was getting fifty dollars, and now he pays her seventy-five. Now a man don't act like that unless he's being robbed."

"What did you see him doing these nights you found him prowling round the place?" asked Brady.

"He was just lookin', captain. He had one hand in his pocket, and I think he was packin' a gat. But he's got a right to do that on his own property. Slippin' from tree to bush, and bush to tree, he was, and watching the house. But when I asked him could I help he says no, for me to go on about my business and when he wants me he'll send for me."

"Who lives in the house besides the old man?"

"Just his wife and son, sir. The son was hurt in the war and don't work none. Of course he don't have to work, the old man's got a pile. But he don't do nothin'—except ride around in that French car he's got. Then there's four servants; this maid I told you about, a woman cook, a chauffeur, and a gardener and general handyman."

"That's five," said Brady.

"No, sir, the gardener and handyman is the same, sir."

"And that's all you know about it?"

"Yes, sir."

"All right, Upton, much obliged. If you hear any more come and let me know. And I'll take care of that Gerlinger kid for you—tell him it's all right, and that he needn't explain anything to his mother."

2

WHEN THE UNIFORMED man had departed Brady turned to Riordan.

"I got a mind to tell the chief to put Smith and O'Malley in uniform, and to get Upton transferred to me," he said.

"But maybe there was a prowl, too, chief."

"Yeah, that's why I don't leave a note for the chief right now. I'm goin' to have a look myself first, right now. And while I'm driving round I think I'll drop in on Juillard, too, and find out about that."

"Who's this guy Juillard, chief? I've heard a lot about him."

"Sure you have, boy, and most you've heard is lies. He minds his own business, and so all the neighbors fake up stories about him. The commonest one is that he lives in a haunted house—you know he bought the old Emory mansion after the Emory twins was bumped off about twenty years ago. He's fixed the place all up new since then though. He's a good deal of a genius, Juillard is.

"He was in the French diplomatic service once, and because he got onto something good and made a heap of money they fired him. Jealousy, I guess. Then he came over here with his wife and boy. During the war the lad drove an ambulance for the French and got shelled up some. Got a wooden leg now, I think.

"Anyway, since the war he hasn't had any ambition, except to find liquor. If the Federal agents could get him to talk they wouldn't have to hunt booze any, for this guy knows where it all is. He's spending all the old man's money he can get making the country drier."

"Hits it up, does he?"

"I'll say. On the road, too—gets arrested for speeding regular. Well, I got to be on my way. I'll see you to-morrow."

Captain Brady was not a true prophet, however. It was not the morrow, but ten o'clock that same night that he next saw his chief aide. At that hour he came into his office at headquarters, threw off his hat, coat, and driving gloves, and, dropping into one of the two armchairs the room boasted, pulled out a cigar and lighted it. After puffing a few moments he relieved Riordan's concealed curiosity.

"Well, boy," he said, "this harnessed bull Upton knows his stuff all right. He had the Gerlinger thing doped just the way it happened, and he sure gave us some business on the Juillard thing. If it didn't look like we was going to be busy I'd get rid of Smith and O'Malley right now."

"Did you cover up the Gerlinger kid?"

"Sure—told his mother my fine sleuths had gotten the prowler two hours after they had seen the evidence, and that the man had pleaded guilty and gone to jail, so she wouldn't have to worry no more at all. The kid was there when I told her, and he came out in the hall when I left and shook hands with me. He's a nice kid, he is."

"Then you drove to Juillard's?"

"No. Then I went home to dinner and climbed into my best suit. And about eight o'clock I went to call on the Frenchman. You see, I happen to know him. He's crazy on criminology and fingerprints, and in the old days he used to come down here not a little. That was when I was on nights, like you are now. After I got boosted up he stopped coming in.

"Well, I made believe I was just around on a social call. We talked of this and that, and after awhile I got the conversation round to burglars and such like, but he didn't rise to the bait. So after a bit I got up and began pacing back and forth while he talked, and then I went over to one of the windows and discovered it was wired. And I asked him what for. He says it is a mere whim.

"So I see I had my work cut out, and I give him the old stuff; how the police was employed to protect the citizens, and how they had a right to ask and be told what was worrying the citizens, even if no actual crime had been committed. And I says that no man is going to have his windows wired unless he was afraid of something, and what was it?

"Still he stalled around. Said the house was full of valuable bric-a-brac, and all that line of talk, but I kept at him and finally he came through—that is, part way through. He says he's been robbed, not once, but a dozen times. And, furthermore, he says he's going to catch the party that did it, and catch 'em himself, and that after he gets 'em caught he'll call me in to make the official pinch. But until that time he's going to work in his own way, and while he appreciates my interest he'll be much obliged if I'll leave him alone.

"He admitted he had the house all wired, and he even took me up to his room and showed me an eavesdropping dingus that he's rigged up, by which he says he can listen to what's going on in any room in the house. And he claims it will only be a matter of time when he hears the crook at work and then all he's got to do is to go and get him. In the meantime, he says, he isn't losing enough for him to worry about, and will I please keep off the case.

"I asked him if he didn't think it was an inside job, and he said he had thought so at first, but that he'd listened on this listening thing of his and had heard the servants talk and everything, and he was sure it was none of their doings, and that was why he was paying them extra wages to stay—because he knew they were honest.

"The only thing he isn't perfectly satisfied about is his listening device, and I told him I had a man who knew more about those things than the man who invented them and would send him out. Otherwise I said I'd keep off the case, like he wanted. Which, of course, was all bunk."

"Who are you going to send out?"

"You."

Riordan laughed. "Why, that's good, chief. I don't know any more about a detectaphone than I do about—about—about why does a flapper bob her hair."

Brady squinted at his aide through the cloud of smoke that was streaming from his mouth.

"I told Juillard," he said, "that while his son was riding round France in a nice flivver ambulance, at least ten miles back from the front, you was sitting out in No Man's Land with a listening dingus that you'd perfected strapped on your head, and that it was so darned good that you could hear the Germans when they pointed a gun at you and so you could duck and not get hit by a sniper—which was why you come back from the war fatter and more of you than when you went in.

"I told him you was General Pershing's own pet electrical expert when it come to telephones in the field, and that you could tell—oh, I fed him all that I could think of.

"And I got him enthused over you. It wasn't so much that he thinks you know all about listening devices as it was that I told him you were the one, lone and outstanding hero of the whole war. And at that, boy, I didn't tell him anything except what I know of your record in spite of your efforts to keep it quiet.

"Maybe I exaggerated a bit here and there, just to get him; but the ground work of what I told him was real stuff, so you won't be embarrassed none when you talk to him. You're to go up to his house to-morrow for lunch, at half-past twelve, and help him ginger up his listener afterwards."

"Did you tell him I was a dick?"

"I sure did. This fellow Juillard was in the diplomatic service, I told you? So why lie to him about simple things like that? He'd find out and distrust you. And I want him to trust you, see? I know you know enough about telephones to savvy his listening system, and not to cross any wires. All you got to do is look it over and look wise, and tell him you'll fix up something and take it to him later. That'll give you a chance to get back again.

"But what I want you to find out this time is all about what's been stolen, from where it was taken, and who he suspects, and what the lay of the inside of the house is, and everything. Get the idea?"

"Yeah; you're a bear for work, ain't you, chief?"

3

THE FOLLOWING AFTERNOON Riordan had much to report to Captain Brady. When he entered the inner office of the detective bureau his chief greeted him jovially with: "Well, and how's the expert listener, eh?"

"You said it," replied Riordan. "Listener is right. Say, chief, when that old Frenchman finally uncorked all I could do was listen. He's a wonder, he is—been all over the world and there isn't anything he doesn't know something about. But at that, I think he's bugs."

"He isn't so crazy as he sounds," commented Brady.

"Maybe not, chief; but I don't want him for a playmate. And I don't want to be the guy that he catches for the thief either—he's got a bad eye when he talks about that pet prowl."

"Yeah? Well, let's hear all about it. What did you do first?"

Riordan laughed. "First thing I did was to get up early, foregoing me beauty sleep," he said. "Went down to the library and read up on telephones, dictographs, microphones, and all that junk. Wanted to refresh my memory and at the same time soak up a few scientific words. And at half-past twelve I showed up at the house for lunch, as you said.

"Old Juillard was nice enough, but he didn't get what

you'd call friendly all through the meal. After we'd got through eating he found some of these funny, thin, French things they call cigars, and we went up into his den, on the second floor. And then he put me through. Asked me what I'd done in the war. Said you'd told him I was a bear, and all that.

"I was as modest as I could be, but I covered the war pretty well. Told him how first they'd let me drive a truck, and after I'd run down too many French trains had transferred me to communications.

"After I'd mentioned most of the geography of France that I'd learned he seemed to warm up a bit, and said his son was in the war, and he mentioned the battles his son had been in—not as a fightin' man, but drivin' an ambulance right in under shell fire and haulin' out the injured.

"He had me razzled for a moment or two, for it seems this here son of his had fought in all the battles—I mean, had run his ambulance into all the battles that I'd never heard of. And when I was attached to General Headquarters I'd got pretty familiar with battles, past and present, and the old war maps, too.

"But I kept my mouth shut and looked as if I'd lost my voice in admiration of his son's bravery, and said 'uh-huh' and 'is that so' at appropriate intervals, and we got along fine."

"You think the son faked his record, then?"

Riordan nodded his head. "He either faked it or he fought in some other war. Why, the stuff he told his father—for instance, chief, he tells one story about taking his ambulance in right behind the combat troops when they took the German guns at Voelklingen.

"Now it so happens I know that country, having been sent in there on a special mission with a little party, and there wasn't never no battle there since 1870 or thereabouts. In the late unpleasantness the French never got within range of the place—though there was German guns there all right. So I knew right then that either the boy had been faking to his father or else the father was stuffing me, to see what I knew.

"But later on it developed that he believed all the boy had told him, and he thought I'd been familiar with all these imaginary battles, too.

"Well, after we'd fought the war over a couple of times we got so we was as thick as two chums, and he began to loosen up about his troubles. It seems he was robbed first time about four or five years ago—two hundred dollars in currency, which he'd left in the library table. Since then he's been touched more or less regularly about once every twenty days; sometimes for money, sometimes for works of art or bric-a-brac, of which the house is full.

"The amounts have varied from as little as nine dollars and a quarter, one time, up to what he said was an 'old master' that was worth a couple of thousand cold—it was a little painting, like a miniature.

"At first he tried to sleuth this guy who was tapping him, and, not having much luck at that, he next began to wire the house. But wiring the house didn't stop the pilfering, so he gradually devised this here listening system he's got—and, take it from me, it's a bear. But he's been tapped just as regular since he's been listening as he was before.

"Just about every twenty days or so this prowl gets in and gets away. He says he's heard him a couple of times, but that when he got down to the place where he'd heard him he'd made his get-away.

"Of course it don't listen reasonable, but after going over the old man's system the thing's got me guessing. I'll tell you what he's got.

"The house is laid out like this: In the basement is a regular cellar and furnace room and a little workshop and a laundry. On the main floor you go into a reception hall from the front door. Off this is a stairway leading to the upper stories, and what you'd call a parlor. Back of the parlor on one side is the dining room, and on the other side, partly under the stairs, is the library. Back of them is the kitchen and serving rooms.

"Upstairs in front is two bedrooms, which Mrs. Juillard and the old man use; back over the dining room is young Juillard's room and the bathroom, and on the other side of the house, over the library, is a big room the old man has fitted up as his den.

"In the rear is a porch and stairs leading to the servants' quarters, which are in the rear of the top floor, the front of the upper story being divided into guest rooms. Back of the house is a barn that's been turned into a garage, and on the second floor of that, the male help sleep.

"Well, in this den the old man has got his listening machine. It looks like a radio cabinet—and, by the way, he's got a radio, first-class one, down in the library. But this listening machine is bigger, only it looks like a radio cabinet. It's got ear-phones instead of a loud speaker, and there's a bunch of dials on the front of it.

"Well, little by little the old man has put microphone receivers in every room in the house, concealing them behind pictures or on the chandeliers, which are the old-fashioned kind, with glass sparklers hanging to 'em, and enough brasswork about them to hide half a dozen microphones in. He's even got the house telephone hooked in to his listening machine; and by turning dials he can listen in on any room in the house or on the phone.

"It's one of the finest pieces of work I've ever seen, and it must have set the old man back about six thousand dollars, or I'm no judge of electrical work of this kind.

"He had me listen on it, and, say, you can hear everything. You can hear the glass sparklers on the chandeliers clink together when a door opens and lets a draft in; you can hear stuff frying in the kitchen on the stove; you can hear people walking about in any room you tune in on, hear furniture moved, and everything. While I was there he cut me in on the wife's room, and she was getting dolled up to go out to a card party this afternoon, and, honest, it was like being a blind man in her room.

"I could hear her lay the hairbrush down, hear her squirt cologne out of a bottle, and hear the swish of her silk skirt as she put it on, and hear her gossiping with the maid, too. It made me blush.

"The old man, he says he's listened on the thing so much he can identify sounds I couldn't even hear, and can tell just what's going on in any room in the house that he cuts in on. And late at night, he says, he cuts in on all of them at once, and then, if he hears a funny noise, he cuts out one room at a time till he's isolated this noise, and then he listens hopefully to see if it isn't his prowler; but it's usually somebody snoring or coughing or getting up for a drink of water or something like that.

"But one of these nights, he says, he's going to hear this prowler in time to get him—and then!"

"Looks like an inside job, doesn't it?" said Captain Brady.

Riordan hesitated before replying. "It does and it doesn't, chief," he answered. "The old man swears the help is honest—says he's tested them in a hundred ways, and listened in on their talk. He's sure they're all right. He's gone at it scientifically, and he makes no bones about saying that he thought it was an inside job, too, at first; but he says he's listened to his wife and son, and can account for every minute of the time they've been in the house, as well as the servants. So he's put away the inside job idea.

"His dope is that some bird, who's a skilled electrician, has found a way to ground the window wires somewhere, and is coming and going when he wants to. Yet he's been all over the wires and they don't show any signs of tampering.

"He says two or three times he's heard a noise in the library, and that's where most of the stuff was gone from, but that when he's got down there there was nobody round, though on one of the occasions fifty dollars that he'd locked in a secretaire drawer was gone and the drawer was unlocked.

"He isn't satisfied with the microphone he's got in the library, and he had me down there to look at it. Just to give me a chance to get back there again I told him I'd build him one that maybe would give him better results."

"Has he got a safe?" asked Brady.

"No; he's got this secretaire thing in the library where he keeps loose cash. It's about as hard for a good man to open as a shoebox would be. One of those old-fashioned things with secret drawers and sliding panels. I asked him why he didn't wire it, and he said he'd tried but couldn't.

"In the first place, the servants move it every time they clean the room, and in the second place half of it is iron with wood veneer over it, and you can't wire it without the wires showing. If you put the wires under the veneer they'd short or else make lumps; and he hasn't tools to channel out the iron to hold insulated cables. So he's relying on listening.

"And, believe me, he can tell some on that listener too. He left me in the library, and I walked around and did different things while he went up to his den and listened; and when he came down again he told me everything I'd done except make faces. Told me just what part of the room I'd walked about, what I'd picked up and put down, and everything."

Brady sat silent awhile, thinking. Finally he looked up.

"How about the household?" he asked. "What do they do?"

"I got that," answered Riordan. "They're a regular bunch—been living together all alone for a long time, and dropped into routine. The wife, she has breakfast in bed, gets up about ten and fusses round with the servants and her own household duties till lunch time. In the afternoons she goes out on social calls or to parties, or putters round the house or garden.

"After dinner she and the old man sit around and chat awhile, and then maybe they go to a show once in awhile. Mostly, though, he goes up to his den about eight o'clock. She sits round and reads, or has a few people in, and goes to bed about half-past ten or eleven.

"The old man, he starts the day just before lunch, when he gets up to eat. In the afternoon he putters round the workshop in the basement or goes out in the automobile, or goes downtown to attend to any business he may have. Home for dinner. After dinner, as I've said, he sits around with the wife till about eight, when he goes to his den and starts up his listening. He listens all night, till dawn, when he goes to bed and sleeps till lunch time.

"The servants keep usual servants' hours—up early and busy all day, and out in the evenings and home before midnight. That's the rule.

"The young fellow, he gets up for breakfast if he hasn't had too bad a night before, or he has breakfast in bed. In either case, he's up and about by ten. Loafs around the house all morning, has lunch with the family, and then climbs in his car and goes societying about for the afternoon. Home for dinner.

"Sits round with the family till about half-past seven or eight, when he takes himself upstairs to figure out what he'll do for the rest of the night. Makes up his mind about half-past eight and takes a bath, then dolls up and gets in his car and goes out. Gets home when he gets home, usually about one or two, and goes to bed."

Brady considered this a long while, frowning. Then, suddenly, he sat erect in his chair and looked at Riordan.

"Did you say young Juillard took a bath every night?" he asked.

"That's what papa tells me. I said something about Saturday nights to him and he smiled. 'Every night, almost to the dot, at half past eight, my son takes a bath,' he said.

Supposed the boy wanted to freshen up and look rosy for his night's pleasure."

"When was the last touch-off?" asked Brady.

"Sixteen days ago—it's getting near time for another one."

"They ever less than twenty days apart?"

"Oh, yes, sometimes only a week apart. But mostly about twenty days, or nineteen, or twenty-one. The old man always stays home and listens sharp about that time. He's getting ready to get on the job extra strong now."

"And the boy takes a bath every night at half past eight?"

"That's what he said."

"And old Juillard still leaves money and things around—in this secretaire thing?"

"Yes. He said at first he was going to put in a modern wall safe, but before he got around to it this prowl sort of intrigued him; and now he leaves the stuff there as bait. He figures he can stand it, anyway. In fact, I think if this guy would come and tell him how he does it, he'd pension him and pay him regular."

Brady laughed harshly. "I'll bet he don't," he said.

Riordan looked at his chief. "You got an idea, haven't you?" he commented. "I can see the fire in your eye. Yet I'm darned if I can see what I've told you to get lit up about."

Brady shook his head. "I just got a fool idea, boy, that's all. I wouldn't have had it if you hadn't done such a good job up there at Juillard's this afternoon. You got a head on you, you have. Don't know what I'd do without you. Well, I got to be going home—it's long past my time. To-morrow maybe we'll start something. Good night to you."

4

BUT CAPTAIN OF Detectives Brady did not go home. Climbing into his car in the police garage, he drove to the Federal Building and for a long time was closeted with certain inconspicuous appearing men who went in and out of unmarked doors along the upper hallways. There were several conferences, and it was two hours before Brady appeared to have won his point and left the building.

Getting into his car, he drove to one of the more elaborate down town restaurants, where he dined well. Toward the close of his meal the head waiter came and stood by his table, answered many questions that the head of the detective bureau asked and finally walked away with a five-dollar tip in his palm.

From the restaurant Brady drove to several of the road-houses scattered along the highways leading from the city, and at each place he held brief conferences with either the proprietors or floor managers. These worthies, knowing their places were outside of Brady's bailiwick, were willing enough to answer his questions, for they all realized that it would do no harm to have a friend down at police headquarters, even though their chief troubles might lie with the sheriff's force.

All this took time, and it was near eleven when Brady tooled his car into the driveway leading to the Juillard home and, alighting, rang the doorbell. There was a considerable wait, during which Brady peremptorily pushed the button several times; but at last Juillard himself opened the door. Recognizing the captain, he bade him enter.

"Sorry to disturb you so late, Mr. Juillard," said his caller, "but I've got something on my mind. Let's go into the library, if you don't mind; where we can talk."

The Frenchman led the way into the somber room, turning on the lights and drawing close together two armchairs. He waved Brady toward one and settled in the other himself.

"This man Riordan, of yours, captain, he was here to-day. He seems a very good man."

"Understood your electric dingus, did he?"

"He comprehended it at once and thoroughly, captain. He is going to help me perfect it."

"Well, that's good. I always understood he was a shark at that sort of stuff. But that isn't what I'm here to talk about, Mr. Juillard. I want to ask you a question, and I want you to think before you answer it."

"Assuredly, captain."

"Well, it's this: do you want to catch this prowl that's robbing you?"

Juillard opened his mouth to make immediate reply, and then closed it again. Something he saw in Brady's eyes gave him pause for thought. For a long time he was silent. At last he said:

"Yes, captain, I want to catch this—person."

"Do you want this person put in jail, or do you just want to find out who it is?"

Juillard looked at the floor a long time. Finally he gazed directly at his caller.

"Captain Brady, breaking and entering in the night time, under your law, is a felony. A householder, should he kill the robber, would be held justified in your courts, even if he did not kill him in actual combat. I do not intend to kill this robber, captain, but I have long promised myself that when I caught him I would make him wish I had killed him, instead of what I shall do to him. And I have promised myself that after I have done this thing to him, I would turn him over to the police."

Brady nodded his head. "Well," he said, speaking seriously enough, "I figured it was like that. I guess we'd better catch him for you. I guess you'll feel better, after it's all over, that you didn't catch him yourself."

"Then you have a suspicion in your mind already?"

"I wouldn't call it a suspicion. I just got an idea—something come up since I saw you last night, that gave me a hunch. I may be wrong. But I want to try out my idea. Give me your check for five hundred dollars."

Juillard pursed his lips and looked at the ceiling. Then he rose, walked to the secretaire, opened it and took out his checkbook. Returning to his chair he drew a fountain pen and wrote out the check, payable to Brady, and tendered it to the detective captain.

Brady, in turn, reached into his pocket and drew forth a wallet, from which he counted five hundred dollars in currency, mostly bills of twenty-dollar denomination, though there was one fifty-dollar bill in the bundle, and several fives, a couple of twos and a one-dollar certificate.

Thrusting the money into Juillard's lap, he took the check, put it in his wallet and returned the wallet to his pocket.

Juillard counted the money and smoothed it out into an even packet and then rolled it up.

"That stuff I gave you," said Brady, "is all counterfeit. I had a heluva time getting it off the Federals this afternoon. I only got it on my promise to get five hundred dollars real money in exchange, so if any of the counterfeits get into circulation they can take care of them through the banks and nobody will lose anything. That's what this check is for.

"As a matter of fact, I don't think more than one of those counterfeits will ever be passed; so you'll get your money back—probably within a week. You'll have to trust me for that."

Juillard pursed his lips. "You want me to leave these counterfeits then as bait for the robber?"

"You got the idea, count. Simple, isn't it?"

"But, captain, I am very desirous of catching the robber."

"Yes, but it's better we catch him, as I told you. And this trick will do it."

"And if you succeed, then what? He will not be arrested as a robber—"

"Nope, you're right," interrupted Brady. "He'll be booked for passing counterfeit coin. That's a Federal offense."

"But suppose he is as clever at passing these counterfeits as he is at getting into my home?"

"You leave that to me. I'm taking the chance."

Juillard considered again.

"Suppose," he asked, "I succeed this time and catch the robber while he is stealing this counterfeit money?"

"The party's all yours then, count. All you got to do is to

send for us and give me the phony money back when you get round to it and I'll give you your check back."

Juillard rose from his chair. "Very well, captain," he said. "I will do as you wish. I will place this money in the secretaire, some in one place, some in another. Perhaps it will work. But I shall not give up my own efforts to catch this robber."

"That's fine," answered Brady. "If you get him first, you call me when you're through with him. If I get him first, I'll call you. But I'll do this, Juillard, if you want—I'll make you a side bet of anything you want that you don't get him, and that I do."

Juillard went to the door with his caller. As they said good night he smiled.

"I will take that bet, captain. I will bet you a bottle of claret."

Brady laughed and shook hands. "All right," he said. "Better go down to the cellar to-morrow and pick it out. Good night, sir."

Then he climbed into his car and drove to his home and slept the sleep of a contented man till it was time to rise for the next day's duties.

5

FOR THE NEXT several days Captain of Detectives Brady showed no interest in the Juillard case. Sergeant Riordan, coming on in the afternoons to relieve his superior, mentioned the matter casually once or twice, but receiving nothing more than an "uh-huh" from Brady in reply, did not press the subject. He knew his chief too well.

For his own part he was not worrying greatly, for he had obeyed orders in visiting Juillard and getting all the details of his household, his woes and his listening system, and he was content to let his chief do what he wished with that information. He had plenty of routine matters to keep him busy.

Of course, he was interested in Juillard's problem, just as he was interested in the study of any unusual crime or series of crimes; but beyond promising himself another visit to the Juillard home, with a new microphone, he had no definite plans ahead as regards the Frenchman.

So things went for five days—or nights, as Riordan counted the passing of time. The fifth evening, about ten o'clock, as he was just finishing reviewing the reports of the men on the first night relief, of which he was in charge, his telephone rang. Lifting the receiver from the hook he was informed by the exchange board man that the person on the line had asked for Captain Brady, and had insisted on getting Brady. Then the exchange operator put the insistent one on.

"This is Peter Rexford, out at the Green Mill," said the voice. "I want to talk to Cap'n Brady. He was out here last week and he told me if a certain party come in and did something I was to call him in person. The party's here and I want to talk to the captain."

"This is Riordan, Rexford," answered the sergeant. "If you want the chief, try him at his house."

"Oh, hello, Riordan. Glad I got somebody I know on the wire at last. Listen, I been calling Brady's home, but he don't answer. And this is something he's fussed about. There's a party here he wants, see? And he told me to tip him off."

"I see," said Riordan. "Gimme a tip as to what it is, will you? I probably know the case. Maybe I can come out and get the guy. I don't know where the chief is, if he isn't at home."

"It's—" came the voice over the wire, and then there was momentary silence followed by the sound of shots plainly audible over the telephone coupled with screams and the noise of upset chairs and tables.

Riordan slapped the phone back on the hook, reached for his coat and hat and dashed out through the front office yelling:

"Come on, you birds—shooting match out at the Green Mill. One of you tip the sheriff's office, the rest of you get out there—I can take four of you in my car."

Down in the police garage a shouted word or two above the confusion of men tumbling into automobiles sent a couple of motorcycle men whizzing out first, their sirens screeching as they sped along.

Close behind them, and almost keeping up with their break-neck pace, was Riordan, piloting his big touring car like a fire driver, and giving four of his fellow detectives one of the rides of their lives. And behind him were other cars, each carrying its load of detectives or officers, now that the alarm had been spread through headquarters.

The Green Mill, one of the largest road-houses near the city, nestled beside one of the main highways two miles from the corporate limits. It was a big, rambling story and a half structure, with spacious grounds, and a broad drive-way leading up to its main entrance.

As Riordan swung his machine from the road to this, and applied brakes so he would come to a stop just at the front door, he noted that the place was exceedingly calm. Yet less than fifteen minutes before he had heard the popping of shots over the telephone. As his ear slid to a halt at the entrance way, he and his companions tumbled out and rushed inside.

Riordan noted the two motorcycle men standing over at one side of the main lobby, before a doorway about which was grouped a small crowd of curious folk.

Shouldering his way through the group he reached the motorcycle men, who at once motioned him past and then closed up behind him to keep the crowd back. Riordan opened the door they were guarding and stepped inside. He found himself in a small, office-like room, which was fairly well filled with people. A man turned as he entered, and Riordan recognized him as Rexford, the proprietor of the place.

He greeted the detective sergeant pleasantly. "You made quick time, Riordan," he said. "Funny thing, that shooting just as I was telephoning you trying to get Cap'n Brady. And he was here all the time. He's over there in the corner, see him?"

Riordan's eyes, roving over the assembly, had already spotted his chief.

"Yes, I see him—anybody hurt, Rexford?"

"No. This fellow didn't get a chance to unlimber good before Brady and his gang fell on him. They've got him over there in the corner. Gosh, I never see so much excitement in so short a time in my life—and then it was all over. Why, Riordan, before the people from the dance hall could run over to the cafe, where the shootin' started, Brady and those Federals had the whole thing hushed up and this fellow in my office."

Riordan went over to Captain Brady and reported.

"Happened to hear the shooting over the telephone, chief, and came out. Rexford was phoning, trying to raise you. If everything's all right, guess I might as well go back."

Brady grinned. "Leave the boys here till the sheriff's men get out. It'll tickle them to find a lot of bulls have beat 'em to it in their own territory. You can take this bird and those two boys with him back in your car—I'll follow you right in with the rest of our party. Take him up to the office and hold him there."

"This bird" proved to be a youngish man, very pale of countenance and nervous of disposition. He was handcuffed to "those two boys," whom Riordan recognized as Federal men.

"Well, come on, let's go," he said.

The prisoner and his two guards got in the rear of Riordan's car. When he was half way back to the city limits he pulled to the side of the road to let a caravan of shrieking cars and motorcycles go by, and then continued his way.

"Sheriff's gang going out," he said, laughing over his shoulder. "Had to recruit 'em first. But you gotta admit, once they get together, they make a fine show going down the road."

Back in Brady's office at the detective bureau the prisoner and his two guards sat on the lounge. Riordan took up post midway between them and Brady's desk, and they waited the arrival of the rest of the party.

"What's it all about," asked Riordan of one of the Federal men.

"Near as I can make out, the prisoner here's a bad man," said the agent, grinning and winking. "All I got against him is possession of alcoholic beverages, contrary to the Federal statutes. What you got on him, Bill?"

The other Federal agent also smiled. "Not much," he said. "All I got against him is personating an officer of the United States Army."

Further questioning was stopped by the entrance of Captain Brady, the elder Juillard and a lean, tall, gray-haired man of unusual size, whom Riordan recognized as one Mike Kelly, Treasury agent and special government investigator. They had met once before, and nodded curtly to each other.

Everybody found chairs and then all turned toward Brady, who was evidently the master of ceremonies.

6

"JUILLARD," SAID BRADY, pointing to the prisoner, "is that man your son?"

The Frenchman looked squarely at the captive.

"Non—no, he is not my son," he replied.

"You've had him in your house, living with you, as your son—at least since the war, have you not?"

"Yes, he has been in my house. I have called him my son. But he is not. I will tell you. I have adopted him, many years ago, in Paris. I have give him every kindness that a father could—but he is not my son. His name is Juks Cauburg, his father died on the guillotine. His mother died of grief. Out of pity I adopted him."

"Would you like to say anything in his behalf?" asked Brady.

Juillard considered.

"I will be fair," he said. "He is a brave man. Not only did he face grave danger in France during the war, but in my house he has undergone grave dangers. He knew I was watching for the thief, he knew I planned to maim the thief when I caught him—yet he stole right from under my watchfulness. I will say he is a brave man."

Mike Kelly spoke up. "Sorry, Mr. Juillard, to spoil one of your fond illusions, but this party here wasn't very brave in war time. When he left your house and you gave him money to sail to France, so he could enlist in the ambulance service, he didn't go. He lived on what you gave him for awhile, and then later he got a job driving a truck for the shipyards.

"In that way he dodged the draft—he was working in a necessary industry. He lost his leg when a load of plate fell when they were hoisting it off his truck with a derrick. He didn't get any nearer to the war than the moving pictures down at the Auditorium."

Juillard winced. "But I had letters from France, in his handwriting," he said, with a tremor of failing hope in his voice.

"Sure you did," said Mike Kelly. "During the war, and before it, every ship that left New York carried over letters to be mailed in England and France and sent home. There were a lot of pseudo-heroes, and the stewards did a land-office business taking letters over to mail back. It was two dollars to mail a letter in England and five dollars to get a French army vise stamped on it. Yes, you could get letters from most any part of the front in those days."

Juillard's face paled. "Well," he said, "this man, then, risked something when he robbed my house, in the face of the efforts he knew I was making to catch him."

"Sorry, Juillard," spoke up Brady. "But he didn't risk a thing. He found out what you were doing and he arranged so that you were actually helping him."

The Frenchman leaped up. "I help him? When I sat up all night listening for him? What do you mean?"

"Just that," said Brady. "Whenever he robbed your secretaire, or anything else in the house, it was between half past eight and a quarter of nine at night, when you were in your den listening. You helped him by leaving stuff around for him to steal—bait, you called it. He knew you'd be listening, but he also knew you couldn't hear him."

"Couldn't hear? Why, captain, your man Riordan there can testify to what I could hear over that listening device. I can hear everything!"

"What can you hear when there's water running?"

The Frenchman frowned. "I can hear the water."

"Sure," said Brady. "And that's all you can hear. Everybody who knows anything at all about the listening do-funnies knows that when there's water running from a faucet you can't hear anything else. This bird knew it. So every night at half past eight he took a bath—or said he did. He knew all you could hear then was the water running into the tub.

"He knew you couldn't hear him open the bathroom door and sneak downstairs and do his burglary and then sneak back. After that he didn't care how much you listened. The minute Riordan told me about that bath habit, I knew what the case was.

"That was why I gave you those counterfeits to plant. I wanted to prove it to you. You saw him out at the roadhouse with the money—are you convinced?"

Juillard slowly nodded his head. "What a fool—what a fool I have been," he said. "I should have called in your police at first, captain. I do not mind the money—no, that is not it. But I mind being a fool, and imagining all the time I was so wise."

"You should have called the police," repeated Captain Brady. "That is what the police are for. That is what you pay taxes for, to have the police. Well, what'll we do about this bird now we've got him?"

"I do not want to prosecute him, captain," said the Frenchman. "I thought at first I would. But—"

"Leave him to me," spoke up Kelly. "I got enough on him. Attempting to pass counterfeit money, possession of liquor, posing as an injured army officer out at the roadhouses, possession of counterfeit money. I can put him away for keeps. But I'm not going to. Since he isn't your son, Mr. Juillard, I've got a much better way.

"We'll just turn him in for deportation. If he's not your son he can't claim any sort of naturalization; and I don't think he'll make a fight anyway. Take him over to the Federal Building, boys, and lock him up for the night. To-morrow's another day. Well, I've got to be going—I sure enjoyed your party, Brady, and glad I could have helped you. Good night."

Kelly, the Federal men and the prisoner left. Brady reached into his desk and then turned and tendered Juillard the check for five hundred dollars he had received some nights before.

"I'll be up for that bottle of claret one of these days," he said, smiling dryly.

Juillard looked at Riordan.

"My friend," he said, "you are interested in such things. Some day you come to my house and I will give you all of that listening device of mine. Maybe in your business you can use it. For me it is foolishness; to be forgotten. Gentlemen, I thank you very much, and I am glad there is no more damage done. As for me, I am sorry—sorry for a lot of things, but—life is strange, is it not? I will go now, I thank you."

After the Frenchman had departed. Riordan turned an inquiring eye at Captain Brady. His chief laughed.

"Yes, I planted it," he said. "Then had the young fellow shadowed. Knew it would only be a matter of time. He got the stuff last night—to-night Juillard and Kelly and I went out to the Green Mill. When he pulled that money on the waiter we started for him and the poor fool started to shoot. But there were too many of us. You know the rest."

Riordan nodded. "Yeah—and I know I don't know so much either. I ought to have doped that bath-every-night stunt the same as you did."

"Tell you what you do, boy," said Brady kindly. "To-morrow morning you put your ear against the door at home and listen. You can hear what's going on in the next room almost as plain as if you were there. You keep on listening till somebody turns on the water somewhere in the house. Then see if you can hear anything but the pipes gurgling. Convince yourself and you'll learn something.

"But at that you 'made the case.' I'd never have doped it if it hadn't been for the line-up you got from old Juillard. Boy, you and me can get most anything, if we stick together on it! Well, it's been a great night and I'm tired. So I'm going home. Be good and you'll be happy."

THREE OUT ON CHRISTMAS

Sergeant Riordan Had Determined To See
The Thing Through, But He Didn't Figure
On A Certain Hitch That Occurred

1

"A PLAIN HARNESSED bull can have a good time on Christmas," quoth Captain of Detectives Brady, enunciating his words thoughtfully. "He can make believe not to see the kids when they throw snowballs, he gets smiles and cigars and maybe a drink or two—of cider—from the people on his beat; he can steer a souse home instead of to the hoosegow, and in a lot of ways he can enter into the spirit of the day, as you might say.

"But us dicks—God help us. All we get out of Christmas is nothing much to do, or else the coroner calls us in to see if some guy is still dead, or maybe we got to break up a party somewhere that's violating the law. No, sir, a dick can't have a Merry Christmas—not if he works. That's why I always try to shut down Christmas, and just have a few of the boys on call."

Sergeant Riordan, who had just entered his office, preparatory to taking over affairs for the first night relief, nodded.

"There's a lot of truth in that, chief," he said. "I remember now when I was on beat—"

"Yes," interrupted Brady. "An' I remember when I was pounding the pavement, too. But what's the use. We're dicks now. I'm going out to the wife's brother's for Christmas, and unless something breaks tonight that looks bad, you might as well take to-morrow night off, too. Fitzgerald says he'd just as soon work, so I'll let him sit in. If something real bad breaks, they can get both of us by phone."

It was Christmas Eve, and the arrangement suited Riordan nicely.

"That's good of you, chief," he said. "I'll spend the evening with the mother—she'll like to have me home for a change."

The door from the outer office opened, and one of the outside men announced:

"General Ridgeway, sir."

Then, without waiting for Brady's response, he stepped back and motioned the caller within. One did that with General Ridgeway, when he called on public servants. He was, perhaps, the city's most influential resident.

Brady rose to greet him, and pushed forward a chair.

"I'm only here for a moment, captain," said the caller. "Got a little job for one of your men. Like to have you take it, in fact. You see, Mrs. Ridgeway is giving a mask this evening, and there'll be a lot of people there. She's a bit nervous, and telephoned me to get one of your men to come up. Probably no need for it, but you know how the women feel about crowds. I'd like to have you come up, captain—I can promise you a good time, and—er—ah, some Christmas spirit, too."

"That's good of you, general," replied Brady, "but I'm afraid I'm too old to mix with the young folks, and a bit too rough. But Riordan here—he's my right-hand, general—is just the man. Young and handsome, as you can see, and a bear with the ladies. He's refined and educated, too—made two trips over the ocean, he has."

Riordan blushed, and the general laughed.

*Riordan's open palm landed a hearty
slap on the other man's cheek.*

"Quite a traveled gentleman, eh?" he inquired.

"Two trips," said Brady, laughing. "The first one from Ireland when he was a baby, and the second some years back, when he and General Pershing and some other good men went over on a matter of business. Better shine your boots and go up, Riordan; I'll make arrangements here."

"It's a mask," said the general thoughtfully.

"That's all right, general," interposed Brady. "Riordan, here, played Santa down at the Salvation Army hall last night, and he's still got his costume."

"That will be very good, captain, I'm sure," said Ridgeway. "From what I know of the originality of thought on the part of the young men in our set who will be there, I can't imagine a better costume, or a more inconspicuous one. I'll wager there will be close to a hundred Santa Clauses at Mrs. Ridgeway's mask. And I'm sure the sergeant will prove a success—both as an officer you have recommended, and as one of our guests. Here's an invitation to present at the door. Eight o'clock, sergeant."

"There," laughed Brady, after their visitor had departed. "You'll get some Christmas after all, my boy. You know what a Ridgeway *soiree* is—best in the land. All you got to do is watch your feet and keep your mouth shut. Run on home now and get dolled up in your red suit and white whiskers, and I'll put one of the boys in here for the night. And have a good time Christmas, too—I'll see you the day after."

So it happened that Sergeant Riordan, a few minutes after eight, was the eighty-second Santa Claus to enter the Ridgeway mansion and present an invitation card to the sober butler in the big hall, and to be shown to the cloak room and then turned loose in the midst of ever-increasing merriment. Unostentatiously, and drifting here and there about the main floor of the big house, Riordan made a survey of the premises and the guests; and then, catching General Ridgeway in the crowd, he persuaded that worthy to take him on a tour of the upper floors as well. Once having learned the plan of the residence, he left his host and returned to the main ballroom and the corridors radiating from it.

He chatted with men and women he did not know and never expected to meet on terms of social equality again; he danced with one or two masked maidens and matrons, he drank sparingly of the punch in the smoking room, and idled about here and there; seeing nothing that roused his professional instincts.

In fact, he was having such a good time that he was almost on the point of forgetting the duty that had called him to the mask, when an incident occurred that turned him instantly from a mere guest at the party to a hunter in quest of his prey.

He was standing at the entrance to the conservatory, talking and joking with a matronly witch, when he felt something dropped into one of the spacious pockets of his Santa Claus costume. There was a mirror directly in front of him and behind the woman with whom he was conversing, and instantly glancing in that he saw a serving maid walking away from him.

There was nobody else near him, so he knew she must have been the one who had made him the unexpected gift. The reflection in the glass showed only her back, and, scanning that swiftly and minutely for some mark of identification, he noted a small hole in her left stocking, just above the ankle, as the only mark that would differentiate her from the half dozen other serving girls in cap and apron and uniform dress that were constantly passing to and fro among the guests.

Bringing his conversation with the matronly witch to as early and graceful a termination as he could, he stepped into the conservatory, sought out a corner behind some palms, where he would not be observed, and, reaching into his pocket, drew forth the object the serving maid had placed there—a small, bangled, silver bracelet. To its owner, aside from the matter of sentiment, it might have been worth ten dollars; as stolen property, to be disposed of, it would scarcely bring a dollar. Whoever had taken it was a poor judge of values, and probably was an amateur thief.

Of course it was instantly plain to Riordan what the system was—there were at least two thieves present. One was the serving maid with the hole in her left stocking;

the other was a man in Santa Claus costume, to whom she was transferring her pilferings. The problem for Riordan, therefore, was to find the bogus Santa Claus who was the receiving end of the conspiracy.

With over fourscore counterfeit Kris Kringles at the mask, this was far from a simple task. Studying the matter, Riordan soon reasoned that the receiver of the maid's thefts would not likely be one of the more active Santas, who were continually romping about in the throng of guests, but would be a sedate sort of St. Nick, who would be standing about, more or less "on fixed post," as police parlance would have it.

He therefore disregarded the palpably younger and livelier Christmas saints, and moving slowly but methodically about the chambers, surveyed the men in red coats and white whiskers who were idling about, some openly bored, near the doors or in corners of the rooms.

Yet these more stationary Santas moved about, from time to time, making his task no easy one; and their great similarity of costume added to the difficulty. He managed to drop into converse with several of those under his scrutiny, but got no enlightenment for his efforts.

For an hour he thus pursued his quest, making no very great progress. Then his eye suddenly caught the flicker of a red coat vanishing through a doorway near the entrance hall. Making his way as quickly as possible to the same doorway, he found the entrance hall vacant; but, glancing up, caught the sight of a black patent leather boot disappearing around the turn in the great staircase that led to the second floor.

Riordan reached the top of the stairway in time to

see a door halfway down the hall closing. He hesitated a moment, then determined on his course of action, and silently tiptoed down the hallway to the door. Listening, he heard nothing within. Gripping the knob firmly, he turned it slowly, then pushed gently, and felt the door yield.

With the quickness and skill of a second story man he was within the room and had the door closed behind him. The room was empty, but the electric lights were on, and at the farther side of the room was another door—leading to another chamber or to a bathroom. Riordan stepped to the light button and switched off the electrics, and then moved back to the door by which he had entered. He was gratified to note, under the opposite door, a glow of light, and to see a shadow moving back and forth. So, in silence, he waited.

2

PRESENTLY THE OTHER door opened, and outlined against the light within was another Santa Claus, garbed almost identically as he was. The second figure reached up and turned off a light above its head, and for a moment the two stood in darkness. Then the light in the second room was turned again, and the second Santa Claus peered out into the darkened first chamber. As his eyes lighted upon Riordan, he started slightly, then visibly pulled himself together.

"Oh, hello," he said. "I hope I didn't intrude into your room?"

"I was just thinking maybe I'd intruded into yours," said Riordan. "The belt to this plagued costume came loose, and I came in here to fix it, and then the lights went out."

"That's funny," said the second Santa Claus, "they were on when I came in. It's so warm downstairs that the grease-paint on my face was running, and I came up here to fix it."

"My own war-paint is sort of gummy, too. Guess I'll come in there and doll up, also."

So saying, Riordan stepped across the room, but his approach seemed to disconcert the second Santa Claus.

"I'm awfully sorry," he said, "but, really, there isn't any more—I used all there was in the tube."

"Lemme have a look," countered Riordan roughly. "Maybe I can squeeze enough out."

He entered the second room—a bathroom—and looked about. There was a suit case in one corner. Seeing this he closed the bathroom door behind him, turned the check lock, and faced the second Santa Claus.

"Open it up and let's have a look."

"Really now," objected the other man, "I think you're a bit impudent."

Riordan's right hand shot out and landed a hearty, open-palm slap on the other man's cheek.

"Open it," he said, "or I'll muss you all up!"

"I shall call the general."

"I wouldn't call anybody if I were in your shoes. Open that suit case or I'll spill you all over the place."

"But it isn't my suit case."

Riordan's left hand landed, with a harder, open-palm slap on the other cheek. The man reeled a little, but caught himself from falling by grasping the pipe leading to an overhead shower.

"You have no right—"

"Listen, I'm a police officer. Open that suit case or I'll stuff you down the drain in the bathtub."

The second Santa Claus wilted pitifully. Slowly he turned, dragged the suit case from its corner, and opened if, bending over it. It was filled with silk scarfs, lace wraps in crushed disarray, and an assorted collection of small jewelry—rings, brooches, bracelets, stickpins, and one or two watches.

"How'd you get in here?" snapped Riordan.

"I work here."

"Yeah? That's evident. How'd you get in here—quick, now?"

The man ducked as if expecting another blow.

"Honest, officer, I work here. In the kitchen—cook's helper. They don't pay nothin', an' it was me chance. Lemme go, will you? You got all the stuff. The general would kill me!"

"How long have you worked in the kitchen?"

"Three weeks."

"Huh; got the job to pull this, eh? What's your name?"

"Bill Jones."

The open palm descended on the cheek again with a resounding whack.

"What's your name, I said?"

"Peter Weston, honest, that's it, officer."

"Where'd you come from?"

"I live in the city—111 Church Street."

"Where'd you do your last stretch?"

"I never done no stretch."

Two open palms, one after the other, made the second Santa's head wobble.

"I never done no stretch, I tell yer—it was reform school at Coopersville."

"That's better," said Riordan. "Now, listen to me, you rat! I'm going to talk to you like a man. You talk straight, and maybe I won't send you up. Who's the jane with you?"

"There ain't no jane."

The second Santa Claus picked himself up out of the bathtub, whimpering.

"I'll tell yer," he moaned. "Only don't you hit me again. I can't stand it. I'll tell you all of it. She's a frail I picked up, see? She don't know nothin'. It's her first job. Damned poor stuff she's picked, too. But she don't know how to get it. She's been out of a job, an' I been feedin' her. She didn't want to do this, but I told her we had to get some money some way to get away and get another start. She's a good girl, officer.

"She argued against it. She won't even tell me where her room is. Just come in on this just one—said maybe the rich people wouldn't miss the stuff, anyway. Her name's Jennie Spargo—at least, that's what she's told me. I told her if this job panned out enough, we'd leave the city and go down the coast and get a job in some resort. Made her come in on it, I did; told her she had to show her gratitude some way for me feedin' her."

Riordan considered this awhile, and looked the stuff in the suit case over. It was, professionally, a poor assortment—there wasn't a hundred dollars' worth of stuff, at prices a fence would pay, in the whole lot.

"How'd you get the Jennie girl in here," he asked.

"Spoke for her," answered Weston. "They was wantin' some extra maids."

"You're a fine sheik. I got a mind to stuff you down the pipe just for luck," said Riordan. "But don't cower like that, I'm not going to. Tell you what I'll do. I could put you away for three years for this—you know that, don't you? Well, just because it's Christmas, I'm not going to. I'm going to give you a turkey dinner instead. Now listen to me closely.

"You and me are going out of here like we were friends. We're going downstairs together and out the front door, to get a breath of air. There's a coupla harnessed bulls outside, watchin' the automobiles that the quality came here in. I'm going to turn you over to one of 'em as a vag, see?

"He'll take you down. You'll lie in jail over Christmas and get the Christmas feed. Next day you'll come up in court, and most likely the judge will feel good natured and give you a floater—chance to leave town. You take it, see, and beat it. If I run across you in town after that it will be three years. Got all that in your bean?"

"Yes, sir."

"And, remember this—you make one false play on the way out, one squawk, and I'll give you a real beating—as well as the three years. Now close that suit case and bring it out into the next room and shove it under the bed, and then come along with me."

Riordan unlocked the bathroom door, turned the light on in the adjoining chamber, and waited for his charge to obey his instructions. Then he turned toward the door to the hallway.

"But me clothes," objected Weston.

"You can send for your clothes from the jail. Now come along, and, mind, you step pretty."

They went downstairs like devoted friends, Riordan with his arm about the other's shoulders, and out through the front door. Under the portico, outside, Stacey, of the uniformed force, was chatting with one of the carriage men. As they passed him, Riordan thrust out an arm and, laughingly, said:

"Come along, officer, couple of Santa Clauses want to give you a present."

They made a laughing group as they moved off into the shadow. Once there Riordan unburdened himself.

"Stacey, I'm Sergeant Riordan, of Brady's department. You got to take my word for it if you don't know my voice. I want you to take this thing here down and vag him. He'll plead guilty day after Christmas. No bail, see? If he puts up a howl, let me know, and we'll change the charge to something better."

"Yes, sergeant."

Riordan paused and watched the policeman and the second Santa Claus go down the street, and then returned to the Ridgeway mansion. He hunted up the general, drew him to one side, and then upstairs to the room he and his unfortunate companion had just left.

"General," he said, "I got a couple of sneaks in here. I'm sorry I didn't 'make' them before they got this stuff." He drew the suit case from under the bed and dumped its contents on the counterpane. "I'll have to leave it to you and your good wife to get this stuff back to the people that lost it—you might start some sort of a rough-house game and then switch off the light, and say you found it after the excitement. I'll have to leave that to you. It's all here, you can take my word for that."

"We'll start some blind-man's-buff, sergeant; thanks for the suggestion," said the general. "And I'm surely much obliged to you. I'll attend to getting these things returned. And Captain Brady shall hear of your good work. You say there were two of them? Have you arrested them?"

"They're taken care of, sir. I tried not to have any disturbance made. They didn't know who-all they got this stuff from, or I'd have made them return it on the quiet. Now, if you'll start this game you were speaking of, sir, I'll have a look around and see that nothing else is wrong."

"I'll see Mrs. Ridgeway right away, sergeant. Later you must tell me all about it. But now I want to thank you—personally."

His hand dived into his pocket and then into one of the pockets of the Santa Claus suit Riordan was wearing, and he left the room. Riordan reached into the pocket and drew forth a twenty-dollar bill.

"He's a good sport," he said, addressing the door, as he, too, went out.

3

DOWNSTAIRS HE WENT back through the main hall to the dining room, and took his stand near the door leading to the serving room. Presently the increased laughter and joyous shouts from the other rooms told him that the general and his wife had already started the merriment that was to end in the return of the purloined things. But he took no part in this.

After waiting a moment he pushed through the swinging doors of the serving room, to find a group of maids and other servants standing about, drinking punch and nibbling at cakes. He walked about them uncertainly and owlishly, as if he had imbibed of too much of the punch himself, and spotted the girl with the hole in her left stocking. Beckoning to her and smiling, he said:

"Come here, Jennie, Santa Claus has a present for you."

The girl looked at him, frightened, but her fellow workers pushed her forward.

"Go on, Jen," they said, "see what he's got."

Riordan drew the twenty-dollar bill from his pocket and waved it in front of her.

"Come along, Jennie, out in the hall," he said. "Santa Claus has something for you."

The others laughed. He heard a remark about "the old sport's loaded," heard somebody else say: "Jennie's made a hit," as he backed through the door. The girl was thrust through after him, and he grasped her by the wrist.

"Be quiet, and no fuss. I got your pal," he said. "Come along."

The girl paled, but made no resistance. He led her quickly across the dining room, pushed open one of the French windows, and drew her after him onto a balcony, then closed the window behind them. Farther down the balcony similar windows led to the library, and into its dark quiet he led her. There were a couple of logs still glowing in the fireplace, and in the half light beside this, in the corner of the room most distant from the merriment they could hear faintly through the closed doors, he forced her into a chair.

"I've got a story to tell you, girl," he said, speaking slowly. "Once upon a time there was a nice girl who lived out in the country, and she wasn't satisfied with life. She ran away from home and came to the city. But in the big town she didn't do as well as she expected, and pretty soon she fell in with a beast who took advantage of her, and taught her to be a thief. What do you think about a girl like that?"

The girl bowed her head and burst into tears. She sobbed violently at first, then more quietly. Finally she twisted her dainty apron into a wad and wiped her eyes, though she still gulped spasmodically.

"What—what are you going to do with me?" she asked hoarsely.

"Well, that depends. What's your name—not Jennie Spargo, but your legal name?"

"Call me Jennie."

"No. If you want me to help you out of this, you've got

to be on the level with me. You've got to tell me the truth. What's your name?"

"What difference does it make?"

"Because I can't talk to you right if I don't know your name."

"My name's Grace."

"All right, Grace. Now, where do you live?"

"I won't tell anybody where I live."

Riordan looked at the glowing logs. The girl gulped down some sobs and looked at him. Suddenly she gave a little laugh.

"My name's Grace Putnam," she said.

"Fine," said Riordan, turning toward her and smiling. "Now we're getting along. I know all about it, Grace. I was a kid myself once. I didn't think my father or mother knew very much about kids, or what they wanted. And I ran away from home. Later on I came back. My father had died—but my mother, my mother, thank God, still trusted me. She's all I've got now, Grace. I've never married. Mother and I have a little house out in the suburbs, and every morning when I get home—I work at night, Grace—she puts on a wrapper and comes down to the door and lets me in.

"And then I tell her about the day's work, and what I've done that I'm proud of, and of what I've done that I'm not proud of—and she forgets the unpleasant part and says about the other part: 'that's what I know my boy would do.' And that makes the whole day worth while, and I go to bed happy. Your father and mother, Grace—they're the best friends you've got."

"Oh, I know that," said the girl, and fell to sobbing quietly.

"Where's your home, Grace?"

"Halseyburg," she answered.

"I know the town—out in the apple country. About seventy miles out. We can get there."

The girl looked up quickly. "What do you mean?"

"Just that, Grace. I've got a car outside. To-morrow's Christmas. I'll drive you home, and you can give your mother and father the best Christmas present in the world—a sight of yourself. When did you write to them last?"

"Two months—oh, you can't mean it?"

"Sure I mean it. I'll take you home. We'll tell them nothing. This twenty dollars here is yours. You can split it between them. Tell them you earned it, and want them to buy something with it. But the best thing of all will be when you tell your mother you're going to stay home—that you've had enough of being on your own."

"But you don't know—"

"Yes, I do. You've been a thief. But you didn't want to be. You fought against it. This beast that made you a thief— he's in jail. But he won't talk—and the only name he knows you by is Jennie Spargo. She's a myth—all gone. The stuff you stole will be returned to the people you stole it from, and they won't know how they lost it or how it happened to be found. That's all fixed. You'll go home with me?"

She looked at him, hope and fear in her eyes. He pressed the twenty-dollar bill into her hands, and then reached inside his red, fur-trimmed coat and drew forth something which he laid in her lap. It was his detective sergeant's shield.

Her eyes grew wide as she saw what it was, and she shrank back from it. Then she looked up into his face and deep into his eyes. And then for a long time she looked at the glowing embers of the fire. At last she gave a little sigh and, picking up the shield, wrapped the twenty-dollar bill about it and held it out to him.

"I don't deserve it—I don't deserve your mercy," she said.

He took the shield and the money, thrust them in his pocket.

"You'll let me take you home, Grace? I've got a sister, a little older than you. She'd want me to take you home. And my mother—she'd want it, too."

"But I've got nothing to show—"

"That's just pride, Grace. You don't want to admit you've failed. But your mother will understand. They want you home, Grace; and you need them. Go on out to the servants' quarters and get your wraps. I'll be at the trades-man's entrance with my car—it's a little roadster, and the curtains are on it, so nobody will see you driving about with Santa Claus. Here—go out the library door here, and turn to your right and down the hall. I'll be waiting outside, Grace—to take you home."

The girl regarded the fire for some moments, then looked up at Riordan, and smiled. "I'll be there," she said. "And I can never tell you how much I thank you."

Riordan, once around the corner in his car, did not have long to wait; but even in the dim light of the street lamps he could see the girl's face was flaming.

"Oh, the things they said," she exclaimed.

"Never mind—they might have said far worse, and you not around to hear them. That's all over with now. First we'll go to your house—to where you're rooming, and get your things. Tell me where it is."

"I'll tell nobody where I live," she replied quickly. "No, not even you. Drive to the corner of Locust and Twelfth Streets and wait there; I'll run up and get my grip."

He shrugged his shoulders and started the car on its course. At the designated corner he stopped and she got out.

"Here," he said, "take this twenty-dollar bill and pay your rent—I want you to go home square."

She pushed the money away again. "The rent's paid," she answered. "Paid till the end of the month—I earned some money when I was working as a waitress—before I lost my job. I've had a place to sleep; it's been the eating that was hard."

Then she vanished. Before she came back, the sky, which had been only flecked with clouds, darkened and snow began to fall; lightly at first, and then with increasing vigor. It would be a "white Christmas," after all, and Riordan, somehow, was pleased.

4

SHE WAS SO long in returning that he was beginning to have misgivings and to wonder if he had been a fool, but at last he spied her figure coming through the swirling flakes, and he opened the door and climbed out to meet her and to take her grip and toss it in the luggage compartment in the rear of the roadster. Then he clambered into the car again, made the curtains secure and, starting the motor, set off on his seventy-mile drive in the night.

Through the city and out in the suburbs the going was easy enough, and as they went along she told him the story of her city adventures—a common enough tale, of a type with which he was too familiar. The night's proceeding was the first really illegal one, and she again expressed gratitude that she had found him so ready with mercy and kindness.

"It's the time of the year for that," he said, to cover his growing embarrassment at her praise; and then settled down to the business of driving, for the snow was now sweeping down with almost blizzard intensity, and was being drifted across the road by the wind. But his headlights bored into the storm, and he kept on, though at a more moderate speed, now that he had passed from the more or less sheltered streets onto the open highway.

Twenty miles from the city they stopped at an all-night coffee shop, and he left the girl within drinking her second

cup and munching doughnuts while he went out and put
chains on the wheels, for the going had become extremely
difficult. Then they took up their way again; the girl settling
down in her corner of the seat and dozing while the car
swayed and swerved over and through the drifts. Riordan
was forced to give all his attention to the problem of driving, for the storm showed no tendency to lessen.

It was the hardest drive Riordan had ever made, and for
much of the distance, battling against drifts, the big roadster made little better than ten miles an hour. But always,
under his skillful manipulation, the car ground steadily on,
and at about five o'clock he picked up, with his spotlight,
the sign he had been looking for at a cross-road: "Halseyburg, 8 Miles." The wind, sweeping across the junction of
the roads, had swept the highway at this point relatively
free of snow and he stopped the car.

The girl sat up with a start, rubbing her eyes. Then,
recalling where she was, she smiled wanly.

"Eight miles more and we're home, Grace," Riordan
said. "And now the time's come for a little talk. We got to
have the strategy of this home-coming all right. Do you
think I can smuggle you into your house without the folks
knowing it, so as to surprise them?"

"My room's in the back," she answered. "Last letter I had
from mother, she said it was 'still waiting for me.' When I
was home and used to go out on larks, I could climb in the
window—if one of the boys would give me a lift."

"The window's probably shut and bolted to-night—with
all this storm."

"There's no bolt on it."

"Well, maybe we can do it. What I was sort of figuring

on was getting you into the house first, and then going to the front door and pulling a bit of Santa Claus stuff on your folks—with this costume it ought to go good. What sort of a man is your father—easy-going?"

"Why, father's the sheriff. Everybody knows him. You probably do—why, what's the matter?"

She had felt him stiffen, and seen the kind expression leave his face, though it was but slightly illuminated by the faint glow from the lamp on the instrument board inside the car.

"Santa Claus stuff is all off," he answered. "Sheriffs and cops don't believe in Santa Claus. And, besides—"

He hesitated.

"Besides what?" she asked.

"I guess I'd better tell you, Grace. You'll understand. It's this way: Your father being sheriff—I ought to have recalled the name, I know it well enough—your father being sheriff, makes a difference. You see, girl, the average man would be glad enough to have some—well, let us say some kindly cop—bring his daughter home. He'd think nothing of it.

"But a police officer—well, that's different. You know police officers—and peace officers, too, for that matter—don't reason like other people. We know what cops do, what kind of people they mostly meet, and where they find people. And if a police officer, like me, was to bring you home to your father, the sheriff, he'd think—well, he'd think the very thing I don't even want him to dream about. Do you get me?"

"I—I think I do," the girl answered soberly. "Father is

hard that way, too. He thinks everybody is guilty of something."

"That's the idea exactly. You've got it. Every police officer, by the very nature of his calling, is looking for *guilt*, not innocence. And if your father knew that a dick had brought you home—well, it wouldn't be such a heckuva Merry Christmas as it ought to be. And if I tried to smuggle you in the house, chances are I'd—oh, well, we've got to think of something else."

"The mail train gets in from the north at half past six in the morning," said the girl, after a few moments' thought. "People from the city sometimes come out on that—especially for holidays."

Riordan nodded his head. "Guess that'll have to be it then," he decided. "We'll drive to the depot. You sit in the car till the train comes, then get out and get a cab home. We'll leave Santa Claus out of it."

"No cab—there isn't any; and then you can see the house from the depot," laughed the girl.

"All right, you'll walk home then. You'll be warm enough waiting in the car here, and you'll be hidden, too, if any village gossips are up and prying round. Now listen, I want you to take this twenty dollars. No, don't make any protest. I won't miss it—old Ridgeway gave it to me last night when I told him I'd caught a couple of sneaks in his place and recovered all the stuff.

"Now you take it, and use it to make a play with when you get home. You'll need it. Remember, you're making a new start in life, and you got to have something to start life on. And you want to look at it this way—that I'm betting that twenty that you've learned a lesson and are going to make good. Here—put it in your pocket, and don't say a word about it. There, that's right."

"You're awfully good, mister—"

"Never mind the name, Grace—the less you know the less apt you'll be to talk in your sleep. This is just a little Christmas joy for me, see. Now let's go."

He started the car and turned into the cross-road, driving as slowly as possible to kill time. Yet when they reached the depot, still deserted, and drew up in its lee, there was still the better part of an hour to wait for the train; provided it was on time and not delayed by the still raging storm.

The day was beginning to break, and the mantle of white on the ground reflected what little light there was, so that Halseyburg's chief characteristics were dimly visible. Grace pointed out the courthouse, looming over all other buildings, the spire of the Methodist church, and the big barn, behind which was her own home, though the house itself was invisible. Halseyburg was a typical country county seat, and was showing no signs of early activity, especially as the day was a universal holiday.

"You know, Grace," said Riordan, as train time drew near, "I'm a good deal of a softy. I got an idea I want to see this home-coming of yours. Not that I don't trust you—it isn't that—but I'd feel better if I saw you go into your own door. Maybe I'll see the folks welcome you—that would be fine. You sit here till the train comes. I'm going to get out and ramble round. Maybe I'll find a tree behind which I can hide and get a peek at your house. If anybody sees me, I'll make believe I been to a party and am late getting home—which is the truth."

"Why not come home with me—father'd like it."

"No—we've been over that. I'd have to tell him who I was—or somehow he might recognize me. That would spoil the party. No, you leave me have my way. And if you see me, don't you bat an eyelash—promise me that. You don't know me, see?"

"If you want it so—you know what is best."

"That's the girl. Well, a Merry Christmas to you, Grace—and be good."

She was sobbing as he climbed from the car and shut the curtained door behind him. His own eyes, in fact, were not dry—perhaps a flake of snow had been blown into them. He made his way quickly across the street, a dull red blot against the background of white, and turned round a corner, circling the block. Then he moved on to the next.

Grace's home proved to be a comfortable-looking colonial house, with green shutters screening the windows from the storm. No light gleamed from it anywhere, and there were big trees in the yard. From behind one of them, Riordan thought, he could get the view he somehow felt impelled to share—the glimpse of her home-coming.

But to reach the tree from the front would leave tell-tale tracks. A quick survey showed him that it could be reached more strategically from the rear—behind and around the big barn. So he circled the block, reaching the rear of the big outbuilding.

He climbed over a fence and began slipping along in the shadow of the big barn. His foot caught in some buried trash or tangle of weeds, and he fell headlong into a drift. Laughing quietly, he picked himself up and cautiously continued his way. At the very corner of the barn, what looked like a drift turned out to be a snow-buried saw-horse and some logs, and he sprawled full length again, tearing the leg of his Santa Claus costume and losing the round, red hat.

Regaining his feet and his headgear, he located the strategic tree he had first picked out and made a bee-line for it. Reaching its shelter, he tramped the snow down behind it and, crouching in the hollow thus formed, peeked cautiously out around the trunk. He had a clear view of the front porch and the door, on the panels of which he could barely discern a brass sign, bearing the unwelcoming notice:

SHERIFF

No Peddlers Wanted

He drew back his head and settled down to wait, turning up the imitation fur collar of his red coat to keep the driving snow from his neck. It was decidedly cold, and was growing brighter. He wondered how late the train would be and peeked out again.

5

"WELL," INQUIRED A hoarse voice behind him; and turning quickly to see from whence it came, he lost his balance
and sprawled once more in the snow. A powerful hand
closed on his shoulder and he was jerked to his feet, facing
a tall, spare, stern-looking man, who gave him a searching,
all-embracing survey.

" 'Morning—Merry Chrismush," mumbled Riordan.
"I'm Shanta Clawsh."

"You're drunk and trespassing. What's your name?"

"Shanta Clawsh—Merry Chrismush," said Riordan,
swaying backward violently, but failing to release the grip
on his shoulder.

"Where do you live?"

In the distance a train whistled.

"North Pole. Lost m' reindeersh, hie, an' I'm lookin' for
'em," stammered Riordan.

The train whistled again, nearer.

His captor jerked him forward.

"You come with me, and we'll find out about this," he
ordered. "I saw you sneaking down along the side of my
barn. Come along."

Resisting not too greatly, Riordan was led to the front
gate and along an intersecting street. The train whistled
again; Riordan could hear its bell clanging now, and the

scream of the airbrakes as it slowed down, for the station. He laughed—suppose it had had no passengers for Halseyburg, and had swept through town, merely tossing off mail sacks? He had never thought of that possibility. He was so happy that it had stopped that he was unaware of his destination until his captor paused to open a door in the basement of the courthouse, over which were the cheering words:

COUNTY JAIL
No Admittance

He was pushed through the door into a room, the rear wall of which was merely a line of steel bars, with a padlocked door in the center. His captor closed the outer door behind him.

"Now, my friend," he said, "try and talk sense. If you do, perhaps you'll go home. What's your name?"

"Shanta Clawsh."

"Snap out of it! What's your name?"

"Shanta Clawsh, I tell you. Shay, lemme go to sleep, will you?"

Up above them, somewhere, a telephone rang. The bell jingled long and insistently. Riordan slumped onto a bench and huddled himself in a heap. The telephone bell still rang.

"Here," said his captor, "get in there for a minute, I've got to answer that phone."

He opened the padlocked door and Riordan stumbled through it, dropping on a cot. His captor swung the door shut, slipped the padlock through the hasp, but did not lock

it, and went out a side door. Riordan heard him climbing
a wooden stairway.

Instantly he was on his feet. Peering about, he saw he
was the only occupant of the small jail. Behind him two
smaller cells opened off the larger one he was in, their doors
open. The windows were barred.

Riordan reached through the bars before him and lifted
the padlock from its hasp. Bending down to the cot, he
tore a piece from the dirty blanket upon it, and with a key
from his pocket rammed and stuffed the fragment into the
lock. Then he replaced the padlock in the hasp and flung
himself on the cot again.

Presently the sound of footsteps on the stairs came to
him, the door at the side of the outer room opened and
his captor entered.

"My wife's just telephoned me my daughter has come
home," be said. "I'm going over to the house to meet her—
she's been away—but what's all that to you? I'll be back
presently, and then we'll find out who you are."

"I'm Shanta Clawsh—Merry Chrismush," mumbled
Riordan.

The sheriff went out, locking the outer door behind him.
Riordan lay still for three minutes, then rose grinning.

"It worked—nicely," he said to the empty cells. A
moment later he had lifted the padlock from its hasp and
was in the bare chamber. Diving into his pocket, he drew
forth his penknife, opened the larger blade, broke the point
from it and, using it as a screwdriver, soon had the plain
lock removed from the door opening onto the street.

Placing the lock on the cot where he had been, he came
out of the cell, put the padlock back in its hasp and jammed

it shut, despite the cloth wadding, and then, after a preliminary peek through the crack of the partly opened front
door, left the jail and streaked to the depot. He passed
nobody on the street and was sure the station agent had
got merely a confused glance at him as he leaped into his
car, started the engine and was off into the driving snow.

At four o'clock Christmas afternoon. Sergeant Riordan,
of the detective bureau, resplendent in his dress uniform,
walked into Captain Brady's office, where Fitzgerald was
keeping holiday watch. Stepping over to the telephone, he
called the city jail.

"This is Sergeant Riordan—send down that fellow
Stacey vagged last night—yes, send him here."

Hanging up he turned to Fitzgerald. "You better run out
for an hour or two and get you a feed," he said. "I'll be here
till six. Take your time."

"Thank you, sergeant."

The prisoner was brought in. He wore ordinary clothes,
having sent to his lodgings and discarded the Santa Claus
togs he had worn when brought in.

"Got your baggage with you?" snapped Riordan.

"Got no grip—travel light."

"Say 'sir,' when you answer me."

"Yes—sir."

"Have you anything in your room that you want?"

"Got everythin' with me—sir."

"All right. Now listen to me carefully. If I ever see you
again in this city, remember there's a charge of burglary
in the night-time hanging over you, and that means no
less than three years, and maybe ten, for a man with your
record. I'll be here in this office until six o'clock; that's one

hour and forty-five minutes. When I leave here I'm going to look for you, and if I find you—here's a pass by the door. Get out, turn to your left and go downstairs and you'll find the street. And Merry Christmas and be damned."

"Thank you—sir."

The door slammed behind him.

Riordan lighted a cigar and reached into the report basket. Glancing over the slips, he placed one aside and put the others back. Then he read the one again:

> December 25.
>
> Sheriff Putnam, Halseyburg, reports escape of prisoner. Six feet, wore Santa Claus costume. Expert jail breaker. Had high-powered auto, painted maroon color. Notify sheriff if captured. Phoned 9.24 A.M.

Riordan tore it up and tossed it in the wastebasket.

Just before six Fitzgerald returned.

"Had a Merry Christmas, sergeant?" he asked.

"I had a bird," said Riordan.

MISTER SOMEBODY ELSE

A Crime Wave Hits Town And
Brady And Riordan Roll Up Their
Sleeves And Work Like Horses

1

THE TELEPHONE JINGLED sharply. Captain of Detectives Brady put aside the South Sea romance he was reading and looked at the clock. It was half past eleven at night. He placed the book upon the table and crossed his sitting room to the telephone.

"Yeah," he said.

The voice of his chief aide, Sergeant Riordan, on duty during the first night relief at headquarters, came to him over the wire.

"Sorry to wake you up, chief, but I guess you'd better come down."

"All right," answered Brady, hanging up, and again looking at the clock. He put on a sweater, then his shoulder holster, examined his revolver, threw on his coat and went out into the hallway. There he donned a naval pea-jacket, and going out to the garage was presently backing his roadster to the street.

Once squared away he lost no time obeying traffic rules, and thirteen minutes later came to a skidding stop in front of police headquarters. Leaving the engine running and lights burning, he hurried inside and was whisked to the second floor on the elevator.

As he entered the detective bureau he noted that only the night clerk was in the outer office, though a circle of

*"I'll get him just like I've already got the fellow
who stuck up the filling stations," Brady said.*

chairs indicated where there had been, some time previously, a ring of more or less idle sleuths sitting round gossiping.

Pushing the chairs aside he made his way to his own office, there to find Riordan sitting alone at the big desk. Jerking a chair to a position beside him, he sat down and leaned forward.

"It's been a large night, chief," said Riordan. "First, there were three stick-ups of filling stations on Eastern Boulevard, one right after another in a row—first, at Twenty-First Street, second, at Thirtieth and the third, at Forty-Third. Telephone wires cut at each one. That was about nine o'clock. We got the first call about nine twenty, and the motorcycle men went out at once. When the second one came in I sent a load of dicks out.

"Half an hour later there were three more filling stations in a row stuck up on the north side of town—same way, and all in a row leading out of the city. Cap'n Charles, downstairs, sent all the motorcycle men that were left, and

I rounded up another wagonload of dicks and sent them out *there*.

"About half an hour afterward the Central Garage, down in the heart of town, was stuck up. The first load of boys had got back from Eastern Boulevard, and I rushed 'em down there. By the time they got back and the boys from the north side had got back, and we had begun to check up and see what we had, the clerk of the Belmont-Grand called up and said would we please come over, that the place had been cleaned good. The whole gang's over there now.

"Besides all which the sheriff's office has just called in to say that three road houses have reported nice fat jobs. I thought maybe you'd like to be here for the next one."

"I knew things had been too quiet to last, boy," commented Brady. "Well, what you got on the filling station jobs?"

"That's what makes it good," said Riordan. "They were all—all seven of 'em—done by the same party. Youngish looking fellow, with curly hair, wearing coveralls and a cap. 'Bout six feet tall and pretty heavy, somewhere around one hundred and seventy-five or one hundred and eighty. Regular white hope, he was. And a good workman, too.

"He drives up and wants just one gallon of gas. After he's got it, he pulls out a dollar bill and goes inside with the filling station man to get his change. Of course, all the filling stations at that time have only one man on the job, and there's no other customers in sight. Once inside he sticks the filling station man up, empties the till, which is full of the day's receipts, jerks the telephone loose and then makes the filling station man walk out with him and stand in sight while he starts his car.

"He picked a good time—most of the joy-riders had already gone out, and the after-theater crowds and business hadn't started.

"Down at the Central Garage he varied the program. The regular night man was away, having been called home when his wife fell downstairs or something, and only the washer was in the place. He drives in, gets two gallons of gas and flashes a five-dollar bill. He goes into the office with the washer to get change and cleans the till, same as at the other places.

"Then, with the washer still covered, he makes him get in the car with him and drives down the water front. At River and James Streets he stops and tells the washer to walk down toward the river and not look back; but as the fellow steps from the car, this bird trips him up and he falls on his face in a heap.

"The fall partly stunned him, but he heard the car put into gear and gets up just in time to see it driving off. It goes south a block and turns the corner. The washer runs after it, and when he gets to the corner he finds the car, at the other end of the block, standing there, dark but with the engine running. There's nobody in it, of course. The washer gets in, drives it back to the Central Garage and telephones for the cops, and the desk downstairs wises me up.

"We got the car out in the garage—it was stolen at five o'clock, or thereabouts, this afternoon, from Sanderburg's Secondhand Market. The license plate on it was '66-166,' but the bird had changed the numbers by sticking black court-plaster over the open part of some of the '6' figures, so the plate looked like '68-188.' He was clever, he was."

Brady nodded his head. "How much did he get?"

"He got plenty—between thirty and fifty dollars at each of the filling stations, and about two hundred iron men at the Central Garage. He got better than four hundred dollars for the seven jobs."

The office door was thrown open and two of the detectives stumbled in and then checked their rush at sight of Captain Brady.

"Well," snapped that officer.

"Me and Halloran just got back from the Belmont-Grand, sir," said Stacy, the other of the pair. "We left the other boys there, sir, while we come in with the report. The clerk says he was alone in the lobby, the news-stand man having just shut up for the night and gone home, and the bellhops all happening to be out, when a heavy-set, youngish fellow, well dressed, hurries in, leans over the desk and pokes a gat in the clerk's stomach, telling him to hand over what's in the drawer.

"The clerk said he was going to stall, but he didn't like the business air the stick-up had, so he opens the drawer, intending to give him a lot of small change. Once the drawer is open, the guy leans over the desk and scoops out the bill compartments and then turns and beats it just as one of the bell-hops comes down the elevator. He got about two hundred dollars, sir. When the clerk and the bell-hop got to the street, the guy wasn't in sight."

"The same one," exclaimed Riordan. "Had curly hair, did he?"

"Yes, sergeant, red and curly, the clerk says. Big, powerful guy he was, and hard-boiled. Didn't look hard-boiled, you know, but acted it."

"What's the rest of the gang doing over there?" demanded Brady.

"Checking up, sir, and buzzing the neighborhood. The clerk hadn't figured just how much he lost when we left, sir."

"All right," snapped Brady. "One of you two make out a report on what you got and the other of you look in the picture books and see if you can find a guy that matches up with this one. And stick around out there, and when the rest of the gang get back, tell 'em I want detailed reports on what they got, and for them to stick around, too."

The two sleuths saluted and withdrew. Brady reached for the telephone.

"Gimme the sheriff's office," he barked. While he was waiting for the connection he held both transmitter and receiver in one hand, pulled out a cigar with the other and bit the end off. Then taking the match Riordan offered, he lighted the brown roll and puffed vigorously. The phone clicked and, taking the transmitter in his free hand, he said:

"Sheriff's office? This is Brady, down at headquarters. Say, what's this you got on them road house jobs? Oh, all sneaks and lifting, eh. I thought maybe they were stick-ups. No, never mind, good-by."

He slammed the receiver on the hook and put the phone down.

"Them road house jobs had nothing to do with this," he said, waving a hand at the outer office, where he could hear some more of the detectives entering. "They were all leather-lifting. He wanted to tell me all about 'em, but we've got enough of our own work. Well, boy, when do you expect the next one?"

"The way they've been coming, chief, it's about due now," said Riordan with a short laugh. The words had scarcely been said when there was a knock at the office door. Brady tipped back in his chair, reached the knob and threw it open, and then climbed to his feet hastily.

"Well, Mr. Mayor," he said, "what can we do for you?"

Riordan, too, had risen, and was pushing a chair forward for the city executive.

Brady closed the door behind the visitor and waited.

2

"WELL, CAPTAIN," SAID the mayor, "you can't do very much, I guess. But the fact of the matter is my brother-in-law has been robbed. Rather curious case, I'd say. He and his wife had been over to my house for dinner, and later on in the evening some people dropped in and we decided we'd all go for a drive. There were too many to go in my car, so my brother-in-law went home to get his. Then he came back and we all piled into the two cars and drove out in the country.

"Coming back we stopped at Snyder's Villa to get some—some refreshments—and as we were going out my brother-in-law drew me aside and said he'd been robbed. He had his money in a wallet, along with some papers he was a bit fussy about, and the wallet was gone."

"What's off about that, Mr. Mayor?"

"Why, this, captain. Aside from our own party, we weren't in a crowd anywhere to-night. Out at Snyder's place we had a private room—I didn't just want to go into the public dining room, you know. We drove up to the side entrance and made arrangements with the doorman before we left the machines. Aside from the waiters—two of them—I don't think there was anybody near enough us all evening to steal that wallet from my brother-in-law's coat pocket.

"And I'm pretty sure the waiters didn't, because they knew me. One doesn't rob the mayor, you know, even when he is at a roadside inn."

"What makes your brother-in-law think he didn't just lose the wallet, sir?"

"Two things, captain. First, he's always very careful of that wallet, on account of the personal papers he carries in it; and then because it had a wide rubber band on it, and that hinders it from slipping out of his pocket even when he bends over."

"Did you report it to the sheriff's office, sir?"

"No—I thought I'd come straight to you, and you could take whatever steps you thought best. We're not anxious for notoriety, you know."

Captain Brady nodded. "The only reason I suggested the sheriff's office, sir," he said, "is because there's been a bunch of road house jobs to-night. Four or five wallets and purses lifted. I'll tell 'em about this one, maybe it may help 'em on the others. What was the description of the wallet, sir?"

"Black seal leather, with the initials 'K.B.G.' on the inside of the flap. Aside from personal papers there was about eighty dollars in it."

"Do you happen to know where your brother-in-law might have been between the time he left your house and when he came back? He might have been 'touched' then."

"Hardly likely, captain. He went straight from my house to his own. He walked—it's only a matter of six blocks. There he got his car. He drove down to the Central Garage for some gasoline and then came directly to my place."

"All right, sir, I'll have the boys do what they can. Anything else, sir?"

"No, thank you, captain. By the way, aren't you on rather late?"

"I'll say, sir. We've had six filling station jobs and a couple of swell stick-ups. So I thought maybe I'd better stick around."

"That's the stuff, Brady—always on the job. Well, good night."

After the mayor departed Brady looked at Riordan and then burst out laughing.

"It's good, ain't it?" he exclaimed. "As if we didn't have trouble enough of our own his honor's got to drag in a road house job for us, too. Oh, well, it's all in the game. Tell you what you do, boys—you get in your bus and roll over to the sheriff's office and tell 'em about this one, only remind 'em that it's not for publication. Maybe they've got a line by this time and perhaps we can help 'em. I'll be here till you get back."

Riordan left his chief, and Brady yelled through the door behind him as he went out for the bureau clerk outside to bring him in the night reports as far as they were made up. Separating the accounts of the holdups from the others, he studied the former in detail. He was still reading them and absorbing their details when the office door opened and Emmett and Drake, two of his men, entered.

"What you got?" he barked at them.

"We got this suit of cover-alls down in an alley near where the stick-up's car was found," said Drake, holding up the garments. "The guy evidently ducked in there after he'd thrown that garage man out and took 'em off, and then walked out in citizen's clothes when the coast was clear. They're big enough for a giant, sir."

"How'd you happen to find 'em?"

"Well, sir, me an' Emmett thought maybe we'd better look around near where that car was. So we went down there and frisked the doorways and the alley in the middle of the block. Looks like these was big enough to fit that guy, from the description we got."

"My gosh, you really used your heads and worked, didn't yuh?"

Brady's tone was friendly, though the words might not have been. He was pleased that his men were alive to their work.

"Good enough," he continued. "Hang 'em up on the hooks over there on the back wall. Anything in 'em, or any marks?"

"Not even a cigarette paper, cap'n."

"All right. Go on out of here now and leave me be."

When Riordan returned he found Brady standing by the cover-alls and fingering them carefully. Brady told him of the find and then asked if the sheriffs men had anything.

"If they have they don't know it, chief. Gee, they're a lot of dumb-bells over there. Say, listen, they've buzzed every fellow who was touched at the road houses, and they still think the jobs were done at the country joints."

"Huh?"

"That's what I said. Listen to this, chief. Them three road house jobs was all pulled at the same time, and, by dead reckoning, the one the mayor's brother-in-law was in was also the same time. That is, that's what the reports show. Each one says that as the party was preparing to leave the place and start home he reached for his money and found it gone. And you know everybody piles out of them road houses about the same time—in time to get home by midnight.

"Each one of 'em says he had a dance or two before they had the last round of drinks, and maybe they was jostled and touched then. Now I put it to you, is it reasonable that there was four dips working the road houses at the same time in one night, and only touchin' one party in each place?"

Riordan screwed up his eyes and looked at his aide.

"You got a long head—like a horse. But at that, boy— say, you got the names of the three parties aside from his honor's relative that was stuck up?"

"Yes, sir."

"Well, listen to me. You put a couple of the boys on each one of them early tomorrow morning. Have 'em buzzed, see. What I want to know is where they went before they went to the road houses. The boys will get a lot of other stuff, but what I want is where they went before they headed for the country highways. Get me? And I want it by noon to-morrow. I'm going out now, and I may not be down early in the morning. But I'll be here at noon, and I want those reports then. You arrange for that. Good night."

Ten minutes later Brady drove his roadster into the Central Garage, climbed out and lifted the hood. The night mechanician, a fat, bald-headed man, came over slowly to see what was wanted.

"She don't hit right," said Brady. "Misses on one of 'em. Needs a new spark-plug, I guess."

The mechanician examined the engine, tested the ignition with a screwdriver, and shook his head.

"Seems to be hitting all right now," he said. "Maybe you had your spark set wrong."

"Gosh, I might have at that," replied Brady. "I had her speeded up some tonight, chasin' these confounded stick-ups. Guess I forgot to retard it when I got back to the legal rate in town. Gimme a quart of oil, anyway."

The fat, bald-headed man moved slowly away, to come back presently with the lubricant, which he poured into the crank-case. Brady tossed him a half dollar, and when the man brought him the change said:

"You were stuck-up, too, weren't you?"

"No, not me," the bald-headed man replied. "It was the rack man, back there. I was out. Wife fell downstairs and one o' the neighbors called me home. Joe there was tendin' bar when it happened."

Joe, the wash-rack man, came forward, grinning.

"Yep, captain, it was me," he said. "Golly, but that guy was hard. I was durn glad when he told me to get out of his car too."

"Wife hurt much?" asked Brady, turning back to the bald-headed man.

"I guess she's hurt, all right. But no bones broken. Doctor says her leg is strained. That darned brat of hers left his toys on the stairs, and after she put him to bed she stumbled over 'em."

"Your boy?"

"Naw; hers. She was a widder when I married her."

"Take her to the hospital?"

"No, she's to home."

"Doctor any good? Think he knows if she's got a broken leg? I'll send out one of the police surgeons if you say so."

"Guess the doctor's good enough."

"Who's your doctor?"

"Young feller in the neighborhood. One of the neighbors called him. I didn't just get his name. Selby, or somethin' like that."

"I suppose there's been a million dicks in here to see about the stick-up?"

"No, only four."

"That all? Show me how it happened, will you?"

"You show him, Joe," said the bald-headed man wearily.

3

JOE WAS ONLY too glad to oblige. He led Captain Brady about the garage, showed him the cash drawer, the position the robber had occupied, and even what he said were the tracks of his car in a pool of grease and oil near the door.

"Did you telephone your boss?" asked Brady.

"Sure, as soon as I got back. Nickerson, he came right down. He said he didn't care very much, as he was insured. Thought it would be good advertising. Said he bet everybody in town would come in tomorrow to get gas or oil and snoop around."

Brady went back to his machine, against the side of which the bald-headed fat mechanician was leaning.

"Nice clean job, wasn't it?" he commented. "Oh, well, we'll get the guy. We get all of 'em."

The bald-headed man made no reply.

"You don't think we'll get him?" asked Brady.

"I dunno—that's your business."

"Well, I'll bet you I get him—just like I've already got the fellow who stuck up the filling stations to-night."

The bald-headed man raised his head. "You got him already? How'd you get him?"

"On description," said Brady. "Had six good descriptions of him. Sent the boys out to the pool halls, and it wasn't more than half an hour before a couple of 'em brought him in. He hadn't even had a chance to spend the little money he got."

"He didn't get much then?"

"No, the filling stations have been touched so often they don't keep much around nights."

"Humph, some of the dicks what was in here thought he'd got a lot," commented the bald-headed man. "They thought it was the same guy did this job."

"Not a chance," said Brady. "The young fellow who tapped the filling stations was a sport. He took a chance. The fellow that did this job was just a cowardly skunk. Why, look at the difference. The guy who did the filling station jobs was out in the open, where any passing cop could have seen him and taken a shot at him. And he had to make his get-away on the main traveled roads, knowing that the motor cycle men would be right out after him.

"The bozo that came in here was just a stiff. He worked under cover, and he was so scared he took Joe there away with him. And then, when he told Joe to get out of his car, he was so scared he tripped him up and ran—even left his car behind him round the corner. No, the guy that did this job didn't have any class at all."

"What you think about the hotel job, then?" asked the bald-headed man.

"What hotel job?"

Brady's voice showed surprise.

"The Belmont-Grand," said the mechanician. "Didn't you hear about that? Somebody robbed that to-night too."

"Is that so? I hadn't heard of that. I been out on these other cases. Did he get much out of the hotel?"

"I heard he got over a hundred dollars."

"Chicken feed," said Brady scornfully. "Why, any fool ought to know how much they keep in the Belmont-Grand. That place would be *good* pickings for a real guy. A hundred bucks—what did he do, rob the news-stand or the flower girl?"

The bald-headed man shook his head. "I dunno what he did—I just heard somebody robbed the place and got a hundred dollars. One of the dicks who was in here was talkin' about it."

"Talking to you about it, was he?"

"No, he was just talking—to one of the other dicks, I guess."

Joe, the wash-rack man, who had come forward and was listening to the conversation, laughed at this.

"He's kiddin' you, Bill," he said. "This is Captain Brady. You don't figure he's so dumb he don't know what's going on, do you?"

"I knew it was Cap'n Brady," said the bald-headed man. "And maybe he is kiddin' me. An' maybe I'm kiddin' him, too."

Brady looked from one to the other and laughed. "I got to kid sometimes, boys," he said. "I'd go crazy if I didn't. And kidding is the one thing I haven't had any of to-night—up to now. Well, I guess I'll go home and hit the hay."

He stepped round to the other side of his car and opened the door, and then paused.

"You phoned your wife to see how she's getting on?" he asked.

"No, ain't got any phone. Besides, she's in bed and couldn't answer if I had one."

"Want me to drive you out there?"

"No, I got to work till seven in the morning."

"Nickerson won't mind if you go home—I'll square it with him."

"No—thanks just as much, cap'n. There's a neighbor woman in the house, and if anything goes wrong she'll go out and telephone me. I was away so long to-night I still got a lot of work to do."

"All right, old man. Hope the old lady will be all right soon. Good night."

Brady backed his car out of the garage, swung it round on the street, and drove slowly off toward his home. When he had gone several blocks he stopped, sat still thinking for five minutes, then shook his head and started on his way again.

4

CAPTAIN BRADY SLEPT late, for him, the next morning, and it was in the neighborhood of ten o'clock when he drove his car into Sanderburg's Secondhand Market and hailed the proprietor.

"Hey, Sandy," he said, "how come that you let that stick-up man get away with one of your cars yesterday evening? I thought you kept 'em all chained down, except when you were showing them to a customer."

"I do keep 'em chained, cap'n," replied the dealer. "And I'd 'a' had that one chained up again only Bill Foster, from the Central Garage, was over here workin' on it for me. He does all my little jobs, you know. He didn't start work on it till about five o'clock, and had it round the corner beside the lot fixin' it. When he got through I was up at the lunch wagon gettin' a bit of supper and he left it loose. When I came back it was gone. Say, how long you goin' to hold it down to the police garage?"

"Not very long—maybe a day or two, till we clear this case up. Know anything about this Bill Foster, do you?"

"Know he's a darned good mechanician. And reasonable. That's all I want to know."

"How long has he been doing your work?"

"Oh, on and off, maybe half a year. Why?"

"Thought maybe he stole the car."

"Ha! That's a good one, cap. Him steal that flivver! Why, he's got one of these big Rolls Easy busses. What'd he want of a flivver?"

Brady laughed, chatted a moment or two about inconsequentials, and then drove to the Central Garage, where he sought out Nickerson, one of the proprietors, and for a few moments talked about the hold-up of the night before. Then he asked casually:

"Say, Nick, where does this Bill Foster live? Your night mechanic, I mean. Sanderburg tells me he's pretty good on fixing up cars, and maybe I got a job for him on his spare time."

"Him? Oh, he lives out in Fairview addition. Got a little cottage out there, with a shop in the barn in back of it. Corner of Grant Avenue and Eighty-Sixth Street. You can't miss the place; there's no other house right around there. But why take the job to him? We do repair work here, you know."

"It isn't a city job, Nick; I'd have to pay the bill myself. And I'm no millionaire."

From the Central Garage Brady drove to the office of the *Daily Globe,* and had a few minutes' talk with one of the boys in the circulation department. Then, with some slips of paper in his hand, he left and drove to headquarters. Once in his office he telephoned the Women's Protective Division and asked that one of the younger operatives be sent down to him for duty.

It was Miss Carlson who was assigned to him. He gave her the slips of paper he had received at the *Globe* office and then explained what he wanted.

"You go out to Fairview addition, Miss Carlson," he said,

"and up around Grant Avenue and Eighty-Sixth Street. I want you to solicit subscriptions for the *Globe*. I don't care if you get any or not—these blanks will let you out if you do. Make all the houses around there, and gossip with the women folks.

"What I want to find out is whether a Mrs. William Foster, who lives in the house at the corner of Eighty-Sixth, was hurt last night by falling downstairs. If she was hurt I want to know what doctor she had, and who telephoned her husband to come home. Get me? I want all the gossip about Mrs. Foster you can dig up, and I want it quick. If you happen to hear anything about old man Foster himself drag that in, too. Now run along, and get back here by noon, or thereabouts, if you can."

That disposed of, the captain busied himself with other matters, going through the night reports, checking on pending cases and looking after the thousand other details of his job. He was just winding up this assorted work when his doorman entered with a sheaf of papers.

"Here's the reports on those road house jobs you wanted," he said.

Brady took these eagerly, and, spreading them out on his desk, began to read them slowly, making notes on a pad beside them as he did so. As he worked a satisfied smile spread over his face, and presently he reached for a cigar, lighted it, and leaned back in his chair, evidently in great good humor. He was sitting thus, rubbing his hands together, when the door opened again and his chief aide, Riordan, came in.

"Hello, chief, you look happy," the younger man said.

"I am, boy—but what brings you down so early? Didn't you get enough last night?"

"Yeah, I got enough, all right. Maybe too much. To tell the truth, chief, I was so worked up over those cases I couldn't sleep. So I thought I might as well come down here and see if maybe I couldn't help you."

Brady shot a quick glance at his aide, but Riordan's face was sober enough.

"You got something, have you, chief?" asked Riordan.

Brady tapped the reports before him.

"I got something," he answered. "I can't prove what I've got yet, but I've got a hunch. According to these reports on those road house jobs, every one of these here citizens that reported he was robbed was, earlier in the evening, down at the Central Garage with his car. Something to be fixed or to get oil. Now what would be easier than for a crooked garage man, when, his customer was looking at the engine, to slip his hand in the customer's pocket and get his leather?"

"Who do you figure did it?"

"You hold your horses—I got to get just a little bit more first. Here it comes now."

Miss Carlson bustled into the room. Riordan placed a chair for her. "Well, captain," she said, "I sold three subscriptions to the *Globe*, and here's the money and the orders. Besides that I got an earful for you.

"Here it is. Mrs. William Foster, 8602 Grant Avenue, put her little son Claude to sleep last night—or rather she put him to bed—right after supper. Then she started to go downstairs to do up her work before she went out to the movies.

"Claude, it seems, had left his 'choo-choo cars' on the stairs, and Mrs. Foster stepped on them and took a ride down the whole flight of stairs, landing at the bottom in a heap. A Mrs. Matilda Jernegan, who lives at 3451 Eighty-Sixth Street, was in the Fosters' kitchen at the time, waiting for Mrs. Foster to come down; and when she heard the racket she ran out in the hall way and found the poor woman had fainted.

"She dragged her in to the living room and put her on a lounge, and then she ran over to a Mrs. Maxton's, the nearest neighbor, and telephoned for Dr. Oswald C. Selby, the neighborhood surgeon. He came over and wanted to send Mrs. Foster to a hospital, but she said she wanted to see her husband first, so Dr. Selby telephoned the Central Garage where Foster works, and the husband came home. He wouldn't stand for the wife going to the hospital; so the doctor fixed her up there at home as well as possible and he and Foster carried her upstairs to bed.

"Then they sent the Foster kid over to Mrs. Maxton's for the night, and Mrs. Jernegan stayed with the Foster woman. Foster went back to work. The neighbors say he's a good man, has a nice little auto repair business out there and that the couple seem to get along well together. I met Dr. Selby while I was out there, and he says the Foster woman will be all right in three or four days, that she was lucky and didn't break anything, only sprained a leg or two. Is that enough?"

"You did fine," said Brady. "I'm very much obliged to you. Hope I can get you to help me on the next job. Run along upstairs now."

When she left the office Captain Brady threw his cigar violently into the spittoon beside his desk and swore.

"What's the matter, chief," asked Riordan grinning.

"It's all blown up—that's what's the matter. Why, I'd have sworn this Foster guy was the stick-up. Everything pointed to it. The cover-alls over there on the wall are just his size. He was out of the garage at the time and his alibi sounded fishy. Except for the curly hair, which you could lay to a wig, he answered the description.

"He was tinkering with the car the stick-up used—the one stolen from Dave Sanderburg. And last night, when I went down there, he stalled me all the time. And when I said the guy that did the job was a cheap bum, he got hot under the collar, though he tried to conceal it. I'd have made him good and mad, too, only that fool wash-rack man in there butted in and spoiled my work. And now it seems his alibi is perfectly airtight, and I haven't got a thing to work on.

"Damn it, anyway. Why, I thought when I set that Carlson woman on the trail I'd cinch it—and all I've done is to blow the whole case up."

"Too bad, chief," said Riordan, and then he laughed.

Brady looked up and his face got red.

"Funny, isn't it? Go ahead and laugh, and have a good time. Say, what 'a' you got to laugh at, anyway? You had the case fresh on your time, and all night to work on it. Why didn't you turn up something?"

"Oh, I dunno, chief. Maybe I did."

Brady's anger vanished at once, and his eyes became keen and clear.

"Boy, what you got," he asked.

"I got to ask you a question first, chief. What really made you think this Foster party was the man we wanted?"

"What's that got to do with it? Foster's out of it now."

"Go on, answer, chief. I want to see how you worked."

"Well, I'll tell you. It was his alibi. It was too good. Except for the wig, he'd pretty near answer the description—big man and hard-boiled. A fat man looks big and hard-boiled when he's behind a gun. And this fellow was away from the job at just the time. And the whole thing could have been pulled by him. The guy who drove the flivver knew how to handle a car. And the Central Garage was a good place to duck into after touching off the Belmont-Grand.

"The whole thing looked like a good frame, all except the alibi and the way he stalled. But no man's going to make his wife fall downstairs to get an alibi—what are you laughing at again, you hound?"

Riordan doubled up in his chair. "And when you got them reports this morning, about them fellows who was robbed in the road houses, you were pretty sure, weren't you, chief," he said, when he had controlled his mirth.

"You're right I was sure. Every one of them had been down to the Central Garage earlier in the evening, for one thing or another about their cars. Yes—I'd forgotten that. I figured their wallets had been lifted down there, and they hadn't discovered it till they went to pay their booze bills out at the road houses. You're right—but what do you know about those reports? You didn't see them."

"No, I didn't see them—I had the boys telephone me out at my house as soon as they got through buzzing the parties. That was why I couldn't sleep—I was listening for the phone to ring. You and I were working on the same line, chief."

Brady sighed. "I don't wonder you laughed—you knew what a fool I'd been all along. Oh, well; we all make mistakes. What you got—now come clean."

5

RIORDAN REACHED IN his coat and drew out a long, black, seal leather wallet and tossed it on Brady's desk.

"Think that will interest his honor?" he asked.

The captain snatched at the object and opened it, and on the flap read the initials "K.B.G." Inside were one or two letters addressed to the mayor's brother-in-law. Brady folded the wallet, put it in a drawer of his desk and leaned back in his chair.

"I give up, boy," he said. "I tell you what I'll do—and I mean it. We'll take this wallet over to the mayor, and I'll resign and tell him to give you my job. I'm getting old—I guess I'd better quit before I get publicly disgraced."

"Now, chief, be reasonable," said the younger man seriously. "That was just luck, me finding that wallet. Anybody might have found it where this here dip threw it away, after he got the money out of it. You give it back to the mayor, chief, and tell him you found it."

"No, I never sail under false colors."

"Listen, chief, me and you has always worked together, haven't we? What one of us got was just the same as the other getting it? Well, it's the same on this job. We was working together on it, too—only you didn't know it. If you hadn't done what you did, I wouldn't have been to get any of this stuff. You gave me the tip at that. But if I'd told you what I wanted to do at the time, you either wouldn't have let me, or you'd have tipped your hand—"

"I gave you the tip," interrupted Brady. "What do you mean?"

"Why, you got the start on the case. Emmett brought you the cover-alls, didn't he, and that give you the hunch to look over this Foster party down at the Central Garage? And after seein' him, your hunch got stronger, didn't it, and you played it right on through?"

"Yes—but you saw it blow up, didn't you, when the Carlson woman came in?"

"No, I didn't see anything blow up."

Brady sat bolt upright in his chair. "Listen to me, boy, you come through right now or I'll beat your head off," he snapped.

Riordan smiled. "I'll tell you, chief," he said. "I played a mean trick on you last night, I guess. But it seemed best to do it, 'cause we always work our cases together. You know what I told you about those road house jobs not being done there at all, but being done in town before the parties went out? And you thought that was reasonable, and started working on that line right away?

"Well, when you went out I followed you, and when I saw you turn in to the Central Garage I knew we both had the same idea.

"But I didn't know how you were going to work it out, and I didn't want to get in your way. So after I saw you had Foster and Joe in the front of the garage, I slipped round to the alley in the back and sneaked in the rear door and got me a nice seat in one of the machines that was stored there.

"I could see you playing this Foster party, and I could

hear a good deal of what you said. I was half expecting the fat boy would get rough, too, and I was all ready to spoil the party. But nothing came of that.

"Well, after you went out Foster and Joe Martin—that was the wash-rack man—talked about you. Joe said you were a smart guy and would get this stick-up, and Foster said you were a puddin'-head, and he offered to bet Martin that the man you said you had for the filling station jobs, was the wrong man. They argued it back and forth, and finally Martin, his work being all done, went home in a huff. Foster sat around awhile, and then he goes to work on a car about halfway back in the garage, and I sneaked out the back way.

"There was a trash can right beside the back door, out in the alley, where they throw oily waste and stuff like that for the incinerator, and while I was there I thought I might as well go through it. That was where I found that wallet— and these other three."

He reached into his coat again and threw the wallets on the desk. Two of them were oil-soaked, but one, like the mayor's relative's had escaped defilement in the can, due to its having fallen inside a tire-tube box that had been tossed into the waste along with other discarded rubbish from the garage.

"Well," continued Riordan, "I knew then that your hunch was good, chief. But I figured maybe we could get a little more proof. You see, this bird is no fool, and we're going to need all the evidence we can get. That is, if he starts to fight the case.

"So I came back here and got out the picture books and began looking over the good dips. For a long time I didn't find anything, but after about an hour, way back in the front of Volume IV, which was filled up nine years ago, I found our bird. He got four years, then, for a job down at Jeffersonville—breaking and entering in the nighttime.

"Larry Peterson was sent up at the same time on another job, and was paroled out three years later. Now it just happens Larry went straight after that, and when the war came he enlisted, and he and I were buddies part of the time over there.

"One night Larry and me were in a tight place, and we had to talk to keep our spirits up, and Larry told me all about the time when he was a crook. He was bumped off in the Argonne later. Of course, he'd changed his name, and nobody but me knew he was really Larry Peterson. Well, I got to studying things over, and I decided that if we mussed around this Foster guy very much he'd get wise and blow, so I figured I'd have to do something to stall him.

"So this morning I got me some nice quiet clothes, and when Mr. Foster quit his night job and was ready to drive home in his big machine, I flags him up on the main drag, gives him the sign and climbs in. I told him I was Larry Peterson and that I knew who he was.

"He tried to bluff it out, but I asked him why did he stop when I gave him the sign, and then I told him things about himself when he was in stir that Larry had told me, including a frame they had to escape and how it blew up on them; and he finally thinks I'm Larry. He wants to know what am I doing, and I told him I had a job on that was real money, but was looking for a side-kick I could trust.

"Well, we had a nice long talk, him driving slow and roundabout all the time, and I give him the lay of the job—

which was nothing less than to crack the box in Felix and Blodell's brokerage office, which same would be a pipe for a good pair, and they'll get it some day, too. It appeals to him, all right; but he says the time ain't suitable, as you was fussing round on these here stick-ups, and he has a sneaking idea maybe you thought he was mixed up in it.

"He said he'd had the thing planned for a long time, but it didn't break right till last night, when this here wife of his fell downstairs and give him an airtight alibi. You see, after he and the doctor had carried his wife upstairs, he beats it right out, figuring that in the excitement the women folks won't make any special note of the time; parks his big car down by the Belmont-Grand, swipes the flivver which was handy and is off—and back to the garage later in his own machine, just as natural as life.

"I remembered what he'd said to Joe Martin about you, so I told him I knew you and you was an awful fat-head— you got to forgive me for that, chief—and that the thing to do was to stall you and get you busy on something else. He agrees with me, but can't figure any way of doing it. I made believe to think about it awhile, and then I told him I had an A. No. 1 idea, and he says what is it.

"I says: 'I got it, Bill. Maybe this bird Brady will frame a raid on your house for booze or something, to search it, if he thinks you was mixed up in this. What you want to do is to beat him to it. I tell you what you do. You let me steal your car.

" 'You put any tiling in it that you don't want Brady to find, and I'll take the car up to Mountainview and store it with a friend of mine there, and then to-morrow when you get up, you go down to police headquarters and ask for Brady and tell him that since he told you he was such a fine dick, to find your car for you, that somebody stole it out of your barn while you was asleep. That'll give him an excuse to frisk your dump and if he's suspicious of you he'll do it, and in that way you can get a line on him.

" 'If he don't frisk your place, we'll know he ain't on to the stuff at all, and I'll bring the car back and you can find it yourself and then go down and give him the laugh.'

"Well, he fell for it. He had some stuff in the house, all right, that would be hard to explain, and he puts that in a suit case and throws it in the back of the bus and gives me the car. Which same is now in my garage, out at the house."

"You mean to say he actually thought you were Larry Peterson and trusted you enough to turn his bus over to you," exclaimed Brady.

"Sure, we was as thick as two thieves. Of course I had to give him that big diamond of mine to prove I was on the level and wasn't going to steal his wagon—but what of that? I'll get the rock back when we get him."

"And when are we going to get him?"

"When he comes down to report his car is stolen."

"Do you think he'll fall for that?"

"Sure, he's a clever guy and he's sure you're a fathead."

"And you got stuff on him in the car, too? Wigs, for instance?"

"He never used a wig in his life."

"But he's as bald as Pike's Peak in the Rocky Mountains," exclaimed Brady. "And he had long hair when he did these jobs."

"I told you he was good, didn't I? Well, a wig is a tough thing to throw away in a hurry, if he got caught. Bill Foster had the wig idea beaten a city block. When he was Mr. Somebody Else he wore a cap, and under the cap, wrapped around his head, he had a strip of this here long, fake fur you see on cheap coats that the dames wear, only it was dyed a reddish brown. It hung down from under the cap and made it look like he had long, tousled hair.

"If he gets in a jam he snatches his cap off and throws the fake fur into the street. If anybody finds it, it looks like something the cat dragged in, or something off a flapper's coat. And if they get him, he's bald-headed and don't answer the description. Yes, he's good, he is."

Brady rocked back and forth in his chair a moment.

"I'll say you're sort of good, yourself," he commented. "And you weren't so far wrong when you told him I was a fathead either. Do you really think he'll come in, or will he get cold feet when he wakes up?"

Riordan grinned again. "I think he'll come in, chief."

"What makes you so sure about it?"

"Well, I didn't want to take any chances. So I posted a couple of the night men out there—Emmett and Drake to bring him in."

6

THE DOOR TO Brady's office opened and the mayor entered. He greeted both officers, and then asked Brady if he had any developments. "Give his honor a chair, Riordan," said the captain.

After the mayor had seated himself, Brady passed him a box of cigars which he took from the lower drawer of his desk. Then he passed the box to Riordan, and took one himself. After all three were lighted, he leaned back in his chair.

"Mr. Mayor," he said, "there's been a little matter I've been wanting to speak to you about for some time. We're short-handed here. We are particularly shy on executive officers. The other branches of the department have got 'em, but we haven't. Now I've got some men that ought to be put up a peg. There's Emmett and Drake, for instance; they ought to be sergeants. And Riordan here, he ought to be a lieutenant. Don't you think you can jigger an ordinance through the council, giving me that much more help?"

"I don't know, captain. Maybe if you were to catch the men responsible for last night's 'wave of crime,' as the papers are calling it, we might do something."

Brady opened a drawer in his desk and drew out the wallet he had put away but a short time before.

"Think your brother-in-law would like this?" he asked.

The mayor gasped.

"Why, captain! That's the wallet he was robbed of last night."

"Yes, sir. We were short-handed, or we'd have got it sooner."

"Have you got the man who stole it?"

"I think he'll be in presently, your honor. Riordan, here has asked him in."

The mayor looked from one to the other and then laughed.

"What is this, captain, a joke?" he asked.

"You sit tight, your honor, and you'll see—I think this is the party now."

There was a shadow on the office door, and a second later it was discreetly opened by the civil secretary from the outer room.

"A Mr. Foster wants to see you, captain," he said.

"Show him right in."

Riordan slipped over to a position behind the half opened door as Foster entered. A large diamond gleamed from his necktie, and he had the general appearance of an old-time bartender dressed for a picnic.

"Good mornin', cap'n," he said. "Remember last night you was tellin' me how smart you were? Well, I've got a job for you. Somebody slipped into my barn last night and stole my automobile. I'd like to have you get it back for me."

"All right, Foster. I'll see what I can do. It ought to be simple. I'm talking with the mayor just now, will you step outside for a minute, till I get through, and then I'll be ready to take a description of it from you?"

Foster flushed slightly, looked at the mayor a second and

then turned about to open the door—to find Riordan's automatic at his chest.

"Just one move, Bill," said Riordan, "and we'll call the coroner."

"What—what the—" gasped the caller.

"Last night, Foster," explained Brady to the visitor's back, "I told you I'd get the man who stuck up the hotel and the Central Garage. You said I was a puddin'-head. Well, maybe I was, but I got the man, didn't I? Take your pin off him, Riordan, before I call in a couple of the boys to lock him up."

Riordan's left hand moved swiftly and Brady pushed a button on his desk.

Two of the detectives entered, there was a snapping of handcuffs and Foster and the sleuths went out.

Riordan shoved his automatic back in its holster beneath his arm.

"I got to apologize for the gun-play, Mr. Mayor," he said. "But there wasn't much room here, and it had to be quick work."

"That's all right, lieutenant—now you boys tell me all about it. I want to hear how good it is," and so saying the city executive settled back comfortably in his chair to listen.